PARADISE 21

BY

AUBRIE DIONNE

Entangled Publishing, LLC
2614 South Timberline Road
Suite 109
Fort Collins, CO 80525

Visit our website at www.entangledpublishing.com.

Entangled Publishing is a subsidiary of Savvy Media Services, LLC.

ePub ISBN   978-1-937044-02-2
Print ISBN   978-1-937044-03-9

Edited by Caroline Phipps
Cover design by Kim Killion

Manufactured in the United States of America

To Joanne and Andy

Chapter One
Descent

Aries sped through space in her escape pod as if she fled the event horizon of a dying star. The controls blinked warnings around her, but she ignored them, pressing the touchscreen to fire the engines to full capacity.

Let's see how fast this antique can go.

Her sweaty palms slipped on the cold metal as she clutched the restraining bar across her seat. Freedom intoxicated her, coursing through her veins like she drank liquid fire.

She squeezed her eyes shut and screamed, releasing raging emotions held back from years of conforming and keeping her true thoughts silent. Many times Aries had thought her head would implode from the pressure, but instead she'd schemed, plotting the day of her departure down to the last water bottle. As the sound of her voice dissipated, she opened her eyes and peered at the stars as they blurred into streaks of shimmering light.

The time flashed on the screen in fluorescent green: 1638. Aries committed the numbers to memory. She'd have at least three hours before the ceremony and reception ended and her fellow Lifers began searching for her. Her shipmates would check her cell first, then activate the locator embedded in her arm. When they realized she'd jumped ship, they'd stop the engines and count the escape pods. By then, Aries would be a parsec away from the *New Dawn*.

Maybe they wouldn't come. Giddiness bubbled in her throat with the thought of the ship coursing away without her, but she knew better. They'd turned the *New Dawn* around before, and knowing Lieutenant Barliss, he'd have it no other way. Not only was he a high-ranking officer, but she was his chosen mate, scheduled to be bound to him in ceremony next month. Her escape would prevent Barliss from passing on their combined genetic code. There was no doubt that a man who followed the Guide to the letter would come after the woman whose DNA he needed.

The orange bulk of Sahara 354 claimed the horizon on the main sight panel. Aries soaked in the sight of the small, forgotten planet, like the first time she'd seen pictures of old Earth. Although the conditions of life on Sahara 354 were reportedly bleak, to Aries it looked like a haven. Blue and red lights flashed on the panel in front of her, warning her of the change in trajectory as the pod entered the planet's gravitational pull. Aries shut off the thrusters and allowed the vessel to sail into orbit. She glided in space, using the pod's sensors to complete a full scan of the surface, searching for signs of resources or life. Although she had enough food and water for days, they'd only delay an inevitable death if she couldn't find further sustenance.

Time ticked away, seconds she knew she couldn't waste. The *New Dawn* traveled much faster than an escape pod, and she needed time to fake her own death and disappear. The vast wasteland stretching before her only had small pockets of water and plant life. If she didn't choose her landing spot wisely, she'd be plummeting to a real demise.

The sight panel for the exterior cameras beeped, letting her know the pod now glided close enough to visualize the surface. Aries drew up the suggested location with the tip of her finger. The screen displayed a smear of sand cut with jagged protrusions of rock, but the life-form locator told her more. A conglomeration of several beings inhabited the area, and not mere insects or microscopic fungi: human-sized creatures. She dismissed the thought of Outlanders—the *New Dawn* had traveled too far, too fast, for any straggling humans to have made it to this planet ahead of her. Whatever form the creatures took, if they could survive down there, then so could she.

Aries triple-checked her readings before entering the coordinates. She wasn't going to make the same mistake as the last escapee. She blocked a vision of Tria's grotesquely dehydrated skin from her thoughts. Her friend had made a run for a different planet without testing it for compatibility. In Tria's mad rush to get away, she'd landed on a barren rock with a vacuum atmosphere that had sucked her lungs dry in seconds. The *New Dawn* had gone all the way back to find a corpse.

With a nervous touch on the control panel, Aries retested the quality of the atmosphere, the pull of gravity, and the radiation levels. Scouts had explored the territory centuries before astrophysicists had fused together the first chrome plates of the *New Dawn*. Their historical readings had proven accurate for other planets, but Aries still verified the findings for herself. The 354th known desert planet ranked close enough to Earth. Not adequate to sustain a large population or major colonization effort, but adequate to keep a 120-pound woman alive.

Taking a deep breath, she punched in the coordinates. The panels went wild, compiling the information. The computer estimated a new trajectory, and she turned on the thrusters once again. The engines rumbled, pounding deep within her stomach.

The inside of the pod rattled. Lifers never used or maintained the flight pods, so she felt lucky the one she'd chosen worked at all. Would the metal skin on this pod hold together as she entered an alien atmosphere? She could either take the risk, or circle this planet until the *New Dawn* came back to get her—the *New Dawn* with Lieutenant Barliss aboard. Holding her breath, Aries activated the final landing sequence. Even if the descent killed her, she'd rather perish on an alien planet than complete her ceremonial obligations.

The restraining bar of her chair shook violently, and she lost feeling in her arms. The air boiled in the small compartment, and her face burned. If she didn't disintegrate, then her head would burst from the pressure. Tears flicked backward from her eyes while she held on, gritting her teeth. An alarm sounded, reminding her to release the parachute. She tried to move, but the force of gravity glued her hand to the armrest, stretching her skin taut. After counting to three, she took a breath and grunted as she yanked her arm up and pressed the touchscreen, hoping the chute would work.

A bright flash of light blinded her, and splotches exploded under her eyelids. The pod hit the ground, and her world went black.

...

Disappointment weighed down Lieutenant Astor Barliss' shoulders as each member of the congregation filed in. No one knew the whereabouts of his intended. After the first speaker took the stand, Barliss' displeasure turned into astonishment at her absence. She played the game meticulously, like he did, appearing at all the events, performing her job at optimum capacity and sitting in the first pew of the congregation without deviation. How could she miss the pairing of Commander Gearhardt's great-granddaughter with the general's son? An anxious dread settled in his chest as he wondered what conclusions they'd draw about him and his own, absent bride-to-be.

Stars glittered on the sight panels around them as the ship sped toward Paradise 21. Even an important ceremony such as this wouldn't slow or hinder their optimum flight speed. The speaker's voice echoed off the glass, resonating throughout the domed chamber. Barliss focused on the preprogrammed flickering of the candles on the altar, something that could be controlled, instead of the vast unknown stretching in all directions.

The ceremony drew out until he felt like a wound coil waiting to spring. The close proximity of the congregation stifled him—too many people to keep tabs on, too many to control at once. As the couple recited their final vows, he breathed a sigh of relief, eager to stand up and move around the room, ready to talk to the right people and make the right impressions. After the usual applause, everyone rose and gravitated toward the trays of food.

Smoothing one stray hair into the gelled-back hairstyle he wore perfectly, Barliss pushed through the congregation. The throng of bodies cluttered the main deck, each one carrying a delicate champagne glass with bubbling liquid, vintage stuff from old Earth. If it were any other day, he'd allow himself one glass for appearances, but the absence of his intended from such an important occasion made him sick to his stomach.

As Barliss worked through the crowd, he dodged stray comments from his lower officers, ducked underneath a tray of miniature breaded zucchinis, and cut through the couple's extended family, all to give his formal congratulations to the bride and groom. The digital numbers on his wristband accumulated, but he knew better than to leave a ceremony without giving his well wishes. Especially this one. To gain favor with the higher command would put him in a position of advancement. It was all part of the political game, the single sport he excelled at. Only after paying his respects could he start looking for his intended.

"Lieutenant, it's always a pleasure to see you." A man in a white tuxedo broke through the crowd to cuff his shoulder. Barliss gauged the timing of the line. Another ten people waited before him to pay their respects, so he could spare a moment for his old friend.

"Gerald, I trust you're doing well with your new bride. How long's it been? A month?"

"Seems like five years to me." He chuckled, but darkness tinged the corners of his eyes. "How can computers be wrong, eh?" He downed his glass of champagne in one desperate gulp. "You have your own ceremony coming up soon, right?"

"Yes, I do." Barliss stifled his excitement, straightening his collar so his gold lapel pin caught just the right amount of light, and the *New Dawn*'s insignia of a seventeenth-century ship cutting through water rested above his right bicep.

"How you ever got paired with such a beauty…" Gerald trailed off as his own designated life partner came up and clutched his arm.

Barliss sized her up. Thick makeup covered her ruddy complexion, but nothing could cure her limp brown hair and bony nose. No matter how she stuffed the dress, the front would never be filled out in the right places. Not well enough for Barliss' taste, anyway. Her beady eyes always had reminded him of the bats in the loading bay.

"Hello, Tilda."

"Lieutenant Barliss, you look stellar today."

Barliss' eyebrows rose, questioning her appraisal. He made it a point to look stellar every day. He didn't spend fifteen hours a week weight training for fun and games. "So do you, Tilda, my dear," he lied, playing the game.

She giggled and squeezed Gerald's arm.

Gerald winced as if she'd grasped him too tightly. Tilda waved to someone in the crowd and placed a wet kiss on her husband's cheek, smearing her lipstick before slinking away. Gerald gave her a little wave and turned back to Barliss. "Like I said, you're the lucky one."

The compliment was not entirely welcome. Too much attention to his pairing might raise suspicions. Aries embodied beauty itself. With hair like old Earth's sunset, unblemished skin, and curves in all the perfect places, Aries was a prize. Not only that, but her parents reigned as the top two astrophysicists on the *New Dawn*. Barliss' mouth watered just thinking of all the connections he'd attain. He bowed to Gerald. "My apologies. I must take my leave to give my respects to the new couple."

"Of course, my friend." Gerald saluted him by waving the champagne glass in his hand. Drips flung across the room and Barliss stepped to the side swiftly, careful not to get any on his pristine, white, ceremonial uniform.

Gerald called over his shoulder. "I'll be seeing you at the celebration after-party, correct?"

Barliss nodded, but his eyes strayed. "If I can get back to the main deck in time, yes."

It took forever for the line to move forward. Everyone inched over to talk with him concerning his own impending ceremony, asking embarrassing questions about his intended's absence. He reached the end of the receiving line, feeling like a schoolboy who'd forgotten to bring his homework. Damn Aries for this humiliation.

"Congratulations, Mr. and Mrs. Byron Locke. You two make quite the outstanding pair."

"Thank you. Lieutenant Barliss, is it?" The way his name fell off the bride's tongue made him feel like an inconsequential fly. He resisted the urge to squeeze her hand too tightly as she offered it, instead kissing it properly before letting go.

"Yes, appointed five years ago by your great-grandfather, himself."

She scanned the crowd behind him, already losing interest. Barliss scrambled to find a topic to prolong the conversation, to make himself memorable and perhaps win a meeting with the commander.

"Such a lovely ceremony—"

"You're the one paired with Aries Ryder, aren't you?"

He fidgeted with his lapel pin, as if hailing Aries now would make her appear. "That's correct."

"Where is she? I was so looking forward to seeing her today. She was my mentor, you know. She did everything she could to help me prepare for my engineering exams."

"She's..." He paused, loosening his collar. "Not well."

The new Mrs. Locke's face turned cold. "She's never missed a day of work in her life."

"Like I said, she's not well." His answer came out more curtly than he intended. Mrs. Locke stepped back as if he'd hit her and wrapped her fingers around her new husband's arm. Mr. Locke whispered something in her ear. She gave the lieutenant a brusque nod and turned away.

The next pair of guests pushed by him to greet the bride and groom, and his opportunity slipped away. Damn it! This was all Aries' fault. Frustration boiled inside him like hot mercury. Throughout the whole ceremony, all he'd been able to think of was the future, a future he'd carefully engineered through many years of slippery politics and hard work, a future that granted him Aries as his intended. He had to find her to put her in her place, to remind her being his partner came with certain obligations.

Barliss quietly walked out of the main hall, then picked up the pace, sprinting down the main entry shaft to the personal cells at the rear of the ship. The corridors had an eerie stillness to them, as if the commander had evacuated the vessel and Barliss was the last one left to roam the decks, eternally alone.

Of course, his imagination sped on hyperdrive. Everyone was here, clustered on the main deck, attending the ceremony as dictated in the Guide. Everyone except Aries. Barliss' worry turned to anger, hardening like crushed steel inside his stomach. She'd better have a good reason for her absence. As his future partner, she'd stained both their reputations.

He reached her cell in a record amount of time, his ten-mile morning runs paying off. He pressed the hailing panel and waited for a response.

The corridor lay as silent as deep space. He buzzed again.

"Miss Ryder, this is Lieutenant Barliss. Are you well?"

He shifted his stance to lean against the door, as if he could hear through the thick, chrome wall. Except for the ever-present hum of the lights, silence insulted his ears. He looked at his wristwatch: 1638. The ceremony had started just after 1500 hours, so she'd been missing for almost two hours.

He pressed his lapel pin, paging the main control deck, tapping his foot as he waited. It took long moments for someone to answer. Everyone was enjoying themselves at the reception.

"Yes, Lieutenant."

"Activate Aries Ryder's locator immediately and inform the commander. She's been missing for two hours."

"Affirmative."

He buzzed the door again, wishing he'd taken the time to talk with her at breakfast instead of strengthening ties with the upper command. She'd seemed distant these past few weeks, shoving her food in her mouth to avoid talking. Their meals together ended quickly. Barliss had been thankful for the silence at the time. After all, a woman's frivolous banter didn't interest him.

"Sir." The lower officer's voice startled Barliss from his musings. He didn't like the tone of voice or the pause at the end.

"What is it?"

"Her locator. It's not onboard."

"How can that be?" Barliss' tone questioned the subordinate's capacity.

"Either she's taken it off and ejected it, or gone with it, but in any case, it's not onboard."

Those final words resonated in Barliss' head, and he fell back against the chrome wall, stunned.

"Why didn't the alarm sound?"

"I don't know, sir. She must have tampered with the energy cell."

Barliss narrowed his eyes "Well, turn it back on. Try a different frequency. Have someone check the escape pods."

"Yes, sir."

"I'm not finished." His voice snapped on the last syllable like a rubber band. He hadn't suspected Aries had been scheming to escape, because she embodied the epitome of civility, apologizing for her silence during their meals and blaming her distraction on an accumulation of work. She'd taken up that hot chick Tria's workload—too bad that one had been stupid enough to get herself killed.

He adjusted his collar, struggling to keep his tone even. "Notify the commander. We're going to have to reverse direction."

Chapter Two
Life-Forms

Aries awoke to flashing lights and smoke. A wailing siren sounded in her ear, each surge aching in her head. Coughing, she pushed a panel to bring up the screen, but the panels remained blank. Trying to control a jolt of panic, she unbuckled the belt across her stomach and heaved herself up, feeling like a supply container was sitting on her chest. She gasped in dismay as she ran her fingers across a jagged crack slicing the main control board in two pieces. The impact had destroyed the mainframe processor, ruining the escape pod.

She'd known the landing would destroy the pod, but that didn't quell a feeling of vulnerability from washing through her. Aries had stranded herself in a foreign land with no way home. The thought of her parents and the ceremony she'd missed in order to escape flickered briefly in her mind. If her friends and family ever found out what she did, she hoped they would forgive her. To live her life for them would make her miserable — she had to invent her own destiny.

Laughter rumbled up from her gut, light at first, then deepening into triumph. She was free. Halfway stuck in a dune on Sahara 354 was exactly where she wanted to be.

A new light blinked beside her, distracting her from the condition of the pod. Aries brought up her arm to check out the locator. A light on the wide cuff flashed bright green, and she wished she could rip it off. Someone in the *New Dawn* had found a way to reactivate it.

The pod's display had died, but Aries checked the time on the locator itself: 1721. She'd been unconscious for only a few minutes, but still long enough for the locator to complete at least one cycle of transmission.

If they'd remotely activated it, they knew she was missing. The signal had obviously penetrated deep space, although she'd hoped it wouldn't. The ship would have the exact coordinates of the escape pod's landing. That's how they'd found Tria. Besides, Sahara 354 was the only planet in light years that had any signs of life. Barliss knew her well enough to guess she'd planned ahead.

Aries pulled the energy cell out and the flashing stopped. The crash coordinates had been sent, but at least no more would go out as she explored her new home planet. She dropped the energy cell on the dashboard and watched it rattle to a halt underneath the cracked glass of the sight panel. If she left it there, they'd know she'd taken it out. It would be better if she brought the energy cell with her and reactivated the locator when she found a life-endangering situation, like quicksand. If she found a way to remove the whole device without tearing off a chunk of her arm, she could throw it in, and they'd have to assume her body had gone with it. They'd stop looking for her once their retrieval machine pulled it out.

Aries shoved the energy cell in her pocket and grabbed the backpack she'd spent months filling with all the right supplies. She hit the pod's manual eject button, and the lid of the craft popped open, smoking and wheezing.

The heat hit her in a tidal wave. She gasped for breath, thinking of poor Tria. The air scorched Aries' lungs, and she waited for her skin to crinkle or her body to burst. She squeezed her eyes shut to brace for the worst, but she remained conscious. Each intake of breath burned like fire, but then again, she'd only ever breathed regulated air. She had to trust the historical reports. The atmosphere on Sahara 354, although parched, must be adequate.

As the hatch lifted, blinding sun poured in like a thousand laser rays, blazing into her pale skin. She'd read about the sun on Earth and had felt the flames of a lighter on her fingertips, but she'd never experienced such a rush of raw elements. The radiating light infused her with awe, as if a higher power touched her directly.

Shielding her eyes, she peered at the sky, a canvas of cerulean and gold. She'd always wondered what it would be like to stand in an atmosphere. It provided a sense of protection in a blanket spreading above her head, shielding her from the harsh elements of deep space. At the same time, the world felt open and endless compared to the claustrophobic corridors of the *New Dawn*.

Aries stepped out of her broken pod, and orange sand stained her pristine space boots. Her white uniform ruffled in the breeze. Thank the Guide, she had long sleeves covering her arms from the burning sun. The light microfiber repelled heat. As her eyes adjusted to the bright glare, she could make out the plateau of rock from the image on the viewing screen. The pod had landed exactly where she'd told it to. Now all she had to do was get as far away as possible, find a place to ditch her locator, and hide.

After one last look at the steaming wreckage, she secured the clasps on her pack and took the first steps forward. Her boots sank into the ground as if lead lined the soles. Trudging through the sand was cumbersome compared to bouncing along the metal walkways of the *New Dawn* in light gravity. She felt like a toddler again, flailing her arms as she learned how to balance and stand. Although the increase in gravity and uneven terrain made her body work harder, the stretching of her muscles felt good and oddly natural, as if she'd missed a certain pleasure all her life.

Drunk on freedom, she trekked on. A brutal wind hit her face, sending sand particles in her eyes and mouth. Aries coughed and spit on the ground. Her tongue stuck in her mouth like sandpaper.

As a little girl, she'd stood in front of the ventilator, feeling her hair fan out as the air had rushed past the back of her neck. The natural wind on Sahara 354 blew much stronger, a violent force beyond man's control. Being exposed made her feel weak and vulnerable, but also excited.

She dug in her backpack, found her water bottle, and took a swig of mineral water, trying to get her bearings and adjust to the new levels of gravity and temperature. Her eyes stung and her skin burned, but she was free. Bracing herself against the gale, she ripped off a piece of her uniform and tied it around her nose and mouth. Thank goodness she'd cut her hair to shoulder length. Barliss had fought against the new style, until she'd fooled him into thinking she wanted to make the change so the upper command would take her more seriously, to move up the ranks with him. Only then had he allowed her to chop it off.

The wind swirled mini tornadoes in the sand, erasing her tracks. The pod glinted as a silver spot on the horizon. She'd walked far, but the monotonous terrain provided nowhere to hide. Miles and miles of craggy ridges surrounded her, sand heaped in drifts nearly up to their peaks. A look at her water rations told her she was draining her supply faster than she'd planned.

The sun set, just as a new sun rose on the horizon behind her. Perpetual sunlight. She remembered reading about it when she'd targeted this forsaken place, but only now did she understand the relentless heat. How could she hide in the blazing light of eternal day?

Aries grew angry with herself for not planning her landing better. The *New Dawn* would come and the search crews would find her easily with their scanners. She was the only life-form for miles around. She desperately needed to find those human-sized beings and hide among them. Then, maybe she'd have a chance of being overlooked.

Aries dug a hand-held device out of her backpack and clicked it on. The glare of the sun reflected off the plastic screen, making it impossible to read. Sitting in the sizzling sand, she took out her sleeping bag and unraveled the fabric. She draped the cloth over her shoulders like a cape and leaned her head over the mini computer. With her arms outstretched, she shut out the majority of bright light.

The readings didn't make sense. Perhaps the landing had damaged the scanner. The device registered several life-forms approaching, the first only meters away.

Aries poked her head out of her makeshift cover and saw only endless dunes of sand shifting under the gusting wind. She consulted the device again and got the same readings, only now the fluorescent dots crowded closer, surrounding her in a circle. The blinking lights on the screen were spaced with perfect symmetry. She gulped down bile. Whoever they were, they were hunting her and closing in.

She searched the hazy horizon and saw nothing. Crazily, she thought of ghosts, specters from a failed colonization attempt, but of course, ghosts wouldn't register as breathing life-forms on her scanner. Fingers shaking, she packed up her sleeping bag and the device. She cursed herself for not bringing any weapons. Why had she thought the only bad guys were on her ship?

At least she had her pocketknife, something she often used to rewire circuit boards. She switched open the blade and held it out in front of her. It felt like a miniscule defense compared to such a vast land.

"Hello?" Her voice broke on the word, and fear twisted its way up her spine. "Is anyone out there?"

The wind ripped through Aries, sending another wave of grit into her face. Before she could clear her eyes, the sand exploded around her, as if bombs erupted at her feet. Human-shaped beings leaped from holes in the ground. They wore layers of rough hides on their bodies and wrapped around their heads. Carved bones with slits covered their eyes. They towered over her, pointing spears at her neck and ribs.

Aries clutched the knife. The blade shook in her grasp. "I mean you no harm."

The creatures jabbed their spears at her nose.

"I'm just trying to get away from my ship…"

One creature stepped forward. Two stubby horns protruded from the animal hide around his head. He hissed, a primitive, insect-like sound cutting through Aries' inner ear. Her hope for intellectual communication dwindled. She gazed into the bones covering their eyes, half of her not wanting to know what kind of eyes stared at her, but the slits were too narrow to see through.

The others echoed the apparent leader's hiss as if in affirmation of their intended quarry, and adrenaline shot through her limbs. Iridescent scales covered their bodies, shimmering vermillion in the sun. The urge to run bubbled up inside her as she eyed the sharp tips of their spears. Three-pronged claws grasped the weapons. One of them lunged, and she backed right into another. It threw its skinny arms around her and squeezed.

Aries dropped her knife. She thrashed and screamed, kicking her legs, but the creature only held her tighter. The others, however, rather than attacking her, rummaged through her pack, so Aries gave up her energy-sapping struggle. Fighting would achieve nothing, only make her too tired to run if the chance came up. They pillaged her belongings and tossed aside important survival gear like trash. So much planning... spilled into the sand. One creature stepped on her only water locating device, cracking the screen and kicking sand over the circuits. Another ripped her sleeping bag open. Feathers fell to the ground, white on orange sand, as if the creatures had shot a bird from the heavens. Their comrades danced on top of the discarded items and thrust their spears in the air in excitement.

"Stop, you lizard bastards!" Now she would die of hunger and thirst in the middle of a desert, her perfectly packed bag stolen by primitive lizard men. Maybe Tria had had it easy.

The creatures didn't let her go. They signaled to each other in strange swings of their heads and tugged her forward. Aries struggled as she watched the first few disappear into the tunnels underneath the sand. The rest dragged her with them.

"No, no, no." She felt like she was stuck in some twisted bedtime story with a moral to scare small children: *never run away from home.*

A high-pitched squeal erupted from the dunes behind them. The creatures froze, then hissed in unison, but this time there was urgency to the sound, a sense of alarm. Twisting their necks at an impossible angle, they peered behind Aries to the dunes. Aries followed their gaze. She focused her eyes until her head hurt. The desert moved on the horizon, a ripple in an ocean of crimson-orange waves.

Not wanting to find out what was causing that disturbance on the horizon, Aires took advantage of the distraction and elbowed the creature holding her. He flew backward, landing on his tail in the sand. Although his wiry body consisted of lean muscle, she outweighed him, so the power of the impact left him stunned. She braced herself for another fight, but his comrades scurried into the tunnels.

She looked around for her pack, but they'd taken it. Before she could decide whether to follow them to steal it back, the ground opened next to the fallen creature. A mound of glittering scales unfurled before her like a giant spring. Choking on a stench that reminded her of the waste depository, she stared as a worm the size of a ventilator shaft rose above her head, casting an ominous shadow on the land.

The lizard creature clawed the earth in an attempt to get away, but the worm lunged, opening its mouth. Ridges of serrated teeth lined the pink, muscular opening. Its mouth clamped down on the lizard-creature's torso. The worm lifted its head, bringing him upward to the sky. The lizard man waved his thin arms and dropped his spear before the jaws loosened and the worm swallowed him whole.

Aries watched, transfixed. The bristles protruding from each scale on the worm's long throat flexed as the lizard man's body traveled down.

Run, you fool.

Her legs shook and buckled underneath her. Aries scrambled down a drift of sand. She tumbled, head over boots, and rolled down a steep incline. Sand was everywhere, in her mouth, in her hair, and she couldn't tell which direction she'd come from. Behind her, she heard the now-familiar squeal of the sandworm, so she scrambled ahead, sprinting blindly in the opposite direction of the call. The sun beat down on her, mocking her feeble plight as she spent her last ounce of energy.

Gazing fearfully over her shoulder, Aries searched the sand mounds for movement, but the landscape remained placid. Why wasn't the worm following her? Was it taking a shortcut underneath her feet?

She wasn't going to take any chances. Aries regained her feet and staggered until the sand dunes ran together in an endless tide, until she collapsed, disoriented and dehydrated. She opened her mouth to gasp in air, and her lips cracked, letting trickles of blood seep into the sand. As she closed her eyes, precious beads of sweat evaporated instantly from her forehead.

At least I died free.

Chapter Three
Striker

Striker shielded his eyes and crouched near the sand, listening to the wind. As the only human on this godforsaken planet, he'd learned in the past five years to rely on his other senses when the sandstorms obscured his vision. He sniffed the tangy scent of minerals in the air. A spring of underground water rippled through a vein in the earth. Reaching into his backpack with calloused hands, he drew out a long metal stick and thrust it into the ground. He waited, perfectly still, while the rod sank down and the wind whipped his long, black cloak behind him.

When he pulled out the rod, moist sand crusted the tip. He wiped the end on his palm and smoothed the granules between his fingertips. After a moment's consideration, he untied the wrap around his mouth and tested the taste of the wet sand on his tongue.

Today the stars were on his side. Placing his backpack down, he began to untie the knot holding his shovel.

A call sounded across the dunes like the wail of a suffering banshee, rousing him from his fortune. *Sandworm.*

"Damn. Not now." Weighing his options, he calculated the proximity and direction of the sandworm. It wouldn't be worth the risk to stay and dig.

He squinted at the horizon. Large packs of raiders attracted sandworms. He wondered what had drawn their attention, but curiosity in this case could mean death in a sandworm's stomach.

Turning away, he collected his belongings and prepared for the hike home. He'd slid halfway down the dune when a familiar sound sailed on the wind. He froze in mid-step, the sand collapsing around his high boots. Not much fazed him these days, but this call stirred emotions he'd long buried. It was a sound he hadn't heard in years: a human scream.

"Damn it to hell." He had no choice. Humans were damned scarce in the universe, unable to live on most planets. They'd wrecked old Earth centuries ago and had existed ever since in space, floating around in giant colony ships or clustered on the few hospitable rocks they'd stumbled across. To hear another human's voice on this desert planet was more than he could have hoped to encounter. Pulling his hood around his face, he grabbed his water-seeking rod, clutching it with both hands as a weapon, and bolted in the direction of the scream.

He could hear the hiss of the raiders on the other side of the dune, wheezing like a dozen steam pipes. Swallowing his disgust, he crawled up the incline of rippling sand until he peered over the ridge. There was a sandworm, all right. A big one. Raiders were fleeing like ants into their tunnels. The scene was everything Striker should be running from, with one unavoidable reason to stay: a young woman, staring up at the hairy beast like a princess in an evil fairy tale.

He couldn't yell to her, because he knew better than to distract a sandworm while it devoured a meal. Before he could think of another way to get her attention, the woman suddenly sprang into motion, sprinting away. As she disappeared over the adjacent ridge, Striker followed, making sure to give the sandworm a large berth.

His caution wasn't enough. The pounding of his boots in the sand roused the beast from its digestion. It stiffened as if it felt the vibrations, raising its head and turning toward Striker. He froze in place, squeezing his palms around his metal rod.

"Come on, you sucker." He'd never come this close to one before, but he had a plan. He always had a plan.

The worm plunged into the sand. It charged at him like a shark cutting through water, the sand shifting above its path in heaping mounds.

There was no sense in running. Not now. He'd seen the worms overpower the raiders, and their skinny lizard legs could sprint far faster than any man's. He held up the rod and waited.

Just as he'd expected, the worm reemerged four feet away, bursting through the sand with its jaws open, ready to swallow its prey whole. The beasts had excellent distance judgment but weren't one hundred percent accurate. As it snapped its jaws shut on nothing but air, Striker drew his arm backward, then threw the rod at its hide.

To his satisfaction, the pointed end of the stick pierced the outer layer. He'd only seen them from afar and had been guessing at the thickness of the hairy skin. He ran toward the worm, grasped the end of the rod, and pushed it in harder, applying his weight.

The worm flailed in the sky above his head, letting out a high-pitched screech. The rod stayed lodged in its throat as Striker let go, falling to the sand as the beast teetered over him. He rolled on his side and came to his feet as the worm lunged in the direction of his attack, its open mouth gulping for air.

He dived toward it and pulled out his rod, calculating another strike. The sandworm retreated, disappearing into the hole. Before he could attack again, it tunneled through the deep sand, stirring up dust and leaving a foul stench in its wake.

Striker shook his head and let the adrenalin ride through his body until it dispersed. It felt good to finally stab one of the monsters. Triumph soared in his chest, yet he reminded himself he might not be as lucky next time.

Had the young woman made it out in time? He hoped the raiders hadn't caught her. If they'd found her, there'd be no hope of rescue. At least not by his one-man show.

Securing the metal rod to his pack, he raced in the direction he'd last seen her.

...

Barliss' anger radiated off his body like rays from a newborn sun. Underneath his lieutenant's hat, the gel on his sleek, blond hair practically melted. He clenched his teeth together until his jaw hurt and watched out of the main sight panel on the bridge as the *New*

Dawn entered the atmosphere of Sahara 354.

His fiancée's attentions had all been a charade. He, of all people, should have known. There'd been so many mornings of coy smiles over coffee and afternoon walks on the starboard viewing decks. She'd played the game like an expert craftsman, so well she'd led them all to believe she was the model Lifer, the woman others looked up to, and the perfect future mate.

Barliss felt cheated. He hadn't spent years of doing favors and manipulating the system for a runaway bride. She was a key part of his plans for his future, and he wasn't going to let her get away.

Barliss' collar buzzed. He cleared his throat and pressed his lapel pin. "Yes."

"We've located the last coordinates of the escape pod, sir. The commander is preparing the search and rescue crews. He's put you in charge of the first landing party."

"Excellent. I'll be down on the landing decks shortly."

Barliss moved to shut off the communication but the subordinate's voice came on again, full of kindness and sympathy. "And, sir, I like to offer my deepest apologies. I'm sure it's just a misunderstanding."

"It's none of your business," Barliss growled. "Just do your job and let me do mine."

There was a moment of silence before the young man replied, his voice empty of emotion. "Yes, sir."

Barliss switched off his lapel pin so hard, he pinched the skin of his fingers. He changed into his camouflaged combat uniform, then sleeked back his wavy hair and rubbed a radiation-blocking lotion into the hard ridges of his face. He packed his laser gun, a tracking device, and an ultrasonic tranquilizer ray, setting the power to optimum. He stormed out of his room and headed for the docking bay.

The members of the search and rescue team had already belted themselves in their seats on the retrieval vessel when Barliss arrived on the loading dock. A hoverchair, with a white head poking out from its top, buzzed near the operations tower. Commander Gearhardt himself was surveying the operation. Panic and excitement rose in Barliss' throat, and he swallowed it down. Sequestered in the control console for months on end, the commander rarely attended functions. The task of unplugging the various tubes and wires connecting his brain to the mainframe computer took two hours and three medics.

Barliss approached the wispy-haired man in reverence, trying not to stare at his hoverchair or the tiny input holes drilled into his forehead. His skin looked as thin as rice paper and as white as a bride's dress. The man was of the third generation, the grandchild of the founding colonizers.

"Commander Gearhardt." Barliss bowed so low, his lips could have kissed the floor. "My thanks for your help in this matter."

The commander gestured for him to rise. "My dear, loyal Lieutenant Barliss. You have worked diligently these past months, and you will be rewarded. You do not deserve to suffer from another's transgressions."

Barliss stifled a smile, attempting to look modest. Finally, some recognition and assurance this awful turn of events wasn't his fault. These sentiments, coming from the commander, of all people, made him feel as though he'd graduated into sainthood.

The commander reached forward from his chair to put a veined hand on Barliss' shoulder. "This is the second one in a year, Lieutenant. Their impulsive, self-destructive actions trouble me. We're going to have to take extra caution in the future. We're losing too much of our gene pool."

"Yes, sir. I'll see to that personally."

"I'm sure you will." The commander's thin lips pulled in a wiry smile. Barliss feared the ancient man's fragile skin would tear.

"Thank you, Commander. I won't rest until she's found."

The commander pulled a tiny lever near his wrist, and the hoverchair turned. "I've given you the best men the *New Dawn* has produced. I'll be watching your progress."

"I hope you do, Commander." Barliss waited until the hoverchair disappeared in the elevator shaft before he walked up the ramp to board the small retrieval vessel. The crew members watched him with anxious eyes, some with fear stretched taut in their faces. For many of them, this was the first time in their lives they'd left the ship. It was like severing an umbilical cord. Barliss relished in their weaknesses, feeding off their dread.

He smoothed his uniform and addressed the team, projecting

his voice as far as he could, making it echo in the far reaches of the hull. "My fellow Lifers, we are the keepers of humanity's history and the preservers of its future. We transport the last remnants of a once great and mighty civilization. Our cargo is integral to the survival of our species. We carry our memories, our technologies and, most importantly, our genetic code."

Barliss watched their faces, gauging their reactions. He'd struck a vital chord with his words. Some of the men's fear had turned to anger and determination. Resolution shined in their eyes.

Barliss continued, delivering the pitch that would send them searching like a cleaning droid after a puddle of milk. "Aries Ryder's disappearance threatens the success of our mission. With an ever-dwindling gene pool, we cannot carry on the diversity of our species. Whole genetic strands will be lost. Our mission is to locate Aries Ryder, and I want her alive and well." He stared them down. "You have my permission to shoot anything that gets in your way."

Chapter Four
Tiff's Regret

"Don't get in my way if you want to keep that hand, pirate!"

Tiff elbowed a burly hulk of a man as he reached for the last bent fork. The hulk grinned, yellow teeth poking out of his hairy beard. His breath reeked of moonshine. "Easy now, pretty pixie, or do you want to start a fight?"

She tilted her head, licking her lips, and flashed him a half smile. While he leaned in, enchanted, she puckered her lips. Then she pilfered the fork, disappearing into line before he could even think about what kind of fight she'd suggested.

A chain of metallic trays lined up before Tiff as she took her spot. She snatched a cracked plastic cup and examined the sides, wondering if it would hold any liquid. The line moved ahead of her, and she clutched the edges of the scratched tray and prepared to step forward. In Outpost Omega, if you snoozed, you ended up as the recycled food.

Drifter peered over her shoulder, his brown eyes roving down the line. Standing a foot taller than she did, he could spot the evening meal well before she laid eyes on the conveyor belts. "Looks like gray sludge again."

Tiff put a hand on her hip, trying to look as though the bad news didn't bother her. She hadn't expected anything better, but deep down, she knew the man-made space station, floating in the middle of nowhere, and its substandard way of life was wearing her thin, chafing at her skin like a pair of boots two sizes too small. "They'll never get the food generators working like they used to."

Drifter grinned, and his crooked nose wrinkled. "We're getting outta here, sweetheart. We'll find Refuge someday, just like I promised."

Tiff fought the need to roll her eyes and bit back a clever retort. She'd had enough of his broken-record phrases these past five years, enough to make her wonder if she'd made the right decision leaving Striker behind.

The line moved ahead and a wiry hag of a woman pushed a bowl of green-gray oatmeal-like slush toward her. Tiff snatched it up before the person next to her could blink an eye. She kept her knife secured in her thigh-high boot, but no one fought her for the gruel this time. With one hand securing her bowl, she positioned her damaged cup under a spout and pushed the button for water on the keypad on the wall. As rusty-colored liquid sputtered out, she leaned against the metal structure of the water dispenser and watched as Drifter grabbed a bowl of gruel for himself.

They settled down next to the heat conductor. The spaceport had an arctic chill. Ice formed on the ventilator shafts, making it impossible to ever feel comfortable. While she lay in bed, her breath blew out in a hazy mist. Compared to the deep space around it, though, it was a steamy, warm bubble of delight.

Tiff hid a shiver. Weakness of any kind couldn't be revealed, which was why she kept her expression hard and her hair short, needing to blend in with the men. Try as she might, she couldn't hide the girlishness in her features. With her dark-rimmed eyes, spiky hair, and small, pointy nose, she looked like a forest fairy gone Goth. Her black eyeliner hid the fear in her eyes and warned others not to come too close.

The conditions on Outpost Omega worsened each day. With malnourished orphans roaming the streets alongside rats the size of small dogs, another epidemic could sweep through any day. Just thinking about it made her anxious.

The slop in her bowl cooled fast. Her spoon jammed in the gruel, and she let it stick out like a flagpole on old Earth's moon.

"Don't say it." Drifter peered through strings of long, greasy hair.

"I already know what you're thinking."

Tiff tried to stir her meal, but the sludge had already solidified. "I wasn't thinking anything."

"We'll find the map and decode it. I've got Reckon on it. He thinks today will be the lucky day."

"Right." Tiff took a quick mouthful of water. Gulping was the best way to drink the liquid without experiencing the acid aftertaste as it went down. "And while Reckon works on it, we're stuck here, eating who-knows-what recycled waste while our bodies rot inside-out."

"I told you, he'll find it. He's the best hacker in this whole station. He's good with puzzles and thinks the same way Striker does."

"Did you promise him a ride to Refuge as well?"

"I had to, but we'll see if we can't leave him behind."

"I don't like the look of him. His weasel eyes follow me too close." She flexed her leg muscle, feeling the reassurance of the knife's hard metal.

"Hey, babe, you know I take care of you."

Tiff swallowed her scoffing along with her acrid water. Because of him, they were stranded here, the coordinates for an uncharted, private paradise an arm's reach away and forever unobtainable. She knew he'd be angry, but she had to try once more. "If we go back to the desert and rescue Striker, we could make him decode the map."

"No!" Drifter pounded the table with his fist, making their plastic cups rattle. In the clamor around them, the sound was but a pin drop. Still, Tiff cringed.

"I don't want to hear that man's name ever again, you hear?"

Tiff didn't move. She couldn't acknowledge his statement, or she'd be forced to let Striker go, her hope along with it.

Drifter's voice grew calmer. "You know as well as I do he wanted to pack our ship full with everyone on this godforsaken station. If we bring the masses, it'll turn into another Earth gone wrong."

Tiff looked away, watching a young girl steal a man's coat while he slept. Probably another runaway from the orphanage, trying to make her way in their screwed-up world. The hungry kids were Striker's greatest weakness. He'd given away so much of his fortune trying to keep them alive. Striker's soft side irked her as much as it got to Drifter.

His philanthropy would only lead to their ruin. That's why she'd helped Drifter take charge, betraying Striker's trust. Drifter could make the hard decisions when Striker would be too generous.

"Besides, what makes you think he's still alive?" Drifter asked, eyeing her suspiciously.

Tiff met his gaze without guilt. "I just know."

Drifter's fist clenched, and she glimpsed a hint of jealousy in his dark, shifty eyes. He opened his mouth to speak, but a brawl erupted behind them, flinging gruel through the air. Tiff ducked and rolled under the table. She heard people grunting in a fistfight. Someone threw a man on top of the table, sending her cup and bowl to the floor. They needed to find an escape route before it turned into a laser fight.

Drifter caught her leg. "Come on, this way." She crawled underneath the benches, following his dark boots. They made their way across the cafeteria. Her hands and knees slopped through puddles of dirty water, gruel, and oil from the leaky machinery above them. Dirty clothes could be cleaned, but laser holes couldn't.

Tiff followed Drifter to a loading shaft. With one look at the chaos behind her, she reached up and closed the metal grate of the lift. He pushed the exit button on the keypad and they traveled down the elevator toward their docked ship, the war cries fading above them.

Drifter adjusted his belt, a strap of genuine leather looted from a stash of Earth antiques. Soon he'd have to sell that as well, if they were ever going to buy enough fuel to make it out of here. "You didn't eat anything, Tiff."

"I wasn't hungry."

The door beeped, signaling the docking bay, and they stepped onto the promenade. Lined with glass on all sides, the walkway of glinting stars led to the docked spaceships. Although the corridor sparkled like a perpetual midnight sky, it revealed the endless void surrounding Tiff, making prickles run down her spine each time she crossed it.

As they turned the corner, a man ran toward them, boots clinking on the chrome floor of the walkway. His tattered coat flapped in his wake like old flags of lost countries.

The hairs on Tiff's neck rose. She grabbed Drifter's hand. "It's Reckon."

"He's found something."

Tiff reined in a rising thread of hope that maybe she'd chosen wisely, after all.

The gnarly man reached them, halfway to the ship. As he gasped for breath, Tiff noticed a gaping hole in one of his yellowed teeth. He'd probably sold the gold incisor.

"Hey ya, Drifter." His marble eye stared askew while his good eye leered at Tiff. He wiped back his scraggly gray hair. "I've got news!"

Drifter clasped his arm. "You found the map?"

"You bet I did. Hidden in the engine room, beneath the incinerator."

Drifter whooped, his voice echoing off the thick glass and down the corridor.

Tiff squeezed his arm, warning him not to bring any unwanted attention. She looked Reckon up and down skeptically. "Can you decode it?"

The old man's good eye strayed to her legs. "Well, it's pretty mixed up. It'll take more time, which means more money and more supplies."

Tiff stepped forward, grabbing the collar of his tattered cloak. "We've already given you what we have."

"Hold it, Tiff." Drifter pried her fingers off Reckon and pulled her back. "The man's good. You have to give him that. We won't need it where we're going." He elbowed the old man and the two of them laughed.

Tiff didn't get any humor out of the situation. Finding a way out was too good to believe, and when something didn't add up right, she was hard to convince. She'd been burned too many times.

"I'll show ya." Reckon ambled toward the ship.

"Come on." Drifter pulled her along in Reckon's smelly wake. "Let's go back to the *Morphic Marauder* and celebrate."

Tiff would only truly celebrate when they stood on real green grass with a glowing sun above. Only then would she feel safe. Happiness was another matter altogether. She'd lost her chance at that when she'd left Striker behind on Sahara 354.

Safety was all she wanted now, and she couldn't decide if Drifter and Reckon were helping her or standing in her way.

...

The *New Dawn* loomed in Aries' dreams, proving she could never truly be rid of it, as if it were imprinted in the marrow of her bones. Much like a mother's womb, the metal hull nourished and comforted its cargo. Yet inside its confines, Aries could never grow to her full potential. In her dream, dangling moss brushed through her hair as she walked through blooming pear trees. Their soft scent filled her lungs, triggering impossible memories of a bygone time.

The iridescent lights overhead made Tria's hair flow like liquid gold. She was easy to follow among all the verdant leaves. Aries ducked underneath a vine of grapes and stepped over an upturned root. Tria headed for the tomato patch. If they were caught with the ripe scent of freshly grown vegetables on their jumpsuits, they'd both be in a heap of trouble.

"Tria, we can't go too far."

"You're the one that dared me to spy on the commander." Tria flashed a mischievous smile.

"I wasn't serious." Aries bit her lip nervously. Tria was committed to fulfilling the dare. Why had Aries even challenged Tria? Because she, too, was curious about the old man, the one they said had known the first colonists, the one so old he needed the help of the mainframe to keep his body alive, coexisting with the ship in a weird, symbiotic relationship.

"Come on," Tria called. "Are you coming or not?"

Aries had passed the point of no return. If she went back, she'd surely bump into the procession as the commander led the new bio team through crop fertilization techniques. She'd be better off hiding in the apple grove.

She caught up to Tria just as her friend ducked behind a tangle of browning branches and leaves, dying plants biochemists had shoved into the corner for fertilization. "Back here."

Aries stepped through the compost, the earth feeling strange and squishy underneath her boots. Adventures like this filled her heart with nervous excitement and enriched her imagination, two things the community frowned upon.

Her friend stuck out an arm and pulled her into the overgrowth. Aries saw a red skin poking out of Tria's pocket.

"You stole a tomato." Aries' eyes widened in shock. This little rebellion had gone too far.

"So?" Tria pulled it out of her pocket and took a bite. "It's just a tomato. It's not like I'm a space pirate or anything."

Even the smallest offense made Aries uncomfortable, but her friend did have a point. The space pirates stole entire ships. They'd even taken over the last working space station. A tomato was small beans compared to that.

"I wish I could live in here." Aries settled on a log, daydreaming about the past. She peered out from between the leaves. "I bet this was what it was like."

"You mean on old Earth?" Tria frowned. "It's all barren, and you'd die of radiation poisoning in a day."

"No, silly. I meant before all the wars. When there was peace." Her words sounded wistful, and she placed a strand of hair behind her ear sheepishly.

"Humph." Tria scoffed at the notion of humans living peacefully together. Aries should know. They'd shared the same history class for three years. Tria's essays were all about the sinful nature of man, as dictated by the Guide. She wondered how much of it her friend really believed and how much she spouted to pass the tests. Aries settled into silence on her share of the log.

Tria spoke with more compassion. "Well, maybe you'll test high for bio skills."

"Nope." Aries sighed, crumpling a brittle leaf between her fingers. "I've already shown promise in technical engineering."

"Me, too."

Tria surprised her. Aries chewed on her words, thinking about their futures. The thought that Tria would be with her made the idea of working in life-support systems more bearable. She smiled and patted her friend's arm. "Looks like we'll be working together, huh?"

"Yeah." Tria looked away, as if she didn't believe it. Aries wanted to ask why, but they heard voices from the far end of the bio-dome.

"Shh." Tria put a finger to her lips. "The commander's coming." Her eyes held a spark of curiosity and something more, a defiance which scared Aries.

A small group of people dressed in the blanched-out uniforms of bio-engineers paraded through the main aisle of the bio-dome. To Aries, they looked like walking test tubes among all the natural vermilion and russet tones of the foliage. All men with graying hair, they were two or three generations older than she and Tria, and the main reason why she'd never get to work in the bio-dome. Another ten years would pass before their jobs became available, and by then, she'd already be assigned. She wished the group would return to the upper decks and stop intruding in her fantasy land.

"Look, over there." Tria pointed to the far end of the assembly. The commander sat in his hoverchair like a king on a throne, his arms and fingers spread over the keyboards in the armrests, as if he could feel every movement of the ship at his fingertips.

"How'd you know he was coming down here today?" Aries held down a branch to get a better look.

"I overrode the information database." Tria shrugged as if it had been as easy as zipping up her jumpsuit.

"Whoa." Tria's computer skills impressed her. Making a mental note to ask Tria to teach her someday, Aries shifted the branch to get a direct view of the commander. "This is a lot closer than we can get at the assemblies."

Tria smiled. "You bet."

"Do you think he's really over 300 years old?"

"How old he is doesn't matter." Tria's eyes turned frosty. "What I wonder is if he's really the prophet leading us to paradise that everyone boasts of, or just another ordinary old man."

"Tria!"

Her friend stuck her nose in the air. "I want to live my life my own way, and no old man is going to tell me what to do, I don't care if he's 300, or chosen by the Guide, or the King of the Universe."

Tria's heresy stung Aries' composure. No one ever questioned the mission. They were supposed to pass on the genetic line in order for their descendants to colonize Paradise 21. But what if they had a choice of how to live, and where? A whole new dimension of thinking opened to her, a place both frightening and exhilarating. Just as she parted her lips to respond, the chair turned in their direction and both girls gasped, crouching down on all fours.

Aries peeked out from underneath a branch. The commander stared in their direction, his distant, pale-blue eyes focusing on their position. Aries thought she'd melt on the spot, becoming part of the primordial sludge the dying foliage withered into. She thought for certain he'd expose them. And punish them.

The commander paused, his chair floating in midair. Instead of showing anger, his face turned placid and calculating, as if he made a note of them in his mind. With only a few clicks on his touchscreen, he turned away and continued to instruct the bio team.

Tria let out her breath. "That was close."

"What did you mean about him being an ordinary man?" Aries' eyes were still glued to the commander's white head.

"It doesn't matter." Tria waved her hand. "Paradise 21 is another 200 years away. We're not going to be around to see it, anyway."

...

Aries opened her eyes to royal-blue light and reflective glass. She wondered if she'd truly awakened from her dream, because it looked like she was lying in a giant sapphire. The sterile atmosphere reminded her of the *New Dawn*, and a streak of panic shot through her arms and legs. Sitting up, she whipped her head around, expecting Barliss' condemning eyes.

Tubes and wires ran across the walls of the chamber. Panels with unidentifiable symbols pulsed in and out like a sleeping heartbeat. Aries stood up slowly, feeling dizzy and nauseous, and stared at the ornate hieroglyphs, trying to make sense of the shapes. Although she was well-versed in many of the world's extinct languages, the symbols were nothing she'd seen before. This was definitely not the *New Dawn*.

Was it the work of the lizard men? Aries ran her fingertips along the smooth, glass-like walls. The panels throbbed with light at her touch. This technology was too sophisticated to be built by their hands. Had she been taken by an alien race, unknown to humankind? Out of the thousands of scout ships that had scoured the galaxy as Earth had withered, none had found any sign of intelligent life beyond primitive indigenous species.

Someone had put her here and allowed her to roam free. There was no door to the chamber, only a threshold of shadows. Aries searched for a weapon. She'd lost her pocketknife in the fight with the lizard men. The only device she had was the locator from the *New Dawn*, stuck in her arm. The weight of the energy cell felt reassuring in her pocket. A tiny voice told her she could plug it back in. They'd come get her in an instant.

No. Then this whole trip would be for naught.

Aries chanced hesitant steps forward, staying near the wall. The corridor outside the chamber was dim, lit at intervals by the blue, pulsing light. She heard a crash of metal down the passageway to the right and cringed against the cool wall. If she wanted to hail the *New Dawn*, now would be the time. But Barliss would never give her a second chance to escape. She'd be stuck under his control for life. Aries stiffened her resolve and headed toward the direction of the crash. She'd rather be a slave to aliens than a slave to him.

Movement around the corner cast shadows on the gleaming walls. Someone or something shuffled across an adjoining corridor. Aries tried to make sense of the shadows, but whoever it was, they were either crouched down or three feet tall. She could hear tiny clicking noises and couldn't tell if it was the being's actions or its speech. If anything, it didn't seem very threatening. Whatever it was, it had saved her from the desert elements, the scaly lizards, and the sandworm.

Cautiously, she peeked around the corner. A humanoid wearing a long black cloak and a welding mask the size of a small shield crouched over an open panel, the wires spewing electric sparks. The humanoid worked with small, lighted tools, shooting tiny lasers into the circuit board. Aries tried to focus her eyes beyond the sparks, but the light diffused any semblance of what lurked behind the mask. The humanoid was too broad to be one of the lizard men from the desert. She checked to see if its fingers had three prongs, but gloves covered the hands.

Suddenly, her pocket started to beep. Aries clutched her side, realizing she still carried her life-form locator and the device had picked up the presence of the humanoid crouched before her. She thrust her hand in her pocket to turn it off, but it was too late. The humanoid rose from its work, standing a foot taller than she was. It stepped toward her, wielding the tools.

She lost her balance and stumbled backward. The humanoid towered over her, a dark blot framed in sparks. Slipping on the slick floor, she pushed back on her hands.

The humanoid held up a hand as if to stall her, and she scrambled up and turned to run.

"Wait!"

Aries froze, then turned slowly. The figure dropped the tools, metal clanking on the floor, and pulled off his mask. He was a human, with a head of wavy jet-black hair, smoky gray-green eyes, and a face that would have looked like an ancient Grecian sculpture if it weren't darkened by stubble.

Aries blinked, trying to make sense of the situation. She'd expected an ugly space invader and gotten a handsome Outlander instead. He looked different than all the men on the *New Dawn*. His skin shone like bronze, much darker than the skin of her fellow Lifers.

"You're not an alien," she said, trying not to sound like a child, as if he'd tried to trick her with a mask.

"That's right." He seemed to find her accusation amusing, because his lips curled in a sly smile. "Sorry to disappoint."

Aries ignored his apology. It was obviously insincere. Besides, he didn't disappoint in the least. "What are you doing on this ship?"

"I should ask you what you were doing parading through the desert with no food or water."

"I had a sufficient amount of supplies to last for days before those…lizard men surrounded me and stole my backpack."

The man nodded as if he sympathized. "Ah, the raiders. They'll steal everything you've got and eat you for breakfast if you're not careful."

Aries thought back to when the creatures had dragged her toward their tunnels. They'd been planning to eat her? She shivered.

"You're lucky to be alive."

She squinted her eyes. "Who are you?"

The man extended his hand. "The name's Striker."

Aries reached out and let his hand envelop hers. His fingers were rough and warm to the touch. Bizarrely, the skin felt more like hardened leather. How did a man's hands get that way?

"And you are?" he prompted her.

"Aries Ryder."

"Well, Aries, how is it you came to be in this little slice of heaven?"

Aries looked away. "My escape pod crashed." She wasn't about to share all of the details. He might try to contact the *New Dawn*, if he didn't like living on this desert planet.

"What happened to your mother ship?"

She thought about all the possible demises of a deep space transport vessels, things like asteroids, a loss of fuel, or a busted engine, but couldn't bring herself to make anything up. He looked like the kind of guy who would want to fix any problem she posed. "The ship is fine. Everyone on board is doing peachy."

Surprise flashed across Striker's face. "Won't they come looking for you?" He nodded at her arm. "That looks like some kind of locator device."

Aries frowned and crossed her arms over her chest. "It is. If I can't get rid of it, they'll come. I know it for a fact."

Excitement flashed in his features. "Great. We have to get you back out on the surface so they can find you."

Her heart skidded. "What do you mean, back on the surface? Isn't this a spaceship?"

Striker looked amused. "You think this ancient hunk of junk is flying right now, as we speak?"

He laughed, but Aries could only stand, dumbfounded.

"This ship crashed here years ago. It's buried underneath several feet of sand," he explained.

Aries' heart dropped to her stomach. "You mean to tell me we're still on Sahara 354?"

"Yup."

"We're not in space, flying away?"

"That's right. We'd better get you up there before your shipmates think you're dead."

He moved to take her arm, but Aries stepped back and put up her hands defensively. "No, you don't understand. I crashed here *on purpose*. To get away from them."

Striker shook his head as if to rid his ears of her words. "Hold on, little lady. You're saying you left your cozy spaceship and crashed on this godforsaken planet *intentionally?*"

Aries looked down. "Yes."

Striker folded his arms across his chest. "Then, there's no hope for saving you. You really are crazy."

"Hey, that's not fair."

"I hate to tell you this, but with the sand monsters, the raiders, the desert heat and no water for miles on end, this isn't the place to settle down and raise a family."

"That's exactly what I don't want. That's what I'm running from."

Her confession seemed to leave Striker astonished. He stood there, mute and looking confused, with his lips parted in an unspoken question.

"You can't turn me over to them," she begged. "You don't understand what it's like. You can't imagine how awful it is, how life is nothing but obedience, what it's like to only be valued for your DNA." She turned away, ready to escape yet another ship.

"Hold on and calm down." He grasped her arm before she could walk away. "Exactly who are you? What kind of ship did you abandon? I'm all ears."

Aries took a deep breath and recited the words directly from the Guide. "I'm a Lifer: a sixth generation colonist bequeathed to a computer-designated mate to propagate the species for the next generation, furthering our bloodlines until the colony reaches a paradise planet 200 years away."

"You're telling me you're from one of those wacko communal transport ships, running from an arranged marriage?"

"Yes." She spat out her words. "Any wasteland of a planet is better than that."

Striker's face softened, his dark brows rising. "Jeez, why didn't you tell me that in the first place? Although you picked one hell of a planet to land on, I get it."

"So you're not going to turn me in?"

Striker waved her fear off like swatting a fly. "Nah."

She sighed and let her shoulders sag. At least someone was on her side. No one had shared her burden, ever. She hadn't had anyone to confide in, not since Tria had died.

He stepped very close to her, his eyes looking directly into hers. "But are you sure this is what you want?"

It was the first time anyone had ever asked what she wanted. She could barely believe it.

Aries stared right into his gaze, her face inches from his. She'd never leaned that close to a man on purpose, but his expression drew her in. "More certain than anything else that's ever happened in my life."

Striker paused as if he considered closing the distance between them. Aries' heart quickened. She felt his warm breath on her lips. Would he kiss her like the Lifers did at the end of the wedding ceremony? Excitement fluttered in her chest like a thousand butterflies startled into flight.

Striker blinked and gestured down the passageway to the chamber where she'd slept. "Come on, I'll find a way to get that locator off without triggering an alarm."

Chapter Five
Revenge

Barliss hated the heat. Heat made him sweat, and sweat was seen as a sign of weakness among Lifers. He couldn't allow his lower officers to see his vulnerability.

His father's voice resonated in his head. "Suck in your gut and pull up your pants. A general never shows signs of slovenliness in front of his troops." He'd always seemed to disappoint the old man, as if Barliss were responsible for his recessive genes.

Barliss stiffened, brushing a grain of sand from his camouflaged uniform. He'd gotten the last laugh and proven his old man wrong. Even though his father was genetically superior, he'd never made it as far up the chain of command as Barliss already had. Barliss had tested low for emotional intelligence, but he'd climbed farther in forty years than his father had in sixty. While he received direct orders from the commander, his father drowned in the bureaucracy, filing life-system reports.

Barliss shook his head in disgust. Although the old man loyally followed the Guide, he didn't have the stomach for politics. He chose poorly with his colleagues and allies. Barliss knew the type of people to gravitate toward: not the do-gooders trying to make the colony a better place, but to those with a penchant for power. He'd become their right-hand man, and they'd rewarded him for it.

Ironically, his greatest prize, Aries Ryder, had developed into his biggest embarrassment. The bitterness tasted sour on his tongue. Barliss spat onto the ground. He wished he could curse the entire desert in a similar fashion.

The squadron leader approached as the search and rescue team pegged tents into the sand. Barliss greeted him formally with a salute. "Awaiting your report, Skyman."

The man looked a generation younger than he was, with his eyes still full of naivety. Although his inexperience irked Barliss, at least this skyman would be easy to control. "Our scanners show pieces of metal on the horizon, sir."

Eagerness rippled through him. "Which direction?"

"Just beyond those dunes."

"Any sign of the locator?"

The subordinate flinched. "No, Lieutenant. The scattered metal is at the exact coordinates last sent from Miss Ryder's locator, though."

Barliss glanced at the man's identification tag. "Very well, Smith. Inform the search teams. We'll set out on an expedition immediately."

"Yes, sir."

Smith darted to the men propping up tents. The heat sizzled around Barliss. His impatience grew like a bad infection as he waited for Smith to return. Each second that passed gave Aries more time to escape. He walked in his usual commanding stride to the tents and spied Smith helping three others hold the nylon tarp down with pegs.

"Smith?"

He looked up while holding the nylon down. "Yes, sir."

Barliss growled under his breath. "I ordered you to assemble a rescue team."

"Copy, sir. As per regulation 658, section B, we must set up these operations tents first to establish a safe base camp for the rescue team."

"No, we don't." He spoke as if talking to a three-year-old. "You need to get off your ass and check out those coordinates!"

"What about the team, sir?"

"They can set up the tents when we get back. They'll just have to tough it out for now. No one's going to die of sunburn." At least not right away. Skin cancer took time to develop, and he'd have Aries before any of his team needed a break.

His voice rumbled in his chest. "Get going!"

"Yes, sir." As Smith trotted off, Barliss gazed over the sand dunes at the hazy horizon. Putting the subordinate in his place pacified him somewhat, but he couldn't shake the feeling Aries had outwitted him. More and more, he found himself craving revenge. Once he found her, he'd teach her not to run away. He'd show her who had the power in their relationship.

Moments later, a hovercraft buzzed behind him. On his way to inform the teams, the skyman had sent the search and rescue vessel his way, complete with supplies. It was none too soon. Barliss didn't want to be left alone with his brooding thoughts.

The pilot saluted him as he stood on the open-air deck of the hovercraft, awaiting further orders.

Smith trudged over the sand, carrying a backpack overflowing with water bottles, batteries and gadgets. "I trust everything is in order, sir?"

Barliss noted the appropriate bootlicking in Smith's tone. The skyman was scrambling to make up for his earlier mistake, yet if he truly wanted the lieutenant's favor, he should have followed his orders in the first place. Was he really the best of what the *New Dawn* could offer?

Smith gestured to the pilot. "Langston's going to fly us to the location, sir."

"Very well." Barliss nodded, slight as a blink of an eye. "Let's get moving."

The hovercraft lifted, spreading waves of sand out like a fan. Barliss held on tightly as the vessel propelled itself forward. Blowing sand stung his freshly shaven face as they moved at high speed, but he ignored the pain as he searched the horizon.

It took a sizzling fifteen minutes to reach the site of the strewn metal. Except for the presence of the debris, the terrain looked like the hovercraft hadn't gone anywhere. Everything on the hellish planet looked the same.

Smith hopped out first, whipping out his metal detector to prove his findings. Barliss was second on the ground. His boots sunk in the sand as he gained his footing. The pilot stayed in the hovercraft. Langston backed away from the site to reduce the spray of sand.

"Right here, sir." Smith waved the device over a heap of orange granules. The metal detector beeped.

Barliss nodded, but not in approval, only as a command. "Check it out."

Smith got down on his hands and knees and dug into the mound. He pulled up a rectangular metal box filled with grit. Turning it upside down, he poured out the sand, then dusted off the cover panel.

"It's a water locator, sir. One of ours."

Barliss stumbled over, cursing as the sand sucked at the soles of his boots. "How do you know?"

"It's inscribed with our symbol, sir."

Barliss leaned down and ran his fingers over the scratched metal. Indeed, the symbol of the seventeenth-century ship was as clear as the replica on his lieutenant's lapel pin and the embroidered insignia on the right breast of his uniform. It was one of their devices, and it was wrecked beyond repair.

"We still haven't found her locator, sir." Smith spoke in a soft voice.

Barliss turned away, clutching the broken metal in his hand. "Keep looking, Skyman. I'm going to get water."

"Yes, sir."

Barliss approached the hovercraft, feeling as though the sand sucked at each step he took. The pull of gravity and the heat threatened his composure, and he fought them like an enemy, pushing his boots through the sand.

Without warning, the sand erupted at his feet like fireworks. Six creatures leaped from the soil and surrounded him and Smith, blocking off their path to the hovercraft.

"Sir," Smith's voice wavered.

"Stay still."

As the creatures held up their spears, Barliss reached for the laser in the holster at his side. He'd had enough of this godforsaken planet, a planet that exposed his weaknesses and had swallowed his bride-to-be whole.

"We shouldn't interfere with the indigenous people." Smith recited the Guide's rule, as if Barliss weren't already an expert.

"Just shut up!"

As the leader came forward, Barliss drew his gun and fired, sending the creature sprawling backward into the sand. The others scrambled into their holes like rats, hissing a warning sound. As they retreated, Barliss kept shooting, downing three more for sport before the rest could get away.

Pleased with his aim, Barliss looked to Smith for accolades, but the man didn't seem to admire his conquest. He covered his head with both hands, wincing at the carnage. *Poor guy's got marshmallows for guts.*

Barliss walked over to the bodies sprawled in the sand. Triumph overpowered his heart. Kicking one over, he bent down to look at the creature he'd defeated with one click of the trigger.

Crude animal hide covered its face, except for the eyes, which were hidden behind some kind of bone mask. Barliss pulled the mask up, wiping his fingers on his pants as if the corpse were diseased. Black eyes framed in scales striped with vermilion and yellow stared blankly up at him. A two-pronged, purple-black tongue hung from its mouth, dangling between two ivory teeth, venom dripping at the tips.

"By god, these bastards are ugly." Barliss lifted his head away in disgust. As he began to turn back to the hovercraft, a glint of silver caught his eye. Tied around the creature's neck on a thin rope rested a diamond.

Barliss fell to his knees, the orange sand grinding into his navy uniform. It wasn't any diamond. He pushed aside the hides the creature was wearing to get a better look. The jewel was a five-karat, emerald-cut, champagne-colored diamond ring, framed by two gray pearls on either side. Barliss tore the crude string and held the ring up to catch the blazing sun. Unquestionably, he held his family heirloom in his fingertips, a ring that had been passed to him by his grandmother, from her grandmother before.

Only a day ago, the ring had claimed a place on Aries' third finger.

The brazen woman may have gotten herself killed. The need for revenge rose, choking him worse than the stinking sand of this desert planet.

...

"Ouch." Aries yanked her arm away from Striker.

Striker raised an eyebrow. "I can't help you if you keep squirming around." He put down the flurometric pliers and picked up the electromagnetic screwdriver.

"Why don't you fry the thing and be done with it?" Although Aries liked the feeling of her arm resting in Striker's large palm, she wanted the locator off her like a prisoner wanted to shed a protonic restraint.

"I have to be careful because it's rigged to alert the mainframe if the seal is broken. You don't want your shipmates joining us down here for coffee, do you?"

"No, I don't." Aries sighed. The thought of coffee appealed to her. She'd known once she climbed in the escape pod there'd be no more early morning cups of freshly brewed Joe. It had been a small price to pay for freedom. But if she didn't have to pay it…"You don't, by any chance, have coffee down here, do you?"

They were perched on rather large pedestals surrounding a white table that seemed to be made from a combination of ivory and glass. Aries stared at the smooth, shell-like walls. She hadn't thought there was much of anything on this ship until Striker had surprised her a few moments ago and pushed on a glass panel set in the wall. The glass had fallen back and a shelf had appeared with more mechanical devices. As if he didn't have enough tools to pry at her locator.

"Nope, although I'd enjoy some, too." There was a wistful gleam in his smoky eyes. He'd managed to break open the latch on the circuit board above her wrist. He poked around for the right circuit to fry.

"What is this place, anyway?"

Striker shrugged, his eyes never leaving the circuits. "I told you. Crashed spaceship."

"Who flew it? The writing doesn't look like any language I've ever seen. These…chairs, if that's what you call them, are too large for humans."

"Yeah, ironically, it's probably one of the greatest finds in the history of mankind. Too bad the owners are long gone."

Aries suddenly felt as though she was trespassing. She didn't want to be stuck in a battle between an Outlander and an alien race with technology far superior to her own. "How, exactly did you get this ship, and what did you do to the owners?"

Striker stopped fidgeting with the tools. He slid off the pedestal and walked toward one of the walls. After scratching a long line in the segment above his head with his fingernail, a panel the size of a window separated from the smooth surface and moved forward several inches. The panel flashed, pixels materializing in static fuzz. It was some type of screen, like the monitor of a computer, but more three-dimensional than anything humans made.

"I've accessed their memory cards. Here's what I found." Striker grinned, looking boyish and manly at the same time. "It will answer your questions while I figure out this locator."

He winked as he climbed on the pedestal beside her. Maybe he did enjoy her company? Turning her head to hide her warm cheeks, Aries watched the screen as the pixels took shape into misty wisps of white clouds.

The scene began to move, like a movie on the *New Dawn*, the camera apparently soaring above a world of rolling moss-green hills and dense forests. The air was clear and clean, unlike the smog-choked scenes of the dying Earth she'd seen in her classes. Crimson light filtered down from the clouds, illuminating patches of trees in a ruddy glow. As the scene continued, the greenery gave way to gleaming cathedral-type steeples, spiraling in silver-lined twists to prick the sunset-colored sky. The buildings were too thin and elongated to be human-made. She wondered what device had recorded this magnificent display as the aerial view descended to the alien city below, resting on the balcony of an impossibly high tower. Strings of white fabric reached toward the sky like strands of jellyfish, blowing in a light wind. The camera focused on the room inside, and it took a minute for the lens to react to the change in light.

"Wait until you see what they look like."

Striker's sudden comment made Aries jump as he brought her back to reality. Her gaze settled on him as he bent his head over his work. She noticed the way his hair curled at the base of his neck, and how the back of his shirt dropped enough for her to see the indent of his broad shoulder blades.

A flash of light brought her attention back to the screen. The tower room pulsed inside with the same sapphire light of the spaceship, illuminating smooth, blue-white walls, an ivory floor, and glass-like structures. A bed of feathers rested above an ivory platform carved with strange, geometric symbols. Aries squinted her eyes, trying to see further in. A lump squirmed in the middle of the plumes.

The camera, if that was what it was, focused on the bed. A white-haired head peered out of the feathers, flashing an opal-skinned face with pearlescent eyes. The creature twitched a slight nose, with flaring nostrils. Lips that looked like they'd been carved from a mollusk shell moved in an "o" shape.

Aries gasped. "Angels. They look like angels."

"Well, that's one way to see it. I always thought they looked more like mermaids with wings."

"They can fly?" The scene suddenly made more sense. It must have been taken by an alien gliding in the sky.

The creature in the bed radiated pale light, casting a luminescent glow through the room to the far reaches of the cavernous ceiling. The pulsing light weakened with each beat. Although its features were foreign to Aries, she could sense a great sadness accompanied by a weariness or fatigue.

"What's wrong with it?" She felt like a small child watching a tragic, age-old fairy tale. Part of her didn't want to know the end.

"Keep watching." Striker poked around with an electromagnetic screwdriver. "The memory-vision will tell you better than I can."

The creature raised an arm, long as an arrow, and pointed with branch-like fingers across the room. The tip of its finger, sharp as a pin and oily-white like the inside of a conch shell, shook slightly, as if from exhaustion or old age.

The vision turned, and the camera-holder paced the length of the room, past a hole in the ceiling filtering the diaphanous red sunlight. Nestled into impressions in the ivory floor were speckled eggs the size of a fat man's belly.

A hand much like the skinny-boned creature in the bed reached out and dusted off the top of the closest egg, sending motes of glitter shimmering in the pale rays of red sun.

"They won't hatch," Striker explained with a sigh. "I've seen hundreds of these visions, and they all show eggs left to gather dust."

"You mean their race is dying out?" All of a sudden, her situation seemed inconsequential. The injustice of her own pathetic lack of choices had consumed her, but the universe held tragedies much more profound. Here she was, running from her duty to maintain the propagation of her own species, when another race lay dying with no offspring.

"That's it, Aries. You're free."

Striker's words barely registered. Aries rubbed her wrist absentmindedly, still staring at the glistening eggs on the screen. The camera hadn't moved in several minutes. Perhaps the alien had placed it down by the eggs.

"Aries?"

She blinked back tears. How could she tell him the vision made her seem small and selfish? She shook her head, unable to speak.

Striker's voice was soft and emotional. "I'm sorry. I thought it would answer your questions, but instead it upset you."

"How long has this ship been stranded?"

Striker shrugged. "The bodies of the pilot and crew were mummified by the desert when I found the craft. The span of time could have been centuries, or millennia. I'm not sure."

"So that's it? That's the end of their race?"

"Maybe they found a planet where the eggs could hatch," Striker answered, as if he'd already thought the question through. "Maybe this ship is the only one that didn't make it."

"Or maybe it was their last hope."

He surprised her by taking her hand. "Come on. I've got to show you what the belly of the ship holds."

Chapter Six
Incubator

"What is it, Lieutenant?"

Barliss slipped the engagement ring in his pocket and turned back to Smith with a frown. "It's nothing. Ugly bastards, that's all."

If they had sufficient evidence of Aries' death, the commander would call off the mission. Barliss wasn't ready to come to terms with the fact she might get her way, even if that meant dying to avoid their ceremony, and he might never get revenge. This ring wasn't true evidence of her death. From what he knew of her test scores and reasoning skills, Aries wasn't an impulsive gambler. She would have planned ahead and come prepared. Heck, knowing now what kind of deception she was capable of, she might have sweet-talked these stupid lizard men into being her slaves.

Barliss promised himself he'd find her, dead or alive. He couldn't sleep at night, not knowing if she'd outsmarted him or perished of her own accord. He wasn't going to leave this filthy sand hole without her, even if it meant he had to drive his rescue team harder than they'd ever been driven before.

A wail erupted over the dunes like the high-pitched screech of the hovercraft's engines in overdrive. Except the planet had no technological devices. This noise had to be creature-made.

"Come on, Skyman. We've got to get going."

The pilot in the hovercraft looked up, only now realizing their search party had encountered native life-forms. Barliss curbed the urge to give him the finger before waving him over. He settled for a curt signal. The vessel's engines revved and it sped toward them.

Barliss grabbed Smith's arm and yanked him up. No one was going to die while he was on duty, not even a bleeding heart like Smith. He wanted the commander to see spectacular reports. Nothing else.

"What about the other metal readings, sir?"

Barliss silently cursed the man's lack of battle instincts. "We need to go back for reinforcements. Stronger weaponry. There's no telling what monstrosity made that sound."

As the hovercraft pulled alongside them, the ground burst open and the land vomited grit. A worm the size of a building broke through, raining sand on their shoulders, nearly burying Smith in the process.

"Come on." Barliss dragged Smith to the craft, hefting him up to the rim and throwing his feet over. As the worm swung its head down, he jumped, dodging the assault. Behind him, Langston fired a laser at its throat. The beast screeched again, whether in frustration or pain, Barliss didn't care. He took advantage of the beast's injury to jump into the hovercraft. "Go, go, go!"

"Yes, sir." Langston kicked the craft into optimum speed and they took off, churning up sand, which seemed to confuse the worm. They were meters away within minutes.

"Whoa." Smith finally found his tongue. "What with the sun, the lizards, and now these death worms, there's no way a person could survive here."

"Shut up, Skyman." Barliss was quick to correct him. "You forget as an engineer, Aries Ryder was trained to work in different environments under all sorts of pressures. You're overreacting, soldier."

He eyed Langston as the man drove the craft. The pilot didn't seem as fazed by the attack. Barliss ignored the stronger man and turned back to Smith. "It's a good thing I'm sending the report to the commander and not you, or we'd all be shipped out of here tomorrow, leaving a floundering young woman to fend for herself and abandoning a great part of our genetic DNA. You should be ashamed of yourself."

Smith's gaze fell to the floor. "Sorry, sir." His face flushed red.

Barliss gleaned no satisfaction from beating someone with no backbone. He sat back and watched the sun as it set on the horizon. Behind him the first sun began to rise, casting a strange yellow-red glow.

At camp, he'd dig up that old bottle of wheat beer brewed by his friends on the *New Dawn*, another perk of knowing the right people. Although it was his last one, he needed it. The situation with the sandworm had scraped too close to tragedy. He'd choose a new team tomorrow, hopefully a few men with spines.

···

Aries allowed Striker to guide her through the bowels of the alien ship, clutching his hand as if he were her lifeline. Which he was. Her entire existence rested on his survival skills and knowledge of Sahara 354. The corridors dimmed the farther they descended, as if the source of light, whatever that was, lost its potency. She wondered how it could still run at all after all of those years abandoned in the sand.

"Don't worry." Striker looked back and flashed a mischievous smile, reminding her of Tria. "I've been working on this ship for years now, studying how it operates. I know my way around it like a fish in a stream."

His analogy made her grin. The only fish she'd ever seen were in the containment aquaducts onboard the *New Dawn*. Striker used phrases from Earth as if he'd actually been there.

"Where'd you come from?" Aries suddenly yearned to learn more about him, to know who her savior really was. "How did you come to be trapped here on Sahara 354?"

"Now, that's a story." Striker stepped over a bunch of fallen cables and picked through the rubbish. He worked through the pile as he talked, throwing away some cables and pocketing others in his long black cloak. "I was exiled five years ago. My shipmates decided they'd be better without me. They stole my ship and left me here in this purgatory to rot, mutinous bastards."

"Exiled?" Aries put the pieces together. "You mean, there was a mutiny?"

"Yup." Striker shook his head in disgust. "Bad luck, if you ask me. That and the loyalty of pirates has gone to shit. Excuse my English. It's been awhile since I've talked to anyone, never mind a lady such as your—"

"Pirates?" Aries stepped back, looking at him from a new perspective. "You're a space pirate?" She put her hands on her hips, challenging him as if he'd told a lie.

Striker bowed like it was something to be proud of. "Born and raised."

Aries looked him up and down. Pirates were supposed to have inferior DNA. Left to die on old Earth, they'd rioted, stealing the last colony ships and overtaking the main space station. Striker didn't look inferior at all. In fact, he was gorgeous, skilled with tools, and possessed a worldly knowledge she couldn't come close to grasping. Barliss was far more flawed than this hunk standing in front of her.

"How'd you get ahead of the colony ship? We've been traveling for hundreds of years."

Striker had a glint in his eye. "Wormhole. Found it while I searched for a planet to shelter life."

He really must be a pirate, then. In an instant, he'd chased away all of her romantic notions. She was conspiring with a renegade! Her mind sped as she rethought her situation. Her repulsion must have shown clearly on her face.

"Oh, I see how it is." Striker threw a length of old cable down the corridor. It rattled to emphasize his words. "You colonists think you're the best and the brightest, only taking the select few with high test skills and ideal genetic code. If you had your choice, you wouldn't even associate with someone like me, someone whose ancestors were left behind to die of pollution and radiation poisoning. Sorry to disappoint you again. My forefathers had to do something. They had to find some way off that putrid rock. What were they going to do, lie down and rot?"

Aries recognized the validity of his logic. "Look, Striker, I'm sorry. You're the first person I've met who wasn't born on the *New Dawn*. It's hard to reconcile you with what they taught me. I mean, for one thing, they said pirates were all second-class riffraff with no moral code."

"Is that right?" He turned all his attention on her. "Saying everyone left behind was immoral kind of eases their guilt for abandoning their fellow man, doesn't it?"

"They didn't just say it. I heard the recorded transmissions myself, in my history class. Pirates overtook one of the central space stations and killed the guards. They severed all communication with the mainframes. My colony hasn't been contacted by another ship in the centuries since. For all we know, the *New Dawn* could be the last colonization ship left out there."

"Where else were they supposed to go? The planet was dead. The space station was the only place humans could live."

"I don't know. All I've been told is they look out for their own good."

He cocked his head. "This coming from a woman who turned her back on her people for her own freedom?"

It was a direct blow. Aries fell back against the wall with the truth of it. Her body prickled with shame and her face heated. She was more selfish than anyone. The Guide spoke the truth about maintaining genetic diversity, yet she'd endangered the future of the race by escaping, taking her unique DNA with her. How could she possibly judge the pirates?

A pang of guilt shot through her. This man, pirate that he was, had saved her from the desert and everything in it. She forced her eyes up to study his pained face. He looked far closer to the ideal man than any man aboard the *New Dawn*. Who were they to decide who should further the species? The first colonists had acted like God, choosing who would live and who would die. But Striker's ancestors hadn't died.

"Aries." Striker walked toward her. "I'm sorry. I've been alone all these years and I'm surprised I can still use my voice, never mind engage in polite conversation."

"No, you're right. I acted selfishly by abandoning them. Here I am, giving you grief when you saved my life." She put a hand to her head as if to ward away a fever. "I'm the one who's sorry. I'm still coming to grips with a lot of things."

"All I know is, desperate people are forced to take extreme measures. Listen, these colonists you describe sound like blowhards, if you ask me. Not only do they make you marry someone you don't want, but they won't let you live your own life. At least the pirates don't care whom you choose, or when you stay, or if you go. Now, I understand the colonists' rules are to further the species, but it's someone else's vision of the human race, not yours. That's my opinion."

He turned around and continued walking down the corridor. Aries watched him leave, wondering why his opinion of her mattered so much. Then she followed him.

His cloak fanned out around his black boots like a shadow. He must have heard her walking behind him, because he said, "A pirate's life can't be any worse than a stir-crazy colonist pilgrim's life."

Aries rolled her eyes. At least he could find humor in their situation. "We're not going to steal anything, are we?"

Striker glanced back and grinned. "Only an age-old ship from the dead."

The thought of stealing a ship from a dead alien species made Aries' skin prickle, like when she watched the caskets of the deceased Lifers shoot into space. Goosebumps blossomed on her body. She'd put her hair up in a bun because of the heat, and now the back of her neck felt naked and cold. She reached back behind her head and undid the pin, letting her hair fall protectively around her shoulders.

The goosebumps didn't go away.

The corridor spiraled down a central shaft, each level colder and darker than the one above. Striker had long, confident strides, and Aries had to jog to keep up, lest she be left behind in the shadows. They came to a glass door leading into a room nestled in the bottom of the ship.

Striker traced a dramatic arc of a symmetrical hieroglyph and the door opened, releasing a mist that pooled over their boots. His gaze traveled the contours of her head, as if he noticed she'd brought down her long hair, but he didn't comment on it. Instead, he gestured toward the door. "Ladies first."

Aries took a breath and walked in. The room was as long and wide as the ship, spanning the length of the main deck on the *New Dawn*. Pillars came down from the ceiling in rows, so many rows it looked like the columns from ancient Rome, only these structures were made of glass.

"I don't understand."

"Look closer."

Aries stepped toward the nearest column. Cosmic dust frosted the glass. She peered through the silver-white at a pale oval-tipped object lying inside. Aries wiped the dust from the case, shedding glitter on the floor.

"Oh, by the Guide." She pressed her fingers harder on the glass. "Are they alive?"

"I don't know." Striker shrugged, although there was nothing inconsequential in the gesture. "Probably not."

He bent over to take a look for himself, his wavy black hair brushing against her cheek. When he turned back to her, his eyes sparkled like a child at Christmas. "I know of a place to take them to see if they'll hatch."

Chapter Seven
Hidden Map

The tent flaps rustled in the breeze. Barliss guzzled his wheat beer, shifting his gaze around the desert camp. Men guarded all sides, but an attack over the sand didn't scare him. His eyes strayed to the sand underneath his feet. The big ones attacked from underground.

"Requesting entry."

Smith's voice startled him. He cursed his jumpy nerves and re-buttoned his shirt. Never could he look less than professional, even in the privacy of his own tent. He was the commander of this expedition, after all, and the commander was never off duty.

"Entry granted."

Smith pushed his way through the tent flaps and bowed. Redness flushed his face, and orange desert sand smeared his white uniform. "Lieutenant Barliss, I have news to report."

"Stand up, Skyman." Barliss waved impatiently. "Tell me what you've found."

Smith pulled a locator out of his pocket. "While I searched for signs of Miss Ryder's equipment, my devices picked up a signal for a mineral deposit." He handed him the locator. "There's a conglomeration of lithium under the plateau on the southern side of camp."

Barliss studied the readings, flicking back and forth between the numbers and a large blob of blue-black dominating the screen.

Currently, the *New Dawn*'s energy supplies were on conservation mode. The first few generations had eaten away at the provisions faster than predicted. The splotch on the locator represented enough lithium to ensure the people of the *New Dawn* could live comfortably for the remaining generations, until the ship reached Paradise 21.

"This is amazing." Barliss shook his head. "Probably the greatest find in all of the *New Dawn*'s history." His eyes darted back to Smith. "Have you told anyone of these readings?"

"No, sir." Smith held his head high. "I wanted to let you know first."

Barliss ejected the memory card of the locator and slipped it into his pocket before offering the device back to Smith. "Well done, Skyman. I'll see to it the commander is notified immediately."

"Yes, sir." Smith bowed. He waited at the tent flap, scratching his head awkwardly, as if he expected the card to be returned to him, or more accolades to come of his work. Barliss estimated he wouldn't push for the credit. Young enough to not challenge injustice, Smith didn't have the cunning to turn his efforts into a greater yield.

"That's all, Smith. Ready the team for the morning shift."

Smith hesitated before ducking out. In that moment, Barliss caught his eye and squinted a warning. The subordinate cowered. "Until tomorrow, sir."

As the tent flaps rustled back into place, Barliss smiled and pushed the hailing button on his communicator. He hid the bottle of wheat beer under his cot and straightened his uniform.

The late hours of night were settling in, and he was surprised to get an answering beep from the central station. Did Commander Gearhardt never sleep? Barliss turned on the monitor, and the commander's pale face glowed on the screen like a ghost. Wires ran from his forehead into the shadows in the control room, reminding Barliss of a spider resting in the middle of his web in the bio-dome.

"Lieutenant Barliss?"

"Yes, Commander. I have new information regarding the status of our operation."

"How diligent of you to contact me at this late hour to keep me updated."

Barliss wondered if he was being sarcastic. He cleared his throat.

"I'm always at your command."

"Right, right." The commander's words sounded faint, as if he'd fade away. "Tell me of the progress and your news."

"A large lithium deposit was found under my watch. Enough to power generations. It can guarantee our colony's success."

Commander Gearhardt's head fell back as if the news had hit him in the face. "You're sure of this?"

"I'll send you the readings right now, Commander." Barliss plugged the memory card of the locator into his computer and transferred the information. The commander's eyes flickered as his brain worked, synapses firing as he reviewed the numbers. Barliss sat back, awaiting recognition and praise.

The commander's pupils regained focus and stared at Barliss. "Excellent work, Lieutenant. As you know, our time is precious. We've already fallen a decade behind on our voyage and are forced to conserve our fuel. More and more of our naturally grown food is dying and the food generators are working overtime. I'll send mining crews down there right away. We'll take all we can before we leave."

"I recommend you put Smith in charge of the mining excavations." Barliss ran his fingers over the end of the memory card in careful thought. "He's done a superb job so far and has great knowledge of the terrain."

By appointing Smith, Barliss succeeded in removing him from his own operation, so the subordinate would have a harder time finding a way to pay him back once he realized Barliss had profited from the findings. On the other hand, the new position might be enough to pacify Smith's desire for recognition and keep the man's mouth shut. Either way, it was brilliant politics.

The commander flicked a finger and a screen beside him came alive with new information. "Smith is appointed. Now the search and rescue progress: is there anything more to report?"

Barliss' neck tensed, but he kept his voice even. "Nothing since my last report, Commander."

The commander nodded, wires moving. "I reviewed your report."

Barliss was surprised and pleased he'd gone through the entire three-page document so soon. "Thank you, sir."

"You believe there's still hope for finding Miss Ryder?"

Barliss stifled an undercurrent of doubt. "I do, sir."

"Good. Our people cannot suffer another blow to their morale. You are always diligent, and your resolve is unwavering."

Barliss bowed his head. "I try."

"Continue with the search crews after the appropriate rest period."

"Affirmative, Commander."

"Thank you for your efforts, Lieutenant. You are a blessing to this crew."

The screen went blank. Barliss let out a breath of relief, but it was short-lived. He bent down and retrieved his wheat beer, tilting the bottle up for the last sip. He'd expected the treat would improve his desolate mood, but it was only a drop in an ocean of aggravation. The conversation with the commander had been going well until his failure with Aries had been addressed.

If he didn't find Aries now, he'd look like a fool.

…

Aries stared at the eggs. They were literally the manifestation of all her dreams come true. She'd wanted to be a biologist for as long as she could remember, but the *New Dawn*'s computers had charted her engineering destiny.

"You're planning on bringing them out and hatching them?"

"Is it so hard to believe a space pirate isn't in it for his own good?"

She could feel her face burning. "You're going to have to give me more than ten minutes to undo a lifetime of the prejudices I was taught."

Striker laughed lightly and put his hand on her shoulder. His voice was calmer. "Let's get back upstairs and I'll make you dinner, okay?"

Aries took in a deep breath but couldn't respond. Everything was happening so fast. First, she'd been on the *New Dawn*, eating breakfast with Barliss, then she'd crash-landed an escape pod, and now she stood on an abandoned alien ship underneath the desert. What next? A dinner date with a pirate?

She'd wanted freedom. She'd gotten a bizarre taste of the surreal.

Striker placed his hand gently under her arm. "Aries, you okay?"

"Yeah, it's just a lot to take in."

"I'm sure." He gave her a sympathetic smile, and she found herself entranced by him. She admired his desire to help another civilization. His optimism was contagious. In a world where everything was preplanned, Striker broke the mold, and she was drawn to him for it.

Striker's hand traveled down her arm to her hand. He squeezed it, sending a blush of warmth through her body. "You'll feel better if you eat something. It'll be delicious. Let's go."

Aries followed him, her emotions running on high. Was he flirting? She squashed the thought. How could she possibly be attracted to a space pirate? An exiled, unsuccessful one at that.

"You see," Striker began, as they climbed the steps to the next floor, "I've been down here for five long, lonely years. I've had a lot of time to watch their home videos. When it's the only channel on and you're all by yourself, your face sticks to the screen like you're hooked on a daytime soap opera. You find yourself wanting to learn more."

"A soap opera?"

Striker grinned. "They didn't let you see those on the *New Dawn*, huh?"

"They censored any videos from old Earth that weren't pertinent to the Guide."

"Of course."

"I'm serious."

"I know you are. It makes perfect sense. Why would they show you a world where you got to choose a mate? That'd provoke mutiny right then and there."

Aries knew what Striker alluded to. She'd heard rumors about the history of old Earth and how people used to be able to choose whom they married. Necessity dictated their lives now. She wasn't about to go off the subject, though. "So what did you learn?" Aries panted to keep up. Striker was in better shape than she was. She'd worked out on the *New Dawn* every day, but it hadn't prepared her for the change in gravity, the extreme heat, or such a gorgeous man.

"That they're a lot like us. Except no war, no violence, no hatred. Only peace."

Tria's cynicism toward mankind came back to her. "I find that hard to believe. How can a species be so perfect?"

"Maybe you should ask how our species can be so flawed."

"This, coming from a pirate?"

Striker laughed. "Under the circumstances, you can consider me to be reformed."

Aries wasn't sure how to answer that, so she brought the subject back to her beloved biology. "These eggs came from a planet that must have had humidity. That means there are water droplets in the air itself."

"I know what humidity is. What's your point?"

"Even if you brought the eggs out, they'd never hatch in the desert. The conditions wouldn't be right for them."

Striker stopped in mid-stride and turned toward her with a glint in his eyes. "Who said anything about a desert?"

Aries gestured vaguely toward the roof of the craft and the desert sands above them. "What else is there?"

"I plan to get off this barren rock. I've been fixing up this ship from scattered pieces in the desert and all I need are a few more parts. I'm going to fly back to Outpost Omega, the spaceport you talked of, twenty-one parsecs away. Before my fickle crew ditched me on this pitiful excuse for a planet, I'd found a wormhole to another galaxy, one with a sun much like the one Earth had. Are you following me?"

Aries found herself leaning in, listening to each word with interest. She nodded. "Go on."

"There's a moon that has oceans, forests, anything you need to sustain a decent population. I named it Refuge. I hid the coordinates aboard my ship. I plan to reclaim my map, relay the coordinates to everyone suffering at Outpost Omega, and travel there. When I land, I'll bring out the eggs. If they hatch, I'll be continuing a long-lost species. If they don't, at least I tried. I figure it'll be payment for taking their ship."

He smiled. "But I hope they hatch. Such a peaceful race doesn't deserve to go extinct. Maybe they could teach us something."

"You've been here for five years. What if your crew found the map? What if they're already there?"

Striker leaned on the wall and crossed one boot over another. "Impossible." He looked so self-satisfied, Aries almost laughed. "The coordinates are hidden in the darkest, farthest recesses of the ship, encoded in three different languages with mathematical enigmas to solve to break the seal. My crew is probably still docked at the port as we speak, scanning the ship in vain for that map."

"You're going to take this ship to go find that ship. Wow, that's quite a plan."

Striker leaned toward her. "The question is: do you want in? You're an Outlander now. No one can make the decision for you. Do you want to stay here, or do you want to find Refuge with me?"

Her first instinct was alarmingly clear: go with Striker, wherever that may be. The engineer training died hard, however. She couldn't factor a man she'd just met into the equation. Her logic wouldn't let her.

Aries considered her options while chewing her lower lip. She had nowhere else to go, but the pirate-run spaceport sounded more dangerous than the lizards and worms of this desert planet. On the other hand, the ethereal images of pale angels and their eggs haunted her, pulling on her heartstrings. A part of her believed her own redemption lay in saving the dying race. Maybe then she'd feel as though her life had purpose, although she'd harmed the *New Dawn*'s genetic mission by leaving. Plus, she could finally live out her dreams of being a biologist, studying the greatest find in all mankind: an alien civilization more advanced than their own. All combined, Striker's plan made for quite a journey, with a paradise moon at the end.

Really, the option of staying with the most interesting and attractive man she'd ever met *wasn't* clouding her judgment.

"All right." Aries looked him in the eye. "Count me in."

Chapter Eight
Coordinates

Aries stared at a scorpion as large as her forearm. It rested on a gigantic porcelain plate shaped like a clam. The legs sprawled out in a strange garnishing around a cracked shell. Its antennae drooped, dark eyes staring blankly at her fork.

"This is dinner?"

"Think of it as lobster." Striker smiled and dusted his own with a granular substance. "You're going to love it."

"The marine tank cracked the generation before mine." Aries stabbed the carapace with a knife and it crunched. "I've never tasted anything from the sea."

"Well this isn't from the sea." He raised his eyebrow and his eyes teased. "It's from the desert. Our favorite place."

"Hmm." Aries plucked out the antennae. "Did you have lobster on the space station?"

Striker split the shell of his meal into two pieces. "Far from it. Just stacks of old videos of life back on Earth. We watched them like prisoners dreaming of a promised land."

"The people of the *New Dawn* didn't want us watching too much of Earth's memories." Aries pulled off a small leg and dangled it above her plate before setting it aside. "The Guide says dwelling on the past only brings more sadness."

"I always thought it would keep us from making the same mistakes."

Aries nodded. "The fact that they were regulated drew me in. I stayed up late many nights, watching videos from the ship's memory bank."

She pulled a piece of white meat from underneath the carapace. Holding it up, she examined it and wrinkled her nose.

"Go on." He stopped, crossed his arms, and watched.

Striker had probably prepared this meal a thousand times in his five-year exile with no one to share it. The thought nudged her heart, and she found herself wanting to try it for his sake. She popped it in her mouth. "Hey, this isn't bad."

"Better than the gruel served at Outpost Omega."

Aries worked out another piece of meat, stabbing it with the pointy utensil. "They don't have gardens there?"

"Most of the fresh plants died long ago. Now the pirates survive on recycled matter produced by the food generators."

"That's awful." Aries sickened at the thought of eating old food. "Those poor people."

"I'm not sure poor is the right word." Striker narrowed his eyes. "They're more desperate than anything else."

Aries could understand desperation. She nodded, chewing another piece. "What are your former crewmates like?"

Striker paused before digging into the scorpion's claw with a little too much force. "Hopefully you won't ever meet them to find out."

"Why?"

His eyes darkened, and Aries glimpsed deeper emotions beneath his nonchalant façade. "Like you said, they're in it for their own good. Even if that means abandoning their captain."

Although he hadn't told her anything she wanted to know, Aries decided not to press the subject. "I'm sorry. No one should have to go through—"

"I'm over it." Striker stabbed another piece of meat. "Now, let's go over our situation and see if we can get out of here."

He reached into his coat and pulled out an unusual-looking palm screen. "To restart the ship, I need a part of the exterior processor. It must have broken off on impact and skidded across the desert. It could be anywhere, covered by hundreds of years of sandstorms. This map shows all of the places I've searched for it."

Aries studied the map of dunes and valleys around the ship. Xs marked Striker's excavation sites. He'd scoured every area within miles of the crash. "Wow, you've been busy."

"Let me put it this way: I don't want to stay any longer than necessary."

Aries ran her finger over the map, thinking. "Do you know what the processor is made of?"

Striker shrugged. "Probably the same material as the rest of this ship."

Aries brought out her life-form locator. "I have an idea." She held it up to the wall, waiting for the substance to register. The device beeped, and the screen glowed with a string of numbers.

"What's it saying?" Striker rose and stood beside her, his body heat warming her shoulder.

"It's just what I thought. This ship is made of a mutated form of calcium carbonate: living matter. The mitochondrial genetic analysis likens it to a seashell from the Earth's oceans. It registers on my life-form locator as an uncategorized form of coral."

"Does that mean you can use the locator to find the missing processor?"

"You bet it does." She flashed a cool smile, but inside she beamed with pride.

Striker looked at her like she'd been named the *New Dawn*'s new commander. "I can't believe it. You've solved our problem."

Aries' smile spread. She'd never felt more appreciated in her entire life. Barliss had always downplayed her ideas, then stolen them for his own when he'd thought she'd forgotten. *Slimy bastard!*

"Come on. Let's go to the surface and test it out."

Striker ushered them down a corridor to a raised platform. Using his fingernail, he traced a hieroglyph, and the walls closed around them on all sides. Aries ran her hand over a series of concentric circles rippling out, the image reminding her of the infinity of deep space, and how one action could affect everything in the universe in some crazy, unpredictable way.

After Striker traced the geometric patterns in a certain order on the wall, the platform lifted.

Aries stared at Striker, steadying herself with one hand on the ivory. "How did you figure it out?"

"I had my fair share of time."

A hatch opened above their heads and the sun and sand streamed in. She breathed deeply. It felt good to be back in the open air. Seconds later, she stood atop the ivory ship, feeling as though she rode the back of a giant torpedo. The tip protruded from the sand, glistening in the rays of sun like a white bone of the gods. Etched in the hull were more intricate designs. A series of blue orbs running down the sides pulsed with a faint light like a distant heartbeat.

"I don't want to stay out here too long." Striker searched the sand dunes, squinting until appealing crinkles appeared at the corners of his eyes. "Too much attention from sandworms and raiders will draw your crew right to us. The raiders and worms can't get in this ship, but I bet the colonists would find a way."

The image of Barliss with his laser gun haunted her mind. "Agreed. I need a few moments to adjust the parameters." Aries' slender fingers flitted over the device, typing in new coordinates and scanning the area.

Striker stepped from the platform onto the sand and began climbing a nearby dune. He pulled out a pair of binoculars from his coat and kept watch. "How did you think of using the life-form locator?"

She stayed at the hatch's opening, nervous to leave the protection of the ship. "I was an engineer back on the *New Dawn*, in charge of the life-support systems."

"Wow." Striker's lowered his binoculars a bit. He looked over them to her. "Impressive."

Aries waved his comment away, although she enjoyed his admiration. "I tested highest in those skill sets." Her voice grew melancholy, and her fingers paused over the touchscreen. "Secretly, I wanted to be a biologist. I read all I could about the natural world. My parents called me a dreamer because the things I studied were all dead."

"They wouldn't let you choose your own profession?"

"Ha! On the *New Dawn* you have little choice, out of necessity." Aries went back to her calculations. "Wait! The locator is picking up something beyond those mountains to the North. It's an exact match to the ship, approximately one meter long and a half meter wide."

Striker slid down the dune and jumped back onto the platform to peer over her shoulder at the screen. "That's it, all right. It's exactly where I feared it would be, the only place I didn't dare to look."

"Why?" Aries tore her gaze from the device to study Striker's face. She'd never heard fear taint his voice before and it made her stomach flip.

"That's the raiders' main den."

Chapter Nine
Red Dawn

The sound of drills filled the air as the mining excavation began in full force. Barliss roamed the perimeter of the site, enjoying the clamor as much as a Wagnerian opera as his crews tore into the sand. The *New Dawn* had dropped a line of empty metal barrels, and they sat like beached whales along the plateau, waiting to be filled with lithium. The canisters reminded Barliss of the pictures from history books, chronicling the fate of sea life as the oceans dried up on Earth. He'd never felt sorry for them, like the others in his class. He saw it as Darwin's theory of evolution, where the more adaptable species survived.

Gleaning lithium from the desert planet made Barliss' spirits rise, as the scent of opportunity filled the air with its metallic reek. The colonists would gouge a gaping crater where the extraction cut into the terrain, and he hoped more than a few of those sandworms and lizard men fell in.

Smith scurried around the other side of the mining operations, calculating coordinates on his palm-sized mineral locator. Barliss welcomed Smith's whining about the destructive extraction procedures. The longer Smith prevented the operation from going forward, the more time Barliss had to find Aries.

As he slid down the sand dune, the diamond point of her ring pricked and scratched his inner thigh. He shoved his hand into his pocket and pushed the ring around until it no longer irked him. He didn't need any more reminders of his failure to control the woman.

Annoyed, he waded through mounds of windblown sand to reach the main operation's headquarters in the center tent. At least walking in this sand against this gravity gave him a constant workout. He'd be even angrier if his abs gained an ounce of flab from this hellish desert vacation. Flexing his muscles to make sure they still hardened in all the right places, he slapped open the tent flap and slipped in.

Langston looked up from a table of maps, navigational charts, and handheld devices. "Greetings, Lieutenant Barliss."

Barliss nodded at his new second-in-command. He followed orders right down to every word, much better than Smith. "Do you have anything to report?"

Langston shifted some papers. "I started where Smith left off. There's not a lot here, just a whole ton of sand."

He smirked, but Barliss didn't find his comment amusing. "Did you find anything new?"

"It looks as though there are three major reptilian colonies in the area." He pointed to sections of the map. "The first is a mile away, the second is over that ridge, and the largest one is over here, six miles from our camp. That's a bustling lizard metropolis."

Barliss leaned down to scan the areas. "You think she's in one of them?"

Langston brushed the ever-present grains of sand off the map. "There's nowhere else for her to go. I scanned the area and there are no metal structures of any kind. Over here is a strange form of living coral, but nothing man-made."

Barliss squinted. His finger traced the region of the map where the coral manifested. "Nothing humanoid?"

"No, sir."

Barliss tapped his finger on the table for a moment, then pointed to the reptilian colonies. "We'll start with this one, the closest one. From there, we'll work toward the second site, and then if we still don't find any trace of her, we'll pay a visit to lizard central."

Langston blinked as if confused. "What do you want us to do, sir?

Ask them if they saw a five-foot, five-inch woman on foot?"

"No, you fool. We're going to blast them all. Exterminate the entire colony. That's the only way we'll know if they're hiding her."

Langston shifted his stance, leaning slightly away from the maps. Barliss could tell he didn't like the idea. Now he'd know what Langston was made of. Would the skyman follow orders, or stick to his principles?

Langston swallowed and met him eye-to-eye. "Yes, sir. I'll form a team. We can leave as early as the second sunrise."

Barliss placed a hand on his shoulder and squeezed hard. "That's my man. Meet you at the hoverships after dinner."

"Yes, Lieutenant." He saluted and stood as straight as a laser's trajectory, waiting for further orders or for Barliss to leave.

"Make sure to charge all the lasers we've got." Barliss walked toward the tent flaps and lifted one up. The sun glared in. "We're gonna have a lizard bake."

…

Alien arms lifted the speckled egg to the dim sunlight trickling in from a hole in the rock-crusted ceiling. Her feather-light robes flowed down her arms, revealing white skin striped with blue and purple veins. The egg shuddered in the diaphanous red-tinged light as if it longed to break open, but the shell didn't crack. She caressed the curve of the shell with her pencil-sharp fingers, the tips making gentle scratching noises against the smooth casing.

A smear of movement blurred in a corner of the room. The camera panned toward it, looking over the egg cradled in the thin arms of the alien making the memory-vision. Another creature glided from the balcony into the room. The visitor fluffed his wings in an intimidating array, causing her to tighten her arms around the egg. He stood taller and had more muscular arms, with brightly colored feathers pointing up on his shoulders. She stepped back and the visitor pursued her. His arms reached out like long tree branches. He tugged the egg from her slender fingers and tucked it under his arm. She fell to the floor, loose feathers fluttering over the vision.

As he flew over the balcony, she rose and followed him, gliding down to a coral ship resting in the town square. The sun shone fainter than in the previous vision, cluttered by blotches of black, a red orb splotched with ink stains. A ship sat in the center of the high, arched structures on a bed of porcelain. Tall and slender aliens stepped in a line, each one carrying a single egg.

"Addicting, isn't it?"

Aries jerked away from the screen. She was sitting on the floor, so she smacked her face against his knee. Mesmerized by the screen, she hadn't seen him come in.

"It's so sad. I don't know why the eggs don't hatch."

He pointed to the sky in the moving picture. "I think it's got something to do with that dying sun."

"You think it's dying?"

Striker stepped closer to the screen, as if he could see the image more clearly. Aries had tried it herself, but the pixels looked fuzzy up close, distorting the picture.

"At first I thought their planet circled close to a weak sun," he said, "but now I'm starting to think the star was swollen."

A sense of dread seeped in the pit of Aries' stomach. She stared at the scarlet sphere as if it were a disease. "A red giant?"

"Yes."

"Oh my. To think, the people on Earth destroyed the planet half a billion years before our sun could burn all its hydrogen, yet here's a species that outlasted their sun."

"Or went with it." Striker looked around, as if their spirits still inhabited the ship.

"I'm not going to let the last of those eggs die. Not if I have a say in the matter." Aries stood up, her voice resolute. "Come on, let's get a move on and retrieve that control processor."

Striker didn't move. "What if your crew decides to go looking for you?"

"What if they look here?" Aries shot back. "I won't be free from them until the *New Dawn*, or I, leave this planet." She flicked her eyebrows. "I bet they're not going anywhere soon. That means we have to."

Aries watched as he mulled over her words.

"All right." He sighed. "It's going to be dangerous."

Aries nudged him with her elbow. "You know me, I plunge into danger."

Striker flashed a smile. "More like danger finds you."

"You found me," Aries countered, stepping close enough to search the green flecks in his irises. "What does that make you? Dangerous?"

"I don't know." Striker turned away. His fingers brushed against the hieroglyphs, and the screen flickered out. "Stupid."

Aries' heart tugged with him as he pulled away. She grabbed his sleeve. "Striker, wait."

He turned toward her with a glimmering interest in his gaze. He'd tricked her. He was playing hard to get. "But I'm staying with you all the same."

His thumb trailed along her cheek, then rested on her chin. His fingers opened and she melted into the palm of his hand, allowing him to touch her like no man ever had. His hand traveled to the back of her neck and he leaned down, brushing her lips with his own.

Was this the mysterious "love" everyone on the *New Dawn* whispered about? It had to be. Aries ached from inside. She pressed into his kiss, wanting to be closer. Her body leaned into his and she felt his lean muscles against her chest. His body radiated heat, warming the front of her uniform.

Striker pulled back and her body screamed for more. He looked confused and lost, as if the kiss had taken him somewhere he hadn't expected to go. Aries gazed up in expectation, but he tore his gaze away, turning to his tools on the pedestal.

"We must prepare."

…

The second sun rose as they set out across the vast sea of dunes. Aries drew out her life-form locator and held it up to the sky. Sure enough, the blinking green light flickered on, registering the coral that matched the ship. She pointed with her other hand. "Due north."

Striker spoke through a scarf wrapped around his head and mouth. "It will take two days on foot."

"Are you sure we have enough provisions?" Aries eyed the bag on Striker's back.

"Enough for two people for five days." Striker looked toward the blazing horizon. "If we stay out any longer than that, we'll have to forage for food and water."

"I'm not planning on lingering." Aries hefted her bag onto her shoulders. She looked at the helm of the coral ship protruding up from the sand one last time. It reminded her of the pictures of fallen skyscrapers back on Earth. She wondered if her need to look back came from an instinctual reference point or a wistful connection. She'd met Striker on that ship.

"Come on. Let's go." Striker led the way.

They waded through soft sand. The sun cast long shadows behind them as it rose on the horizon to claim its long reign over the day. Aries recognized this sun from her first journey through the desert. Larger than the first, a haze of orange-red bled off its rim in a devilish halo. She wondered if it, too, would evolve into a red giant, dooming Sahara 354 to a predestined end.

Her dire thoughts always returned to Earth, as if it were her true home, although she'd never been there. "Striker, do you know what happened to the people left on Earth? After the space pirates took over the central station, the *New Dawn* lost all communication."

Striker pulled back his scarf and put a canteen made from lizard scales to his lips. "Do you really want to know?"

Aries gave him a look like he'd asked if she really wanted to leave the *New Dawn* behind. "The people on the *New Dawn* have speculated what became of them for the past century. Yes, I want to know."

Striker closed the canteen by stuffing the end of a lizard tail down the hole and pulled the scarf around his face. All she could see were his smoldering eyes, touched with sadness. "You must have deduced there wasn't enough room on the space station for everyone."

Aries nodded. "Of course."

"Once the last ship was stolen, and the resources on Earth used up, the space station didn't go back for refugees. There were cameras and a communications link to a headquarters back on Earth. At first, the remaining people kept in contact, telling us about the dwindling numbers, the disease and the devastation."

Striker dug his walking stick into the sand with a hard push. "I watched the videos. Fewer and fewer of them reported in over time, and when they did, their faces were pockmarked with boils and puss-filled welts. They didn't look good."

Aries kept up to his pace with extended strides. She was lucky she had long legs. "The radiation?"

"Who knows?" Striker crested a dune, scanning the landscape. "All of a sudden, they stopped talking to us. Whether they'd all perished or were too angry with the pirates for failing to return, we could only guess."

A sense of irresolution spread through her, as if she'd heard a long, sad story without an end. She felt as though there was more he hadn't told her. "That's it?"

Striker paused, as if deciding whether to go on. Aries climbed to the crest and caught his arm. "What is it?"

He looked toward the blazing sun. "The cameras sent a live feed. Radiation made reception spotty, but the space station still picked up the transmissions off and on. At first we thought it was only garbage rolling around on the deserted streets, but then we saw them huddled by trash bins and underneath toppled cars."

"The people?"

"I guess. We never got a good look at them, but they walked strangely, crawling around on all fours like animals."

Aries shuddered.

Striker tilted his head as if to say he'd told her so. "Maybe they evolved along with the radiation. Maybe it's another species altogether. All I know is no one wanted to go back there, so we eventually shut the cameras off to save energy."

"How horrible."

"The world's a tough place, and the universe is colder still."

Aries fell silent, thinking about Striker's words and the deformed people inhabiting old Earth. She had always held onto the hope that the people of Earth had turned things around, but Striker's story blasted her hopes out of the sky. Maybe he was right: she had been better off not knowing.

"Man, I know how to trash a date, don't I?"

Aries looked up, confused. "What do you mean?"

"Get down!" He dropped to a crouch and motioned for her to follow. Aries fell to her knees and watched him scan the rippling sand dunes. A blast of wind threw sand in a wave across the desert, making it hard for her to see the black dots dancing on the horizon.

"What is it?" She whispered, as if any living soul existed within earshot.

"Raiders, and lots of them." He brought his binoculars from his cloak and looked again. "A freakin' parade."

Chapter Ten
Repo

Tiff leaned against the metal framework of her bunk in the *Morphic Marauder*, squeezing glue out of a tube, applying the white worm to the sole of her space boot. She'd kicked a man so hard yesterday, the three-inch heel had ripped off the leather. After running a finger along the rim to spread the sticky ooze, she put her foot high against the chrome wall and pushed.

She'd have to hold the position until the glue dried, but waterproof boots were necessary where she was headed, and these were a rare pair. Refuge had forests, lakes, and marshes full of fresh water. She planned to be the first to take a dip. Gritting her teeth, she held herself up between the cot and the wall like a gymnast stretched taut on the high bars.

"Practicing your yoga?" Drifter stood in the doorway, chewing a piece of old gum. He'd used up the last package two years ago and kept this final wad as a reminder. He pulled it from his teeth with a grin and tucked it into a corner of his pocket for later.

"Shut up, Drifter. If you'd come with me in the first place, then I wouldn't have needed to fight, and I wouldn't have broken this heel." Men in the twenty-seventh century disappointed her, Drifter included. They'd left all notions of chivalry back on Earth.

"Hey now, I was working with Reckon on the map. You know I

always look out for ya.'"

Tiff cracked her knuckles and looked away, resisting the urge to fight him. "Have the two of you made any headway?"

He crossed his arms in the self-satisfied way that aggravated Tiff's nerves. "We've cracked the first set of theorems, yes."

Tiff couldn't help but look up in surprise. "And?"

"It's only a matter of time."

Tiff blew air out of her nose in relief. "How long?"

Drifter's shoulders rose and fell in a nonchalant gesture. "Give Reckon another day or two, and we'll be hightailing it outta here."

Tiff released her position against the cot and the wall and landed on her feet. Her heel held underneath her weight. It was a good omen. She moved toward him. "You mean it?"

"You bet."

Her anger faded. She wrapped her arms around his neck and locked lips, kissing him fiercely. He put his arms around her and squeezed, his long, dark hair falling around them.

Footsteps clattered in the corridor behind them. "Captain Drifter, sir."

Tiff recognized the voice as the boy they'd found living in the ventilator shafts over their docked ship. She'd convinced Drifter to keep him around, so she hoped he wasn't up to anything stupid. She felt responsible for the kid.

Drifter pulled away from her and turned around. His voice had a tinge of annoyance to it. "Yeah, Loot, what's up?"

"It's Reckon, sir. He's throwing a fit."

Drifter loosened his grip around Tiff. "What do you mean?"

"He's lost it. You have to stop him."

Drifter shot Tiff a wary look. "Come on."

They ran down the corridor to their ship's main deck, pale green lights illuminating their path. Tiff's heart beat hard in her chest as her boots clanked on the metal grid that served as a floor. As they grew closer, Tiff heard Reckon's screams of fury echo down the corridor. She prayed it didn't concern the map.

As they entered the deck, Reckon threw a plastic cup across the room. It cracked on the main sight panel and fell to the floor, bouncing twice before rattling to a halt. Tiff put a protective arm around Loot, holding him close as Drifter ran to stop Reckon.

Reckon beat his fist against the control panel, making red lights flash in warning. Drifter grabbed him from behind and held the old man's arms back before he could do any more damage. "Reckon, what are you doing?"

"Damn son of a-" Reckon fought, but his feeble-boned arms were no match for Drifter's pull-up-shaped biceps. Drifter let him go and he collapsed on the floor at Drifter's feet, grasping his head in his hands.

"What are you talking about?" Drifter knelt beside him and held his head up, staring into his watery eyes. Tiff was glad she didn't have to be the one to talk sense into the man. She didn't want to touch his oily skin.

"He imprinted it. That's what he did."

Drifter looked back to Tiff but she had no idea what he meant.

"Imprinted what, Reckon?"

"The map."

Did her heart stop beating? She wasn't that lucky. Fate refused to allow her off its hook. She shivered, running her hands up and down Loot's boyish arms. She'd never felt so trapped.

Drifter put his hand up to his head as if he couldn't believe it. He growled through gritted teeth. "What do you mean?"

"He put in a code that's linked to his genome. You need a piece of his DNA to match it."

"We'll scour the ship! There must be a piece of hair or something."

"That's not it." Reckon seemed to gain an ounce of sanity as he righted himself on the floor. "It's voice activated as well. The DNA is only the first step."

"Damn." Drifter looked up, as though an answer hung in the air above his head. His eyes brightened. "We could mimic his voice. We must have video logs of him saying something."

"No. He needs to speak the DNA code in order. It's impossible." Reckon's last word resounded through the chamber, damning them all.

Drifter held out his hands as if asking the old man for his salvation. "Reckon, you've got to tell us what else we can do."

"Repo. It's the only way."

Tiff spoke for the first time. "You mean go back and get him?"

Drifter winced.

Reckon spoke, his voice whistling through the hole in his front teeth. "It's the only way."

Emotions whirled inside Tiff's body, rising from her pointed boots on her feet to the spiky hairs on her head. She thought she'd never see Striker again. Part of her dreaded the sight of the pirate she'd help maroon, but a larger part of her surged with a bubbly feeling of hope.

"Loot." Drifter flexed his forefinger, calling the boy over. His voice sounded hoarse and edged with anger. Tiff held Loot back, afraid Drifter might take out his aggravation on the boy.

Loot broke free of her grasp, shunning her motherly instinct, and walked over in a fearless gait. "Yes, Captain."

Drifter's face fell in disgust, his long chin jutting in a pout as if he'd swallowed a nasty bit of recycled sludge. "Prepare the *Morphic Marauder* for takeoff. We're going back to Sahara 354 in three hours."

…

"Over here, come on!"

Aries ducked and ran at the same time, following Striker behind the crest of a sand dune as the raiders crested the adjacent ridge. He pulled an orangey-beige tarp from his backpack and spread it over them like wings. It fell on Aries' shoulders as she lay on her stomach beside him, her elbow touching his.

He gave her a wink. "Camouflage."

"Has it worked before?"

Striker pulled his scarf down to show her a smile. "I'm still here, aren't I? It works every time."

Aries peeked through a crack in the fabric as the caravan of raiders approached, first in twos and then in larger numbers. Their tall, scrawny bodies bounced lightly over the sand, heads lolling from side to side. They carried spears and water skins and dragged dead scorpions by their tails behind them. An animal emerged from the haze, as big as Earth's elephants, with tentacles sprouting from its mouth like whiskers. Two raiders rode its curved back while three others whipped its rump from behind. A waft of musky-scented air rode the wind and Aries had to hold her breath to avoid gagging.

Exhaling, she asked, "What is that thing?"

"Desert cow." Striker passed her his binoculars. "I haven't seen many of them alone. They stay in herds, and you don't want to be around when there's a stampede."

Aries peered through the lens and pursed her lips, watching the beast feel around with its many trunks. It looked like an elephant from some crazy experiment gone awry. She gave Striker back his binoculars.

Child-sized raiders ran zigzagging behind the beast, circling its tracks in the sand. She hadn't considered the fact the raiders had young, like any other species. Suddenly, the lizard men seemed more human to her. "I hope we don't have to kill any of them."

Striker must have spotted the children as well. "We'll be quick. They won't even know we're there."

One of the lizards' young broke free from the caravan, following a snake as it writhed through the sand toward their dune. Aries tensed her arms to bolt, but Striker held her hand. "Don't move."

She hissed under her breath. "He's coming right at us!"

"Trust me." Striker squeezed her hand, and a wave of emotion rolled through her. How could she not desire a man who looked out for her? Who kept her safe?

The snake plunged into the sand, and Aries peeked from under the tarp, watching the lizard-child climb the dune and dig for it, grit flying up and raining down upon their tarp. It made a hollow sound when it hit and Aries cringed, thinking for sure the young raider would hear the difference.

The lizard boy ripped off his bone mask to get a better look, exposing rainbow scales around his eyes, like a gecko. The iridescence in his skin changed color in moments to blend with the dull hue of the sand. Black eyes with no pupils scanned the top of the dune as his head turned almost all the way around like a bird's. She wondered what thoughts flitted behind his big, dark eyes. Did he feel pain or sorrow? Would he ever fall in love?

He dug closer, his webbed claws reaching for the sand above the tarp, and she held her breath. Striker shook his head ever so slightly, telling her not to move. They lay inches from the lizard boy's reach. Aries grasped Striker's hand and held on tight. Together, they waited for whatever might come.

The exhalation of her uneven breath moved the edge of the tarp and she forced herself to breathe out her nose. The youngling snapped his head in their direction and stuck out a blue-black, two-pronged tongue. He licked the air as if he could taste her sweat and fear. Aries' heart thumped heavily in her chest.

Clicking sounds came from behind the lizard boy. One of the adult raiders pulled him off his feet, lifting him by his crude woolen shirt, and tossed him back to the caravan. With one look back at the dune, the lizard man returned to his kin. Aries let out a sigh. So many dangerous things lived on this planet. Death waited for her at every dune.

She turned her head toward Striker. "I would have died out here without you. The first day."

He touched her cheek. "I'm glad you chose my planet to crash on."

Aries held her breath, hoping his touch would turn to more, as it had before, but Striker looked away, watching the last stragglers of the caravan disappear on the horizon.

Aries studied his profile as the wind crept under the tarp and tossed a stray wisp of his thick, dark hair. She wanted to touch his hard-edged cheek, run her fingers along the stubble on his chin. Lying next to him filled her with an anxious energy, as if his body gave off fuel for her soul. The label "pirate" melted away to reveal a man struggling to survive, like everyone else in a cruel and harsh world. She truly saw him for the first time.

The clicking sounds of the raiders faded away, leaving only the sound of the tarp as it shifted in the wind. Aries had so many things she wanted to say, but her tongue felt numb and tingly in her mouth. She reached out and placed the stray piece of hair behind his ear.

Striker looked at her in question.

She'd been thinking all day of the kiss they'd shared. So tentative, and hesitant, the brief moment of contact had left her wishing for more. Now, his face rested so close, luring her toward him like a magnet. She bent forward to kiss him, but he turned his head away. Aries pulled back in a sheepish retreat.

"Might as well stay here and make camp for the night," he said.

His casual tone stung her composure. How could he talk of such mundane things when they'd almost been captured, when she'd touched him so tenderly?

"We'll let them get farther away," Striker explained, reasonable as always. "We're going in their direction tomorrow."

The sting of rejection grew, burning a hole in her heart. "Why?" Her voice came out as a plea.

"Why what?"

Her lips trembled. "Why not kiss me like you did before?"

"I can't." He shook his head, and the air cooled between them—so much so, Aries wondered if the desert had turned into deep space.

He'd teased her with such affection before, it was cruel to take it away. "I don't understand," she said, wishing she didn't care, wishing she could stop all the emotions he'd started in her heart.

Aries caught a glimpse of pain etched in the wrinkles around his eyes. Striker turned away and started pulling supplies out of his backpack. "I can't do this."

"Do what?"

Striker shook his head and Aries prompted, "Can't kiss me, can't trust me? What?"

"I can't allow myself to get tangled up with someone. Not again."

The thoughts of Striker with another woman confused her. On the *New Dawn*, everyone had one lifemate and that was it. "You mean you loved someone before?"

Striker's hand tightened on the backpack. "I trusted someone a long time ago, allowed myself to love, if you will. She hurt me so much I lost my entire life and ended up here. I can't experience that kind of pain again."

"What did she do?"

"She marooned me here. She stabbed me in the back."

Aries clasped her hand over her heart. "I'm so sorry."

He waved her apology off as if it meant nothing. "It's a tough world, Aries. And it's dangerous to love. If I were you, I'd keep my heart well-guarded, because you never know when it will affect your decisions, when it will make you weak."

Aries couldn't take his advice. Watching him talk about his past made her realize she'd already given up her heart.

He had it.

Chapter Eleven
Navigator

Huddled under the propped-up tarp in the blazing heat of the desert, Striker allowed his thoughts to roam to places he hadn't visited in a long time, places he'd quarantined in his mind like the wastelands of old Earth. His mind wandered back to the decision that had changed his destiny, the day he'd hired Tiff.

A light techno beat had charged the air, pulsing and buzzing in a retro syncopation. The heater over the ship's bay sputtered out and an edgy chill descended throughout the space station. Striker worked up a sweat to keep the cold from settling in his bones. He screwed in bolts until his fingers ached and his sleeves dripped oil, fixing up an old family antique.

The ship hadn't flown in over two generations, and he was determined to make it soar. Like any young man trapped on a pirate spaceport full of poverty and crime, he craved breaking free to explore the vast universe around them. Although his father lingered day after day in the same room where his mother had withered away, Striker yearned for a better life. He didn't believe the stories of barren worlds and empty space. Somehow, deep down in his gut, he knew there were places like Earth had been before mankind, bounteous worlds untouched by squandering hands.

Boots clanked on the corridor above the ship's bay, echoing off the thick glass separating him from the void of space. The footfalls sounded light, the gait as quick and bouncy as a deer's. Striker looked up from his work to see a small young woman, barely five feet, with blond, pixie-cut hair spiked around her face and a waist tiny enough to hold in both hands.

"Greetings, Pirate." She leaped off the walkway and landed on her feet in front of him like a ninja come out to play. Her gaze traveled over the metal hull and settled on the engine hanging over her head. "Nice ship."

Striker rubbed a grease stain off the engine shaft the way someone would caress their loved one. "It belonged to my many-greats grandfather before me."

A spark of interest lit her eyes. "So, you're the descendant of Captain James Wilford?"

"Yes. Funny how everyone had a last name back then." The sound of Striker's ancestor's name always flowed oddly off his tongue, like another language of a time long past. Striker had a picture of the man hanging in the three-room cell he shared with his father. In the picture, James Wilford peered out the window of a ruined building, looking both arrogant and courageous. He'd had the gumption to steal one of the last freighters, saving five hundred people from the wastelands of old Earth. He would be appalled at the living conditions now, especially all of the orphans.

"Yeah, and now all we have is shit," she said.

Striker laughed, not expecting her comment or the edge in her tone. "So what brings you down here?"

"I hear you're looking for a crew."

Striker stared with mild interest. "What is it you do?"

Her gaze scanned from his head to his black-booted feet. She must have liked what she saw because she grinned, narrowing her black-lined eyes. "I'm a navigator. Learned it from my brother, before he blasted himself up in space."

"I don't need a navig—"

"Oh, yes, you do. I hear you're looking for some paradise planet. A hefty task. People have been scouring the galaxy for hundreds of years." She rose up on her toes to meet him eye to eye. "Give me a set of coordinates and I can get you there." Her eyes widened, daring him to deny her.

Striker put down his wrench and wiped his hands on a rag. "Listen, honey, I'm sorry to hear about your brother, and I understand you need another ship, but this mission isn't for you. I'm going out there to an unknown destination. No coordinates involved."

The young woman was clearly struggling to mask her disappointment. He could see her hopes crashing down on her, her last chance at a better life. A pang hit his heart. He spoke softly, as if warning a child. "You may not make it back."

"Don't care." She exhaled, looking around. "There's nothing here for me. I'd rather die on a spaceship going nowhere than sit around and watch humanity decay."

How she could fit so much attitude into such a small body, Striker couldn't begin to guess, but he liked it. "All right. You're in."

She nodded with a jab of her head, her spiky hair unmoving, like the plastic grass lining the more expensive suites in the space station. "Just show me what you want me to do."

"Over there." Striker pointed at the far end of the ship's bay to a metal desk. "I've collected a bunch of maps and circled a few of the least-explored quadrants. See what you can find."

"Yes, sir."

"The name's Striker."

She extended her hand. "Tiff."

Striker blinked, squeezing once and letting it go. "As in an argument?"

Tiff narrowed her eyes. "Perhaps, if I don't get my way."

Before he could react, she pushed by him, skipped to the end of the room, and ruffled through his collection of maps, throwing the ones she deemed useless over her shoulder. Striker wondered in that moment if he'd gotten a bargain, or made the biggest mistake of his life.

Looking back on it today, he still wasn't sure.

The desert breeze rustled over the tarp, pulling him back to his senses. If Tiff had never found this desert planet and abandoned him here, he would never have been there to save Aries. The auburn-haired woman lay beside him, her chest rising and falling in a deep sleep.

He studied her high cheekbones and the perfect bridge of her nose, sprinkled with freckles in just the right amount over her porcelain skin. She reminded him of a sleeping beauty, preserved from a past time on Earth, when people had lived in opulence under a fairy tale blue sky. He knew the scientists had never perfected the stasis sleep, but looking at Aries and her flawless facade, he could have believed she had.

She shifted, turning over and pressing her back against his side. A familiar yearning stirred in Striker's gut. The sexual attraction grew stronger with each moment they spent together, becoming harder to ignore. He moved away, disciplining himself to leave her alone. To not cross that line—no matter how much she'd indicated she wanted to cross it.

Questions swirled around in his head, but one pressed into his heart, demanding to be answered: could he bring himself to love again?

…

Parsecs away, Tiff leaned over a lap screen in the *Morphic Marauder*'s control room, surrounded by glowing monitors. She drew circles and lines with a barely-lit light pen. Just as she charted their current path from the mouth of the wormhole, the screen flickered and went blank. Frustrated, she broke the pen in half, the plastic cracking like a toothpick between someone's teeth. Like everything else in her life, the energy cell had died, outlasting its usefulness.

Drifter sat with his feet on the table, twirling a wire that had frayed at the end.

"What's the matter? Can't find the place?"

"No, it's not that." Tiff shot him a baleful glance. "When we emerged from the wormhole, our sensors picked up a band of asteroids blocking our path. An alternate route would take seven more days."

Drifter sat up, chewing his historic piece of gum. "I don't remember no asteroids the last time we flew to Sahara 354."

She shrugged. "They must be new, some waste from a meteor collision or floating debris that moved over time."

"Well, can we go through them?"

Tiff tossed the light pen away and attached her last operational keyboard to the screen, then entered the rest of her data. She paused and looked down at her fingers, as if they'd typed a lie. "The computer says we should go around."

"There's your answer, sweetheart."

"The computer is wrong."

Drifter almost spit out his gum. "What?"

"We can make it through. I see a path right here." She pointed to the screen and then consulted her maps. "If we go around this big one here, there's a clear corridor of space leading out of the conglomeration."

Drifter shook his head, his long, dark hair tangling around his shoulders. "I don't want to risk it."

"Drifter, it would take another seven days to get there if we went around."

"What's seven more days when it's been five years?" Drifter narrowed his eyes. "How come you're so anxious to get back?"

She ran a hand over her spiked hair. "I'm restless to get out of this black void and onto a real world, to start a new life. Besides, what if something happens to him in the next seven days? Where would we be then, huh?"

Tiff wondered if her words were true. So many emotions flooded through her, she couldn't categorize them all, and some, she didn't want to deal with. Part of her had been drawn to that planet ever since she'd left it, as if Sahara 354 had tied a cord to her heart. Even now, as the *Morphic Marauder* sailed to it, the taut string eased.

"If he survived five years of exile," Drifter announced, "then he'll outlive the next seven days."

"I'm the navigator and I say we go through it."

"I'm the captain and I say we fly around."

They locked eyes for a moment before a cracking sound erupted over their heads. The ship tilted, sending Tiff's maps sprawling over the oily floor.

Drifter stood up, steadying himself as Tiff scurried to save her maps. "Something's hit our hull. Damn you, Tiff. You didn't tell me we were already close to the asteroid field."

Tiff pulled herself up to the computer as another crash sounded from the right wing. She brought up the main sight panel and calculated a few coordinates. "Gravity's radiating off the largest crater. It's pulling us toward it, right into the middle of the field." She looked up at him with an apology in her eyes. "We're going into the asteroid field. We have no choice."

"That's great. Just great."

Tiff stumbled over to him and wrapped her hand around his arm. "Drifter, I'm sorry. I should have turned us around sooner."

He shook her off, yanking his arm away. "I've got to prepare the upper weapons turret and try to blast as many of those rocks in our path as I can. You're going to have to do the driving."

Steps rang from down the corridor as someone hurried in panic. She heard Reckon wail. Tiff covered her mouth with her hand, hoping everything was okay.

Loot ran in and stumbled into Drifter as he moved to the door. "What's happening?"

Drifter caught him and turned him around to face Tiff. "Our lovely navigator here's gone ahead and flown us straight into an asteroid field."

Tiff bit her lower lip. "It pulled the ship in before I could turn us around."

Fear flickered in Loot's eyes before he nodded and stood his ground. Patches of dark stubble grew in place of the boyish fuzz on his jaw and Tiff knew he was on the verge of manhood. Yet to her, he'd always be the grubby little boy she'd saved from an air duct.

"What can I do to help?" Loot asked.

Drifter threw his arms up in disgust. "Talk some sense into Tiff, that's what you can do."

Tiff rolled her eyes and began typing, calculating the safest course. "It's no good to talk sense into me if we're all dead." On one of the screens, she could see the field swarming over them, a mass of brown spots cluttering the black, star-studded sky. Some of them remained stationary and others shot through the air like falling stars. She needed time to plot the course and every second counted.

She heard Loot ask Drifter, "Where you going?"

"I'm going to man the upper gun pod. Now, if you'll excuse me."

"Wait."

Tiff looked up in surprise. Loot sounded more like a commander, and an equal, not a boy.

Her boy-man put his hands on his hips. "Who's manning the lower one?" he demanded of Drifter.

"I guess I'll go get Reckon, although his eyesight—"

"I'll do it."

Drifter stood, silently assessing the boy from head to toe.

Tiff pleaded. "Loot, it's too dangerous. If one of those asteroids grazes the bottom of the ship and you're stuck out there in that tower…" She was unable to speak of it.

Drifter held out a hand to silence her. "Let the boy make his own decision."

He was right. She wasn't the boy's mother, and she couldn't decide for him. He'd been making decisions for himself before she'd found him. Who knew how old he really was? Thirteen? Fifteen? His tall, lanky body still looked boyish, with the promise of a man inside.

Loot looked at her and shook his head. "You can't keep me safe forever."

Tiff wanted him tucked safely away forever, so she'd never have to be alone. That wasn't reason enough. The boy had to grow up. "Go." Her voice sounded ragged.

Loot smiled. "I'll be careful, 'kay?"

"Okay."

It was their own personal exchange, stemming from the time she'd found him sleeping in the air vent. Tiff had told him she wasn't going to hurt him, and the first thing he'd said to her was "'kay." She'd said "okay" back, and they'd done it ever since.

Loot left, and Drifter walked over to her and leaned down to place a kiss on her lips, but Tiff pulled away.

"What? All of a sudden you're not my girlfriend anymore?"

Another crash sounded, this time toward the front of the ship, the weakest spot by the glass sight panel. "Shit, Drifter. Get to that turret. Hurry."

Drifter left in the opposite direction Loot had gone. Tiff stood alone in the control room, with all of their lives resting in her hands.

Panic crashed through her, but she tried to compose herself as she sat in front of the multiple screens. If she could get them past the largest asteroid, the ship could reach a corridor of free space and fly fast enough to break free of the gravitational pull.

She charted a course. The giant asteroids were much easier to navigate around than the fragments that were being pulled into the gravitational fields of the larger ones. A path would open up between the large asteroids, but she had to predict the current projection of the smaller rocks crossing the space at the same time. It was the most complicated puzzle she'd ever had to figure out.

Tiff rubbed her temples and forced herself to concentrate. If she adjusted the velocity to reach this point in time, that put her at odds with another coordinate later on. She'd have to drive the ship manually to engage the frequent changes in speed.

Tiff gripped the control stick with both hands. "Computer, turn off autopilot."

Warning signals sounded in her ear. A message ran along the screen: *Unadvised in maneuvering through unpredictable space.* Tiff flicked off the message and brought up the main screen. She trusted herself more than a rickety computer has-been, built a hundred years before she'd been born. Two green lights blinked on her right, signaling the turrets were occupied on both the top and bottom of the ship. Shafts of white light shot through the air. Drifter was already firing.

Clutching the controls, Tiff led the ship through the first conglomeration, tilting the ship left and then right. She couldn't avoid every asteroid, so she chose which ones would do the least damage to the ship, leaving the rest of it up to Loot and Drifter. They blasted most of the smaller rocks before they reached the hull, but every few minutes she heard a crash and cringed, wondering how much damage the hits were causing. They needed this ship to get to Refuge. It would do them no good to crash on Sahara 354 and never be able to take off again.

As they grew closer to the largest asteroid in the middle, Tiff recalculated her coordinates. The bulk of the rock loomed on the main sight panel like a small planet. Two other large asteroids half its size flanked it, moving slowly in its gravitational pull. On either side were thousands of small rocks flying at them like cracked mugs hurtled during an Omega cafeteria brawl. She would have to fly between the bigger ones to make it out.

The force of the gravitational pull strengthened, and she engaged the backward thrusters to slow down. It wasn't enough. The *Morphic Marauder* hurtled toward the monstrous asteroid, destined to collide with one of the huge rocks in its orbit. Tiff turned the ship on its side, trying to make it as skinny as possible. The asteroids hovered seconds away, and she realized the ship wouldn't make it through without grazing one side or the other. Drifter perched in the turret at the top and Loot sat in the module at the bottom. She had only a second to decide.

Tiff pulsed the bottom engines, sending the top of the ship toward the jagged edge. Tears welled in her eyes. The warning beeps flashed, and she saw Drifter's lasers shoot in a steady stream, trying to break off a piece of the rock before it hit. The chances were slim, but if she were trapped in that small bubble of glass, she'd have the trigger down hard, too.

Guilt sickened her stomach. It was her fault they'd gotten into this asteroid field, her impatience and impulsiveness. She closed her eyes and waited for the impact to the top turret.

No sound came. Tiff opened her eyes and looked out the main sight panel. A chunk of rock sailed through the space in front of them before Loot blasted it into dust. Drifter had managed to break it apart. The particles hit the glass and bounced off, careening though open space.

Both men had made it. Tiff swallowed acid in her throat and leaned back in her chair. Drifter had survived. How would she explain why she'd chosen Loot over him?

Chapter Twelve
Sea of Bones

Thump, thump, thump, thump.

The sound of someone running on plastic mixed with the gush of falling water.

Aries sat on the plush, purple carpet of her parents' living room on the *New Dawn*, her fingers digging into the thick fibers. A waterfall plunged into a forest on a screen to her right and her brother ran, smooth as a gazelle, on a treadmill behind her.

He shot her an annoyed look. "Aren't you going to get that?"

"Get what?" Aries straightened up. A feeling of displacement shot through her and she swerved with dizziness. The carpet underneath her fingers felt fake and, for some strange reason, she expected it to be sand instead. A persistent beep sounded in front of her, bringing her thoughts back to the room.

Her brother pressed a panel on the console treadmill, upping the speed. "The door."

"Oh." Aries scrambled up and pressed the hailing panel.

Tria's blue-eyed face stared up at her from the identification screen.

"Hey, Aries. You won't believe it, but I have our future life assignments in my hands."

"Really?" Aries pressed the panel to dissolve the door and the chrome fizzled away like the foam on top of an opened vitamin soda can. A warm, comforting feeling spread through her at the sight of her childhood friend. Her eyes burned on the brink of tears. "Tria."

"You look as though you haven't seen me in years." Tria wore her uniform, her shiny, blue *New Dawn* badge over her right breast. She'd tied her hair up in a bun, but stray wisps of gold poked out, catching the fluorescent light. "Don't you want to see your life assignments?"

"You bet."

She handed Aries a slim piece of paper cut from a fancy, thick stock. Aries knew this had to be important to use any paper at all, never mind premium white stock. "I was walking by the main deck when the orders were issued. It took a lot of convincing to let me bring yours to you. Go on. Tear the seal."

Aries studied the fancy golden sticker with the *New Dawn* symbol and her fingers slid under the envelope flap. In one second she'd know the exact course of her predestined life: her job, her husband, and her future on the *New Dawn*. She swayed back, overwhelmed, her stomach churning. "We should do it together."

"Of course." Tria held hers up.

Aries' fingers slid forward, tearing the seal as the white paper cut a slit in her skin. A thin red line appeared, so she put her finger in her mouth and sucked while opening the folded document one-handed. She wanted biology and gardening so badly, when the words stared her in the face, she hardly believed them.

Engineering: Life-Support Systems Diagnostics and Management.

A list of the procedures and operations followed and she flipped through it, trailing drops of blood to get to the next life-changing assignment. The words lay there, blunt and fat in black ink. They might as well have been carved in stone.

Life Partner: Lieutenant Astor Barliss.

"What is it?" Tria stared at her as if she'd turned into a ghost. "What did you get?"

"Engineering: Life Support Systems and—"

"I got that, too."

Aries' brother chimed in from behind them, "A most important and honorable job, indeed."

Tria rolled her eyes at him. "Always the diplomat, aren't we, Trent?"

"Don't start that again." Aries put a hand on her friend's shoulder. "Let's not fight. At least we'll be together."

"I know you wanted—"

"Shh." Aries shot a glance over at her brother. "Not now, okay?"

"Okay. Sheesh! You act as though they have microphones in the walls. Who's your life partner?"

His name felt stale on her tongue. "Astor Barliss."

"Oh." Tria looked away. "Isn't he too old for you?"

Aries' brother jumped off the treadmill. "Hey, Lieutenant Barliss is a respectable man and a highly trained official. It's not every day a maintenance engineer gets paired with an elite officer. You should be honored."

Aries' throat tightened and she couldn't suck in enough air. The room pressed in on her, the waterfall gushing in her ears, an unstoppable force.

Her brother moved by her and put a heavy hand on her shoulder. He pressed down, his tone hard and edged with warning. "You are honored, aren't you?"

Aries gasped in a small breath. "Of course." She swallowed and focused on Tria, as if ignoring it would make it go away. "Tria, who'd you get?"

Tria flipped her paper over. Her eyes widened as she read.

"Tria?"

She crumpled the paper in her hand and turned to leave. "I don't want to talk about it."

"Why?" Aries grabbed her arm as she ran to the door. Her life partner couldn't be any worse than a controlling superior officer with a penchant for power. Tria wriggled out of her grasp and pressed the panel. The door fizzled away.

"I'm going for a walk."

Aries grasped her friend's arm. "Wait, Tria. Tell me who."

Tria sighed. "Adam Stenzer."

An image of a man lying eternally in a sleep pod flashed in her mind. Tria would be bound to a sperm donor, not a husband. Aries didn't know what to say.

"You can appeal it." Aries spoke out of hope, not only for her friend but for herself.

"We all know what happens to appeals, don't we?" Tria kicked her boot against the chrome, unable to make a dent.

Tria moved, but Aries still held onto her arm. "Where are you going to go?"

"Don't worry. I'll be on this ship somewhere. We'll always be on this ship somewhere, won't we?"

Aries loosened her grip as the reality of Tria's words hit her. When she didn't answer, Tria took off down the hall. Before she could follow her, Aries' brother pulled her back inside, pressing the door-seal panel. The chrome coalesced into a barrier between her and her friend.

"Hey, it's not Adam's fault he's comatose. It was a freak accident, and he's lucky to be alive. Don't feel bad for her, Aries. Even though odds are he won't wake up, the man's got perfect genes and that's what matters. Her children will be smart and healthy."

Aries turned around and stared into her brother's eyes, wondering if he'd ever questioned the policies of the Guide. Knowing Trent, he'd eaten every word of it up, just like he gulped down spinach because they'd told him it would make him strong. But was this really the best pairing for Tria? Was Lieutenant Barliss the best man for her? Could computers ever calculate wrong?

Trent sauntered into the kitchen and opened a bottle of vitamin water. "With an attitude like that, she's going to get herself into trouble. I'm glad you took the news well." He gulped the beverage down and wiped his mouth with the back of his hand. "You're a true Lifer, and Tria, she's bad news. I'd stay away from her as much as possible, even if you two are assigned to the same job."

Aries never questioned Trent, but to separate her from Tria stirred up so much resentment, she had no choice but to speak her mind. "Why?"

"People talk. Tria's attracted the wrong type of attention from the upper command." He leaned in close, so close his eyes bored into hers. "You don't want to be associated with her, Aries, especially if you're now tied to the lieutenant."

Aries looked back at the door, wanting to be with Tria and not Trent. She took in a deep breath and forced herself to meet her brother's gaze. "Gotcha."

"Good." Trent disappeared into his bedroom and closed the door.

Aries' body loosened in relief. She'd played the game well today, giving the appearance of compliance. But inside, she hurt like she'd been punched in the stomach. She worried about Tria, who didn't want to play the game at all. If her rebellious attitude continued, she'd be contained in the emergency bay and given meds to keep her under control. Aries would rather die than be kept in a prison, and she knew Tria well enough to assume her friend would do the same.

The screen on the wall flickered, the rushing waterfall morphing into desolate wasteland. Misty water and verdant shrubbery became gray, pockmarked rock. A single figure in a space suit stood by a broken escape pod. The spaceman stared back at her and beckoned her to come closer with a curling index finger.

Aries stepped toward the screen, the static from the light making the room seem like she'd walked into an old black and white movie. Her bare feet pressed into the carpet, her toes clenching. The suit's visor clicked open and Tria stared out.

"No, don't do it!" Aries collapsed beside the screen, putting her hands up to the wall. "You didn't test the air!"

Tria's face shrank as the atmosphere sucked the air from her lungs. Her voice was faint as her last breath flew away. "You aren't free yet. Barliss is close and his search is relentless." Her voice turned to a rasp. "Be careful. You're walking right into his slimy hands."

"Tria, put your visor back up. The *New Dawn* will come back for you. I know it."

The whites of Tria's eyes filled with red as the veins burst, spilling blood. Her eyes glazed over, staring at the space above her. Her voice sounded in Aries' head, because her lips no longer moved. "I know, Aries. That's not what I want."

As she fell to the barren rock, the screen faded to static. Aries beat her fists upon the wall. "No!" She didn't care if her brother heard her or if the *New Dawn* officials marked her as insane. Everything felt like it was too late. Sinking to the carpet, she wept.

...

A snarly reptile face, two inches long, hissed at Aries as she woke, flashing its headdress of scaly skin and dancing from side to side.

Aries screamed and scrambled away, pushing sand at it with her heels.

"What is it?" Striker peeked his head under the tarp.

"A lizard! Over there." Aries backed up toward his feet.

Striker grabbed it and held it down with his knee. He pulled out a knife and cut its head off in front of her. "That's what I call breakfast."

The haziness of a disturbing dream kept her from thinking clearly, and she rubbed her eyes, trying to shake the feeling of uneasiness. Although she could blame it on the reptile, she knew the uneasiness ran deeper than a snarly wake-up call.

"You were supposed to be keeping lookout."

"For raiders, yes. For critters, no." He grinned and offered her his canteen. "You slept like you were in hyper-sleep."

"I guess trekking across the desert can make a person tired."

"Understandable." Striker examined the lizard's body as if deciding how to eat it.

Aries sat up and stretched. Her skin felt sore and itchy from sunburn and every move made it worse. "Any more raiders?"

"None since the last caravan."

She watched as he gutted the animal and fried it on a rock with his laser gun. "Good. That last caravan was enough for me. What about those awful sandworms?"

Striker shook his head and scanned the horizon. "The sand is too thickly packed in this region for them to dig through. That's one reason the raiders have made this their home."

"At least we don't have to worry about them coming up from the ground. You're not really going to eat that, are you?"

"You bet. You should try it, too. Our supplies are only going to go so far, and you never know when another meal will walk right into camp."

Aries wondered if it would be anything like the scorpion he'd cooked for her earlier. Small reptiles were the least of her worries. She searched the distance, expecting the *New Dawn* to emerge from the horizon like a flying beast, but nothing came. The dunes were an endless sea of hazy, golden light.

"You seem on edge this morning," Striker said. "Bad dreams?"

"You could say that."

Striker's voice was soft. "Afraid of raiders?"

"No. I'm more afraid of being found by the man who's searching for me."

Striker picked at the lizard's hide. "You never told me what he's like." Although his tone was nonchalant, Aries could see the muscles in his jaw tighten.

She'd never voiced her thoughts, not all of them. Not even to Tria. "His name's Barliss. He's controlling."

Striker tested a piece of meat. "Don't worry. I won't let him find you."

"No, you don't understand. He's bent on ambition. Closed minded, insecure, and self-centered."

Striker stabbed another piece of lizard meat and handed it to her. "Wow, that bad, huh?"

Aries shook her head. She'd lost her appetite. "Yeah. And he'll go to every extreme to find me, even if it means sacrificing some of the crew. His concern for humanity's DNA isn't going to outweigh his desire to pass on his own. If he doesn't have me, the computer may not let him have anyone."

"Listen, he's going to have to get through me to get to you. I won't let him get you, okay?"

Aries sighed. "That's what I'm afraid of. He'll kill you, Striker. I know it. I won't have you die for me."

"No one's dying. You're helping me find the last piece of my ship so we can get the hell out of here." He stared at her with an intense gaze. "Besides, you're worth any risk."

A shot of heat ran through her. His compliment jump-started her heart. She wanted to ask him about the woman he'd loved, but she stopped, unable to form the right question. She envied her, whoever she was, this woman who'd once held Striker's heart. Aries yearned to ease the pain this woman had caused him, just like he wanted to protect her. Could she be the woman to make him love again? Aries took a deep breath before pushing the issue.

"Any risk? But—I thought last night, when you said…?"

Striker ruffled his hair, the black waves resettling in such a way Aries longed to run her hands through them. "I said I didn't want a lover. That doesn't mean I don't value your friendship. You're special, Aries. You're smart and kind. You want to help me save this dying species. You deserve better than Barliss, and I won't let him have you."

Aries wanted to scream at him, *If I deserve better than Barliss, why can't I be with you?*

The question rested on the tip of her tongue. Why couldn't she spit it out?

Striker spoke before she could voice her thoughts. "Now, let's have some breakfast, shall we?"

Aries sighed as disappointment overwhelmed her. She'd missed her chance. But maybe life was better this way. She couldn't handle being rejected twice. She'd storm off into the desert alone, with no ride home. "Scrambled eggs and bacon?"

"More like scrambled scorpion and lizard-strips."

"Sounds delicious."

They ate and packed up camp, stuffing the tarp into Striker's backpack. He smoothed over their indents on the side of the dune with his walking stick, then they followed the same path as the raiders.

Aries had to make sure her clothing covered every bit of her skin. Flakes peeled off her nose and arms from the previous day's trek, and she didn't want any more of her body to burn. Striker's skin was darker than hers, tanned from his years of exposure. The way the sun hit his cheeks and forehead made his skin glow like he was some bronzed demi-god. Again, she wished she could reach out and touch him, but after the scene last night, she decided against it, holding her hands close to her sides.

They climbed a plateau to a large plain. Spindly thickets of grass grew in patches and cactus rose in bulbous forms with sickly, sweet-smelling flowers and prickles the size of her hand.

"Don't eat those." Striker kicked one out of his way as it hung down. "They're poisonous."

"I wasn't going to." Aries turned in the direction they were headed. White structures littered the horizon like an abandoned city. Her eyes squinted against the glare of the sun as she peered out from underneath her raised hand. "What are those?"

Striker turned around and gave her a wistful smile. "That's what I call the Sea of Bones."

"Bones?"

Striker gestured ahead. "You'll see."

As they trekked closer, the white stalks poked out of the ground and curved around in patterns. Aries realized that they weren't frames of buildings at all, but giant rib cages of massive beasts, sprawled out like some doomed migration, all heading the same way.

Aries stepped through the first skeleton, making sure not to trip on the bumps in the sand. "Jeez. What happened to them?"

Striker shrugged. "Climate change? Like the dinosaurs on Earth?"

The skeletons looked far nastier than any triceratops or tyrannosaurus. Their teeth curved out like a wire fence blasted with a laser gun, sharp as diamond points and as thick as her fingers The sockets where the eyes had been lay deeply sunk in each skull and slanted in an empty but still menacing predator's stare.

Aries skirted around the skulls as if they'd come to life at any moment and swallow her whole. A great sense of futility washed over her with the transient nature of all things, large and small. The universe was a vast wasteland with small pockets of life, and even those pockets faded out like dying stars.

"You okay?"

Aries stared into the mouth of one of the beasts, unmoving. Striker had picked his way through most of the bones and waited for her on the open plains. *All I can do is hold on to what I have.* She scrambled to catch up, leaping over a serrated tail.

Striker waited for her with a questioning look on his face.

She shivered despite the arid heat. "It's just unsettling, that's all."

He put an arm around her shoulders. "Everything has its time. The trick is to enjoy life while it lasts."

Aries settled against his hard body and allowed herself to soak up his comfort. She breathed in deeply, smelling the morning's smoky laser breakfast on his clothes. He squeezed her close to him and she put her arm around his waist. She felt so alive in that moment and held on tightly, as if he were all she needed in the world, but Striker ended the embrace and resumed their trek.

The sand turned to hard soil, and the dunes became small mountains of jagged rock. They reached the edge of the raiders' den when the dual suns rose and set. Using the tarp as cover, they crept closer and peered from the top of a ledge.

Hundreds of rawhide tents flapped in the dry breeze, painted with red and blue, the colors of the lizard men's scaly skin. Tethered desert cows stomped the ground and bleated, stinking up the air. Aries watched as raiders darted in between dwellings, carrying buckets of water and sacks on the tips of sticks. They moved in sinuous arcs, graceful as snakes in water, leaving little or no tracks in the hard-packed sand.

Aries brought out her locator, having muted the sound after its last ill-timed alert, and searched for the coral readings. At first it registered all the life-forms, green dots blinking everywhere. She narrowed the search, adjusting the parameters to locate only the material matching the alien ship. It took a few moments to scan the area before honing in on a target thirty meters away.

"Over there." She pointed to the western side of the camp near a pen of desert cows. It appeared the raiders had built a statue using the coral processor as a foundation. Skulls and rocks dangled from sticks, decorated with beads and tinkling pieces of metal.

Striker pulled the binoculars from his backpack and peered through them. "It's right in the middle of their tents. We need a diversion." He handed her the binoculars.

"We could create a landslide from the cliff's edge." Aries brought down the binoculars to look into Striker's eyes.

"One of us would have to stay behind, and it'll take two people to move it. Besides, they're smarter than you think. They'll search for the originator of the disturbance." Striker held his chin in his hand. "I don't want to risk it."

"Oh." Aries' heart sank. The task seemed so impossible. She didn't want to sacrifice Striker for her freedom. She'd go back to the *New Dawn* before she'd cause this good man's death. "How are we going to get that part?"

Striker settled back against a rock cropping. "Sleep on it. Maybe one of us will think up something in the morning."

Aries clenched her fists in frustration. They were so close. Just as she set her life-form locator down on the sand, a deep buzzing sound rumbled in her ear. She scrambled to look over the ledge. Raiders slithered out of their tents in chaos like a brood of snakes, some arming themselves with feather-tipped spears. Striker whipped out his binoculars and searched the horizon behind them. "Damn. Looks like we're not the only visitors."

He handed her the binoculars, although Aries knew who approached. She'd heard that rumbling sound her whole life. Raising the binoculars to her eyes in resignation she looked and affirmed her worst fears. Scout ships hovered over the sand. Focusing on the hull of the lead ship, she could see the painted insignia of the *New Dawn*.

"Are those your friends?"

"More like my enemies now."

Barliss stood on the prow of the lead ship, holding up a laser gun as long as her leg. Aries swore and pounded her fist in the sand.

Striker pulled her back behind the ledge. "We've got to get out of here."

"No." She jerked out of his grasp and turned toward the processor. That smooth object represented her only chance at freedom. "Now we have our diversion."

Chapter Thirteen
Bargaining Chip

The smooth flight was almost surreal to Tiff as she maneuvered through the last pebbles of the asteroid belt. The *Morphic Marauder*'s engines thrusted, and she zipped into the clear space, feeling as though they'd all escaped death. She didn't ease her grip of the controls until the litter of rocks became specks on the horizon behind the ship. Her thoughts were too tumultuous to revel in the victory. The navigational controls clocked Sahara 354 as one more day away.

"Is it over?" Reckon's raspy voice interrupted her concentration. She turned to see the old man hunched over and wheezing like he'd run a marathon. His dark cloak hung half off, as if an asteroid had hit the hull before he could slip the second arm in its sleeve. His wispy, rat-gray hair stuck up in the back.

She sighed in resignation. "Yes."

"I didn't know you were such a risk taker, sweetie."

"I'm not." Tiff restrained a rising thread of anxiety. "A gravitation force pulled us in. It was beyond my control."

"Was it, now?" His beady eyes narrowed, and she wondered if the uncertainties lurking in her heart shone clearly on her face.

Tiff tried not to set her temper loose on the old man. "I would never intentionally put us in danger."

"Where's Drifter?"

She resisted the urge to wince at his name. "He'll be here shortly." She wanted to curl up and hide in the wires under the control panel, but showing such weakness was unthinkable for a pirate. Weakness got men like Striker marooned on desert planets. Weakness got men like her brother blown up in space.

"I know what you did." Reckon pointed a grime-crusted finger with a broken nail at her. "You tipped the ship. You came close enough to risk the upper gun pod."

"Shut up!" Tiff shot him a sizzling stare. "Or I'll push your wiry body into space before you can get a helmet on."

Heavy footsteps stomped down the corridor, and she flicked the switch to autopilot. She didn't know how long this argument would take.

Drifter barged in like a star about to go supernova, pushing his way past Reckon and honing in on Tiff. Sweat soaked his oily, long hair, and he wiped it back from his fierce eyes. "What the hell were you thinking?"

Tiff stood her ground. "I was doing my job, trying to get the ship out of those asteroids safely."

He stared at her incredulously. "I don't know who you are anymore. You could have gotten me killed."

"You're still standing here, right?"

"Yeah, no thanks to you. I could have sworn the ship tilted as that mother of an asteroid came too close."

Reckon cleared his throat and spoke up from behind him. "It did. It swerved toward the right, which was the top, because she had us turned sideways."

Tiff gave Reckon a nasty look and the old man shrugged. "I'm siding with him," he said.

Drifter's eyes lit up with the new information. "I see. You were trying to keep Loot safe, weren't you?"

Tiff had to look away this time. She couldn't deny his accusation.

"You chose that ragamuffin over me, a looting pipe rat you found cowering in the air shafts."

Tiff turned away toward the main sight panel. The glinting stars mocked her. "He's still a boy. I couldn't let him die."

"I see how it is." Drifter walked up behind her and swiveled her chair around so she had to face him. He stuck his nose right up to hers. "You swoon over your old boyfriend all the time and kick me out of your bed, then you chose a teen brat over me."

Spittle leaked from the corner of his mouth and Tiff wondered if it would sizzle and foam.

"It's over, Tiff. Once we're outta here and on that moon, you're on your own. No more free rides on my ship. You're lucky I keep my end of bargains, or else I'd leave your sorry ass in the desert." He tore his face away from her and stormed out of the room, leaving Reckon to stand like an awkward gremlin by the door.

Tiff crunched up inside like recycled metal in a garbage compacter. She'd remade herself so many times she didn't think she had anything left to morph into.

Reckon stepped forward and held out a hand, his raggedy cloak dragging on the floor. "If you're not with Drifter anymore, I'd be happy to take his place."

"Get away from me." The words came in a squeak. She searched the control console in front of her and scooped up her only working light pen. She threw it at him, but it missed and shattered in three pieces against the wall. The old man ducked and hustled into the shadows of the corridor, muttering under his foul breath.

Tiff held her shoulders and tried to keep from shaking. Goosebumps pimpled her skin and nervous jitters ran down her arms and legs. The sprawling vastness of space stretched out before her in an endless slate of black, cold and empty. The feeling of being on her own scared her more than anything else in the world.

…

Reckon settled on the floor next to his cot and typed in the code to open his tool box. The back of his head ached where he'd fallen during an asteroid hit, but Drifter had given him clear instructions and he needed to get his work done before they reached Sahara 354.

"Yeah." He clicked open the lid. "Find a way to steal a piece of DNA and record Striker's voice patterns so we don't have to keep him around. Easy enough to say, but hard to do." Drifter might as well have asked him to clone the exile.

He puttered around in the box, throwing used nanodrives over his shoulder to find one with recording space available. "Yeah, I'll just get him to recite the entire alphabet and count to one hundred. What does Drifter think this is? *Sesame Quadrant with Kyro the Alien Bird?*

Besides, even if he did have him speak every known letter and number, the rhythm would be off and, knowing Striker, the coder would sense that. The only way they were going to get those coordinates was to have Striker release them. Whether or not the man would be willing to divulge them was another matter altogether, and not Reckon's responsibility.

As he reached for another nanodrive, a glossy green case poked up from the pile, catching his eye. None of his scratched-up copies had such a shiny sheen. Reckon picked it up and examined the cover. The plastic had no nicks or scuff marks. He popped it open and handled the glistening nanodrive that lay inside. Had Tiff's or Drifter's stuff gotten mixed up with his? He turned it over and saw a small label with his name written in unfamiliar handwriting.

Reckon scratched his head. Who would leave him a message? He didn't have many contacts back at the spaceport, and whoever had left this must have known the combination for the toolbox and slipped it in when he wasn't looking. The only person better than he was at combinations had been marooned five years ago, left to live the life of a desert nomad.

As Reckon popped the nanodrive into his central processor, a series of codes blinked on the screen, asking for answers. It looked like Striker's work, indeed. Reckon began decoding the string of numbers, his fingers typing fast. It was easier than he'd expected, and he wondered if the person behind it made the code only hard enough to keep from everyone except Reckon himself.

The screen flickered and Reckon secured the door panel to his room before turning back to watch the nanodrive play.

On the screen, a man in his sixties appeared, wearing an old flight uniform from Outpost Omega. He had the prominent forehead and sharp nose of a general, but wrinkles and dark shadows circled his deep-set eyes. He carried an aura of wistful regret, like an old bald eagle with a broken wing. He had Reckon's complete attention. Listening carefully, Reckon upped the volume with a few flicks of his fingertip and leaned closer.

"You may not recognize me, Reckon, but I'm James Wilfred the third, otherwise known as Decoder, Striker's father."

Reckon inhaled sharply. Hadn't the man died years ago? He'd never given any credence to the rumors that Decoder had retired in seclusion, shutting himself in his small cell in the far reaches of the space station. For a moment, Reckon considered turning the message off, in case James Wilfred the third had programmed some type of bomb, but if Striker's old man had wanted their ship destroyed, he would have done it by now. No, he'd meant this message to be heard, and by Reckon's ears alone.

"I'm aware of your mission to find my son. Don't concern yourself with the details, just know I have my sources and know about the map. As you figured out, there's no way you can decode it without him." The old man smiled as if experiencing a happy memory. "My son is too smart to trust pirates with something so valuable."

Reckon clenched his fist. "Get on with it, Decoder."

"I thought, as a coder yourself, you were smarter than that, as well." Striker's father leaned in, as if he could see Reckon sitting there on the floor, and narrowed his eyes. "What makes you think these people are going to take you with them to paradise? Why won't they dump you in the desert like they did my son?"

Reckon snorted and looked away, but Decoder had a point.

"You and Striker must work together as allies if you ever want to see the greenery of paradise. I can give you what these other pirates can't. Bring my son back to me, and you'll have your ticket to the better world. I'm a man of my word, and I can assure you I'll keep to it. Convince these pirates they have to keep Striker until the very end. Watch his back. When the battle begins, remember who your true ally is."

The image flickered out, leaving Reckon with a decision to make. He couldn't break the code on the map, and it was close to impossible to record Striker's voice and gather enough DNA to make it happen without him. He might as well play his cards wisely and convince Drifter to keep Striker safe until they reached the space station. Then he could see which bargain turned out for the best.

Out of the two of them, Decoder had a more solid reputation than Drifter. Reckon would have to balance on a fine line, but he'd done it before. How else had he survived so many years in a bubble-like rat cage teeming with desperation and treachery?

Chapter Fourteen
Sacrifice

Aries leaped over a ridge and scrambled down the cliff side, her boots sliding on loose pebbles as she flailed her arms to gain balance. She chanced one look behind to make sure Striker followed, then threw herself across a gorge in a race against time. Meanwhile, the raiders below them sprinted ahead to the battle in a meager effort to protect their civilization. Aries knew they'd be a scant deterrent to Barliss.

"We have to get to the processor before they do!" She landed on another ledge. She caught a glimpse of the white coral on the horizon, glistening in the rays of the larger sun.

"Be careful!" Striker leaped to join her. He grabbed her arm, halting her. "It'll be no good to us if you break your leg, or even worse, get caught by a raider and can't help me drag it away."

Aries couldn't heed his words of warning. A fierce burst of anxiety had shot through her blood like a bolt of electricity when she'd caught sight of Barliss and the ships. All she could think of was stealing the processor.

Striker pulled her behind a rock. "Wait until the path is clear."

"It's as clear as it's going to get. I'll fight any raider that gets in my way."

"I don't want to lose you."

"We'll both be captured if we don't get that processor." He stopped her by cradling the back of her head with his hand. Blasts erupted behind them as the first set of search and rescue ships entered the colony, but neither one of them moved.

Aries felt a pull toward him, a tug of emotion that resonated deep within her. "Striker, I want to fly away with you. I want us to be together."

Striker leaned in so close, Aries felt his breath on her lips. His voice was deep and husky. "I want that, too."

"Then we have to go now." Aries tore away as the last few raiders scurried past them. She ran across the open plain toward the structure built on top of the processor. Behind her she heard Striker shout. "Aries, no!"

She'd been so focused on the processor, she hadn't realized the fence surrounding the desert cows lay open, the beasts stampeding toward her.

Aries looked all around her, but it was too late to run. She froze in place as the massive beasts came at her, their stomps rumbling in the pit of her stomach.

The first one missed her by inches. Its tentacle-like trunks reached short of her arm. A waft of filthy air blew her hair back in its wake. Another came right at her, belting and bleating as it pounded toward her. Its trunks reached out to entangle her and she ducked and rolled underneath its belly.

She saw a clear path to the processor through the chaos of rampaging beasts in front of her and sprinted ahead, weaving in and out of the herd.

Skulls of all shapes and sizes decorated the structure. The search teams at her back forced her to waste no time, so she threw them all down to the sand. A beak-shaped skull came first, followed by a string of teeth bigger than her index fingers. As Aries pulled the decorations off, she wondered what god the lizard men prayed to and what kind of temple she defiled. Guilt came over her, but she reminded herself another race wouldn't have a chance without this processor.

As she cleared the first layer off the processor, something grabbed her shoulder and threw her back. Aries landed on her butt, the air knocked out of her. A spearhead jabbed at her throat and she rolled onto her side to get away. A raider stood over her, hissing and clicking his two-pronged tongue. Aries picked up the skulls she'd discarded in the sand and threw them at the raider. Each one cracked on the shaft of his spear as he blocked her weak throws. He lunged for her belly and she kicked at his scaly legs, trying to send him off balance.

As the spear came within inches of her, Striker yelled and tackled the raider, sending them both into the dust stirred by the stampede. Aries scrambled up with an alien skull in her hand, her fingers poking through the eye sockets. She raised her arm to throw it, but feared she'd hit Striker instead of the lizard man. Striker gained the advantage, and as he pinned the lizard man's arms and held him down, Aries turned toward the familiar sound of ship engines.

She watched in horror as the *New Dawn*'s search vessels plowed through the dwellings, killing everything in their path.

"Striker, we don't have much time!"

"What do you want me to do, ask him to help us?" Striker fumbled with the raider's clothing, trying to use it to tie his arms.

"Let him go."

Striker cast her a baffled look as the raider wriggled underneath him.

"Look around you. His home is ruined. He's got nowhere to go but to run away."

"Damn it to hell." Striker released him and threw him backwards. "Get on with you, now. Go away." The raider cowered, holding his arm over his head as he scurried away.

They pulled the processor free of the rest of the beads and other debris that could only be the lizard men's offerings. Stripped of its decorations, Aries saw the entire bulk of the processor for the first time. The frame was three times bigger than a computer monitor and carved with strange, loopy writing and pictures of feathered wings. Striker ran his hands across it, wiping away the grit.

Aries' heart raced. "I hope it will still work."

"We'll have to get it back to the ship to know for certain. It looks like it's in great shape, though." He looked back at her and smiled. "At least they didn't bash it in."

Striker ran around it to the other side. "Get your hands underneath it."

A tent erupted into flames behind them and the heat singed her hair. Trying to be tough, she squinted her eyes and shoved her hands into the sand at its base.

"Heave!"

Aries' muscles tightened as they hoisted it off the ground. She wished she'd done more weight lifting back on the *New Dawn*. Her arms shook with the effort like frail twigs.

Striker lifted the brunt of the weight and gestured with his head over his shoulder. "Over there! In the shadows of the cliffs."

Looking behind her, Aries saw the silver hull of one of the hoverships cutting through the black smoke. "They're gaining on us."

Striker smiled despite the weight he carried. "We'll make it."

They carried the processor in staggering steps through the dust and smoke and underneath a cliff's edge, where they hid in a shadow. A ravine behind the settlement, flanked by twin mountains, provided an escape route.

"Look for a place to hide it."

"We're not going to take it back with us?"

Striker hefted the processor higher to get a better grip. "We'll have to come back for it."

"What if the Lifers find it? What if they take it with them?"

"That's a chance we'll have to take. Right now we need to get the hell outta here."

Raiders ran by them in retreat, some carrying their wounded in makeshift slings. Aries froze as she saw a parent carrying a bleeding child in its arms. "Their blood is the same color as ours," she muttered under her breath. "They have families. They're just like us."

Striker was too busy surveying the cliff side. "Come on." He tugged the processor forward and she went with it. "I see a crevice in the rock."

They crossed the fleeing population of raiders and sneaked into a crack in the other side of the cliff. Aries' arms ached as she set down the heavy weight. "Here." Striker threw her his cloak. "Put the hood up. We can't stay here."

When she didn't move fast enough, Striker stepped over the processor to her side and wrapped his cloak around her shoulders. "Do they have life-form locators?"

Reality hit her hard and her skin prickled with fear. "They do. Better ones than I have."

Striker pulled the hood over her head and tied the strings taut. "We have to make a run for it. We'll get lost in the wave of raiders."

Aries reached for Striker's hand. "Striker, wait. If anything happens to us, I want you to know that I…"

Striker put a finger to her lips to silence her. "You can tell me when we're safe. Right now, we have to run."

Before she could protest, he pulled her back into the sun. They ran in the wave of refugees, and she held on to Striker's hand, afraid to get separated. Hoverships appeared in the distance, shooting lasers at the trailing lizard men.

One of the ships glided over them to the front of the fleeing horde, spewing up sand and smoke. Aries covered her mouth, keeping her face down so the hood covered her auburn hair as Striker covered her with his arm.

"What are they doing?" Striker asked her, raising his voice over the noise of the engines.

Before she could respond, the ship aimed lasers at the rock wall and shot the cliff side, freeing a landslide of rocks. The raiders around them ducked as debris fell in front of them, crushing the few unlucky refugees at the front of the exodus.

Aries' hope sank, and terror rose in its place. "They're blocking our escape!"

The other ships closed in from behind and Aries searched the high cliff walls, but they were too steep to climb.

"What are we going to do?"

"Hide in here." Striker pulled her to a crevice in the rock, wide enough for only her to slip through. Lasers fired around them, and a few raiders fell forward. Aries slipped in but clutched his hand, not wanting to let go.

"Where are you going to—"

Striker pulled his hand away. "I'll draw their attention away."

Before she could protest, he disappeared into the masses.

The ships' engines rumbled as they approached. Aries pressed into the rock, trying to slide more deeply into the crevice. She watched Striker as long as she could, until she lost his dark hair in the crowd. The ships touched down, flinging up clouds of sand. The engines stopped, and it felt like time stopped as well. Her heart hung in suspension as she waited for the dust to settle.

A metal edge cut through the haze as the ramp lowered. Barliss stepped onto the ground like a world conqueror, holding an ultrasonic tranquilizer ray with blue static fizzling at its orb-like center. Her blood froze in her veins. If that hit Striker, he'd go down cold. It would take days to wake him up.

Although Barliss looked even more physically fit, with his muscles filling out his perfectly pressed uniform and his blond hair gleaming white in the sun, to Aries he'd never looked less attractive. After spending time with Striker, no man would ever compare, and certainly not one who suffocated every last ounce of her freedom.

Other guards followed Barliss, fanning out to collect the fallen raiders around the ship. "Bring them to the ship," a man ordered. "Lieutenant Barliss wants to inspect them."

She recognized the voice immediately as Langston, the hovercraft pilot from the *New Dawn*. They'd grown up together, enrolled in the same mechanics class. He'd graduated at the top of their unit. Aries knew he could work the life-form locator like no one else.

"This one is human, sir."

Aries' heart skidded.

"A man?" Barliss' rude voice echoed in the ravine. "Bring him here."

Aries watched in horror from her crack in the rock as Langston dragged Striker to the lead ship. Aries crept forward enough to see their faces.

Langston unwrapped Striker's headscarf. "Looks like an Outlander or a pirate, sir."

Barliss pushed his way through the men and shoved his face into Striker's. "We're looking for a runaway. Five-foot-five, slender, with auburn hair."

Striker looked him straight in the eye. "Haven't seen her."

Barliss pulled his head back and sized Striker up and down. "What's a space pirate doing out here in the middle of nowhere, anyway?"

"What's a colony ship doing on an uninhabitable planet?"

Barliss smacked him across the face and Aries gasped, holding her mouth with both hands. Her fingernails pressed into her cheeks. "I'm the one asking questions. Tell me why you're here or I'll blast a hole in your skull."

Striker didn't look fazed by the threat. He raised a brow. "Deserted by my crew."

Barliss laughed deep in his throat. "Some pirate you are."

Aries noticed Langston had stepped closer, studying a device in his hand. He moved nearer to Striker. The scanner beeped and Langston stepped closer, staring at Striker's chest. He pulled something that Aries couldn't see off his cloak.

"Sir, the DNA matches."

Barliss snatched the invisible object in his pinched fingers. A hair from her head. It had to be. He dangled it in front of Striker's face, a glint of auburn. "Want to explain this?"

Striker spat on the ground.

Barliss cocked his laser gun at Striker's foot. "If you don't tell me where she is, you'll be a one-legged man."

Aries knew Barliss would fire, and she tensed as his finger curled around the trigger. Striker stood, ready to die for her, and it was all her fault. Just a few days ago, she wouldn't have given up her freedom for anything in the world, and now, one man had changed her entire purpose by working his way into her heart.

Striker remained placid, as if Barliss only threatened to call him a nasty name. "You'll never have her."

"No!" Aries screamed, darting out from the crevice, keeping her gaze riveted on Striker as she ran toward him. "Let him go."

The distraction gave Striker enough time to knock the laser gun out of Barliss' hand and elbow Langston in the throat. The man doubled over, and Striker pulled free.

The hovercrafts' engines revved as she changed direction and ran, racing across the sand to a rock pile blocking the narrow ravine. She ducked underneath a boulder and slid through a tight place between two rocks.

If she could get to the other side, she could make a run for it and meet up with Striker back at the ship. As she wiggled free of the rocks, one of the hoverships flew over her head, blocking the sun. Barliss stood on its prow, aiming the ultrasonic tranquilizer ray.

Aries had no choice. If she hid in the rocks, they'd find her eventually, but if she reached the adjacent cliff, she could hide in the shadows and follow the ledge until she reached a better hiding place. She dashed across the open space, hoping his aim was worse than his temper.

A laser hit the ground by her feet, spraying sand into her eyes. Another hit the ridge above her. Aries zigzagged, hoping she wasn't an easy target. A third laser hit her square in the back, throwing her down and knocking the air out of her lungs. Lying on her stomach, Aries clawed at the sand with her fingernails, but the shock of the stun gun spread through her body, paralyzing her limbs. As it reached her neck, her eyes blurred and the world spun.

"Striker," she mouthed as she writhed in the sand. She hoped he'd managed to escape. Her heart broke as she realized she'd never see him again.

Chapter Fifteen
Sandy Boots

"Well done, Lieutenant Barliss. You've succeeded in yet another mission, demonstrating the highest levels of excellence." Commander Gearhardt pressed a panel on his hoverchair, and the device brought him within arm's reach. He placed a pasty hand with blue veins on Barliss' shoulder. "Welcome back to the *New Dawn*."

Barliss was surprised and honored the commander chose to attend the initial welcoming ceremony as the search and rescue ships unloaded their cargo and the last of the lithium. "Thank you, Commander. It's only under your guidance such success can be achieved."

The commander smiled so openly, it reminded Barliss of the time he'd watched Gearhardt from afar as the old man had listened to a chorus sing the praises of the Guide. "No lives were lost, you found Miss Ryder, and we managed to mine enough fuel to make up for the *New Dawn*'s lost time."

Behind them, men attached harnesses to the animals they'd brought aboard, elephantine mammals with tentacles instead of trunks.

"You've found a few more species to add to our food supply." The commander signaled to the men with a salute of his frail hand. "Our chief biologist is working on a way to breed them as we speak."

One of the beasts reared on its hind legs, and a man fell off its back to the floor. Three others ran to his aid and tugged the beast away. Barliss turned his back on the scene. He didn't need any more reminders of his least-favorite planet in the universe.

"Are you certain we shouldn't stay another day to glean extra resources, Commander?" Barliss had never before proposed anything to the commander concerning objectives, but he didn't like the idea of leaving that renegade pirate free, even if he was deserted with no ship. When Barliss had recognized a strand of Aries' hair on that lowlife's chest, terrible thoughts had flitted through his mind, murderous cravings that he couldn't shake.

Although the life scanners said Aries was unharmed and untouched, he knew what that pirate had wanted. Barliss wanted to track him down and rip his arms off so he could never steal his future wife again. The fact that Aries had called out to help the pirate angered him even more. He'd have to deal with her rebellious nature when she woke up.

"We have enough fuel to make it to Paradise 21 with extra reserves. We've spent enough time off course."

"Yes, sir, we have. Too much time, in fact." Barliss had little choice but to agree with such a direct decision from the commander.

The commander's bright eye winked at him so quickly no one else in the room could see. "However, it's encouraging to see a lieutenant with such noble concerns."

"You are too complimentary, sir."

"And you, too modest." The commander leaned back in the cushions around his head. He looked as though being away from the mainframe and disconnected to its life-preserving energies weakened him. The chair buzzed and rose higher before turning to the elevator shaft to the higher decks. "Your efforts do not go unnoticed." With one finger raised in salute, he rode away.

Barliss sighed, releasing the emotions he'd been keeping in throughout the conversation. Usually he played the tunes of conversation like Chopin struck keys on the piano, but with the commander, he felt like an amoeba underneath a microscope. Someday the old man would see through his façade and realize his favorite lieutenant wasn't as strong, sharp-witted, or noble as everyone thought.

Barliss flexed his shoulders. For now, he was safe. His career rose by solid increments each day. He had Aries back, and he could use the lithium discovery to frame this mission as a personal success instead of a personal humiliation. Smoothing over the front of his uniform, he walked over to the scout ship and watched as a crystal cylinder floated on air down the ramp, guarded by a team of medics.

A member of the medical team held a life scanner connected to the cylinder by a cord. Barliss stopped them before they could pass. He peered inside the glass, but the foggy lid obscured any details. All he could see was the silhouette of auburn hair splayed out like a sleeping beauty.

"Dr. Pern, is it? How's she doing?"

The head doctor looked up at him as if he intruded on a conversation between her and her readings. She flicked her finger over the touchscreen and the monitor changed to strings of numbers that had no meaning to him.

"My apologies, Lieutenant. I'm quite busy right now. I'll provide a report within the hour."

Behind them, the engines ignited as the *New Dawn* broke free of the planet's gravitational pull. The floor shook under their feet as the intercom came on with a low static buzz. They stood in observance, listening to the incoming message.

"All officers on deck. Prepare to leave orbit."

The doctor cocked an eyebrow as if to prod him into action, but Barliss stood his ground. "Her status, Doctor, if I may."

"She's dehydrated and sunburned, but otherwise her condition is stable."

"Good. When will she be awake?"

"The stun laser hit her square in the back at close proximity." She gave him a frown of disapproval as if she knew he'd fired it. "It will take another four or five hours for the brunt of the effects to wear away. Even then, she may not be able to discern her surroundings or stand up and walk around for another twenty-four hours at best."

"Excellent." Barliss couldn't hide his pleasure and didn't try. "By then, we'll be far away from Sahara 354."

. . .

As Striker crested the dune, long cables detached from the ground all around him, rising to holes in the spaceship's underbelly, like tentacles retracting into a jellyfish.

"Damn it to hell!" he shouted, then wheezed, gripping a muscle cramp in his side. His legs burned from running through thick sand, chasing the ships as they'd sailed away. He'd tried to hold their pace with the hope of overtaking one before they headed back to space to join their mothership, but the desert had held him back.

He'd want to leap up and grip one of the cables, but the holes in the ship were too small for him to climb into, even if he'd succeeded. He'd fall to his death when the last of the metal disappeared.

A sense of helplessness washed over him. The thought of the man in charge having Aries made Striker's blood rage like he'd been infected with a disease. Finally, he grasped the extent of the horror she ran from. He understood her desperation and the totality of the sacrifice she'd made to save him.

Collapsing in the sand, he watched the last vessel rise, stirring up mushrooms of dust in the engines' wake. His heart went with it, the growing distance tearing it from his chest. No matter what he'd said, his loyalty to Aries ran deeper than mere comradeship and mutual interests, and her last act proved it beyond a doubt. If such unconditional love existed, then she was his. To have her ripped from him by a monster of a man was beyond cruel. As the ship became smaller and smaller, he reached his hand up to the sky, as if he could grasp it in his palm and drag it back down. The impossibility of all the obstacles between them clogged his brain and battered his logic so he could hardly breathe.

Overcome with grief and frustration, he pounded his fists into the ground until the skin grew red and raw. He'd find a way to get her back. He could finish restoring the alien ship. Thanks to Aries, he had the final piece he needed, and he'd get it to fly. Then, all he had to do was find the *New Dawn*. Aries had said they were traveling to a paradise planet, but that could be anywhere in the unending vastness of space—another impossible obstacle.

Perhaps they'd left behind a clue to their coordinates. Striker looked over the dunes like a desert wanderer searched for an oasis, but the windblown sand covered all tracks in seconds, and he knew they'd never leave behind a map or a skychart.

Frustrated, Striker clenched sand in his fists, the particles falling in a stream around his legs. His thoughts flew in overdrive, each one banging against metal doors. The *New Dawn* would be gone in seconds and leave no trail. So how could he track them?

The answer came to him so suddenly, Striker shot up from the ground as if he'd heard ten sandworms screech in chorus. Aries had left her locator on the alien ship. If he could reverse the frequencies, he could follow the homing beacon back to the *New Dawn*.

The colony ship was now a small speck in the sky, like the glint off the wing of a silver bird. The farther it flew, the slimmer the chances of establishing a connection. Striker threw himself down the dune so fast he almost toppled head over boots. Regaining his balance, he sprinted to the alien wreck. The smaller sun rose at his back as the colossal giant set in front of him, blinding his path with its glorious sunset.

The white column of the alien ship's communications tower protruded from the sand like a fallen obelisk. Striker wiped the windblown grit off the hatch and traced the correct hieroglyph to enter. Seconds ticked away as the platform rose.

He could no longer spot any ships in the sky. They must have breached the final layers of atmosphere into space. The hatch opened, and the platform appeared. Striker jumped down, boots stomping on the floor. As the floor beneath his feet glided down, he thought of all the possible ways to reactivate the locator. A sliver of doubt stung his confidence and he pushed it away. He could decode anything, even the controls to an alien ship—he'd be able to rework a simple homing beacon.

The locator sat, untouched, in the corner of the table where he'd discarded it after dislodging the cuff from Aries' arm. Striker dug up all his tools, spreading them across the table like a sea of odd treasures. His hand shook as he opened the control box and prodded the wires inside, too aware that he held his only existing tie to Aries in the palm of his hand. One false move would ruin it forever. After running his fingers over the scratches his tools had caused, he carefully reinserted the energy cell.

The green light flickered on and then off again, a distant heartbeat revived. Striker used pinpricks to type in commands on the device's tiny touchscreen. Like anything digital, it had codes, and any code could be manipulated or cracked.

Memories from his childhood came back to him, long nights spent huddled in the heat of the air shaft with his father, playing intricate puzzle games with strings of numbers. "Find the patterns," his father whispered in his ear with immense patience, "and follow it through."

His frustration would grow as his father sat beside him, encouraging him to solve the riddle, calming his aggravation. "The fabric of time and space is all connected, like a giant being, and you must find those correlations if you're to ever work your way out of this station."

He'd work his way toward Aries now. Within moments, Striker cracked the code. The device beeped once, then the light flicked on and off in a rhythmic pulse. The beacon had latched onto a similar signal from the *New Dawn*'s mainframe computer. The device gave him a litany of numbers and letters ending with the most important five digits in Striker's world: the coordinates of the flight path of the *New Dawn*.

Rising from the table, Striker rubbed his eyes. The processor was all he needed, so he grabbed his metal rod and prepared himself to fight anything standing in his way.

…

Warning lights flashed as Tiff angled the *Morphic Marauder* into the atmosphere of the ruddy orange planet. Out the main sight panel, she saw that parts of the ship's skin that had taken asteroid hits were peeling off as they passed through the atmosphere.

"Computer, bring up the diagnostics on structural integrity."

Several outer compartments were leaking pressure at an alarming rate.

"Everyone on deck," she yelled through the speaker system. "Now."

Reckon stumbled in, holding everything he owned in his arms. She gave him a questioning look, but he only shrugged. "I packed, just in case. Don't want this stuff blasting off into space."

"Some faith you have in my abilities." Tiff jerked a lever and pulled a few switches down to close off the outer levels. "Where's everyone else?"

He strapped his belongings to his seat. "Don't know."

She got back on the intercom. "Our ship is falling apart and collapsing under the pressure. Drifter, Loot, you need to get to the control room."

As Reckon buckled himself into his seat, Loot came in with bags of supplies. "Heya, Tiff. I salvaged what I could before we lost the atmosphere in the kitchen."

"Good thinking. Now help me check the levels of the engines. We're falling at a staggering rate."

"You bet." Loot scooted into the chair next to her and switched on two more sight panels. A blur of orange-red gas filled the screen and his face blanched. "Will we make it?"

"We'll make it in." Tiff lowered her voice. "Getting out is another story. Looks like this landing might be the end of the *Morphic Marauder*."

Loot's jaw tightened and his eyes watered. "What will we do?"

Tiff bit down on her lip, feeling as though she'd failed him. She'd wanted to give him a better life and instead they were diving nose-first into a hellhole. "Haven't thought that far ahead, yet. Right now I'm trying to get us on Sahara 354 alive. I'll think of something, okay?"

"'Kay." Loot gave her a reassuring nod.

As she looked back to the blazing inferno on the screen, her thoughts flashed to her brother and the crooked-toothed grin he'd given her before he'd left on his journey to find a paradise—a journey that had ended with an explosion in space so big, she'd seen it from the bubble of the space station. If she disintegrated this ship in the atmosphere, would she see him again? Would he be proud of what she'd become?

"Who's flying this goddamn ship, a monkey?" Drifter jumped on deck with four sets of laser guns strapped to his body.

Tiff hardened her face. "You think you can do better?"

"It's those asteroids." He spat and sat behind her and Loot, buckling himself in. "They've damaged our hull. My ship's not going to survive, is it?"

Tiff gritted her teeth, sensitive to the fact he called it his ship and not theirs. He really did mean to abandon her. "I can't be sure. Maybe we can repair it once we're on the ground."

"A rat's ass we can." Drifter's voice was a growl. "You've ruined my ship."

Tiff squeezed her hands around the control stick. If Loot weren't there, she wouldn't mind crashing his precious ship to show him what a piece of junk it really was and how much he needed her. A warning siren echoed in her ear. She ignored it, releasing the second set of landing wings. Their descent slowed a bit, allowing her more control. Looking at the surface grid on her sight panel, she chose a patch of even sand.

"Everyone, hold on."

The first time the ship hit the ground, it bounced back up, and she wondered how many pieces it left scattered behind it in the sand. Tiff knew they'd have to go back for anything missing, but it was a small price to pay to slow their speed. The second time they hit, she coasted along the sand as it tore at the bottom of the hull, until the edge of the ship rammed into a ridge. They jerked forward on impact, their seat belts holding them in place.

White silence filled her ears as the ship went dead. Dust settled around them.

Reckon broke the trance. "I almost had a heart attack."

"Great." Drifter's face curved into a sardonic smile. "Just great. Now we're marooned on this desert planet like Striker."

"Hold your horses." Tiff unclasped her seat belt. She tasted blood in her mouth from clamping her teeth on her tongue. Swallowing the metallic taste, she stood up. Although her knees wobbled, she forced herself to straighten. At least they were all alive. "Let's check the damage. Reckon, get out your life scanner. See if you can find any trace of Striker. Loot, help me with the escape hatch."

Drifter sneered. "What? Are you making yourself captain?"

"No. I'm filling in until the real captain gets his sense back."

Drifter spat. "I never lost it. I'm telling the truth of the matter here. We're stuck with a busted ship on a forsaken desert hell of a planet."

"You don't know that. You haven't even checked the damage yet." Tiff signaled to Loot to join her. Loot jumped out of his seat and followed her up the ladder leading to the escape hatch, probably eager to get out of their heated conversation. To her relief, the lever and the panel were intact. She overrode some codes and pulled the latch. The door popped open and pure sunlight streamed in. The touch of the sun on her skin lent her hope. If she could get them to this desert planet, then she could get them to Refuge just as well. All she needed was the coordinates and a working ship.

Drifter groaned on the deck beneath her as he climbed the ladder to take a look. "My head hurts like hell."

"Quit complaining." Tiff felt like she had two boys to take care of instead of one. "Reckon, you getting anything on the scanner?"

"Not yet, but I'll pick up life better outside of these metal walls."

"Get your butt up here." A rush of adrenaline shot through her and her face flushed in the heat of the second sun. "We have a repo mission to do."

Chapter Sixteen
Ugly Truth

Aries awoke to searing bright light. She closed her eyes and splotches burst on the back of her lids. Had she floated to heaven? No. She recognized the glint off the chrome walls of the *New Dawn*. She'd sunk to hell instead, her own personal hell, made by her blunders and poor choices.

Itching around the IV on her arm, she wondered what could be worse. What if they'd caught Striker as well? He'd be condemned to death on their ship for the crime of sheltering a runaway. They'd set him adrift in space in a small capsule with little food or water. Although no one spoke publically of such a thing, it had happened before.

She dangled her feet off the hospital bed and tried to calm her dizziness. The door melted away and a nurse appeared holding a needle. "My goodness, you're awake."

Aries didn't recognize her. They'd probably chosen a stranger on purpose. If she had a nurse she'd known growing up, then her caretaker would be more likely to listen to her plight, maybe even give her a chance to run to the escape pods. In any case, she wasn't going anywhere. Not this time.

"Listen, I need to know if another man was escorted onboard. A man not on the *New Dawn* to begin with."

"You mean an Outlander? No, there's no one like that here."

"Never mind." Aries couldn't trust her. Even if the nurse was being honest, they wouldn't tell a lowly nurse about other captives.

The nurse pushed the touchscreen on the wall, probably alerting the higher-ups of her patient's status, then walked toward her with hesitant steps, holding the needle up as if in defense. Aries wondered what they'd told her and how much of the truth she knew.

"You need your rest, my dear."

"Like hell I do."

The nurse took a wary step back.

Aries wanted to overpower the woman and break free, but that would only lead to further imprisonment and a more confined cell. It was better to play along, for the moment. Aries offered her arm. "I'm sorry. I've had a bad day."

"I bet you have, dear." She inched toward the door. The last thing Aries wanted was a guard.

"No, I'm okay. I promise."

The older woman eyed her suspiciously and stepped toward her, needle raised. Aries estimated how hard it would be to overtake her and turn the needle around.

A familiar voice came over the intercom. "Wait. Don't give her that. I need her awake."

Barliss. Aries searched the corners of the room for a camera.

"Yes, Lieutenant." The woman backed toward the door.

The chrome slipped away and Barliss appeared, dressed as if he'd come to pick her up for a date. Instead of a military uniform, he wore a civilian suit, pressed perfectly, and his fedora tilted at just the right angle over his right eye. Underneath the hat, he'd gelled his hair so much it reminded her of wet plastic. Aries' insides shriveled up just looking at him.

"Leave us," he said to the nurse.

"Yes, sir." The older woman bowed slightly and Aries wondered how powerful Barliss had become while she'd been on safari in the desert.

After the woman left, he turned to her and Aries wilted under his gaze. So many emotions lurked there: betrayal, hatred, suspicion. They were all justified. His words were stilted. "Are you well?"

"As much as possible."

She moved to stand, but with a gesture of his hand, he indicated she should remain sitting on the side of the bed. He chose to sit on the chair by the door. He took off his fedora and cleared his throat, running his fingers gingerly along the rim.

Aries knew that nothing Barliss did was tentative. This was all an act. She braced herself for the real reason he'd come.

"At first, when you ran away, I thought you'd deceived me during the entire courtship, making me look like a fool. I have to admit, I hated you for it. The doctors say you suffer from a condition in which you blur fantasy with reality. They reassure me with the correct medication you can—"

"No." Aries surprised herself with the amount of venom in her voice. Now was the time to come clean, to voice the emotions she should have spoken long ago. "They're telling you what you want to hear, Barliss. I'm sorry. I should have told you in the first place I never wanted to marry you. Even if it's never been done before, I should have tried." Her words fell out and a wave of relief spread through her, as if her declaration removed all the obligations clinging to her chest.

He sat there with his mouth half open, and Aries took advantage of his stunned silence. "I want my own life, my own choices." She stressed her next words. "I want off this ship."

Barliss shook his head. "That's impossible. There's nowhere for you to go. You're destined to be here, to be my mate. It was chosen by the Guide."

"What have you done with Striker?"

Barliss scowled. "That man is not of your concern. You'll never see him again, so put him out of your head. You need to think about your place here, beside me." He spoke as if he were correcting a child's insolence.

Aries' frustration boiled inside her. As always, he wasn't listening to her. "I'd rather die than marry you."

Barliss stood abruptly and raised his hand to strike her. With a lift of her chin, she dared him to come at her. She had a few blows saved up for him as well.

The moment hung, sizzling in the air.

Barliss looked away as if he couldn't bear to stand the sight of her. "Then I'll have you put on suicide watch. You're very sick, my dear Aries. I'll see to it you get better, even if I have to administer your medication myself, every day of our lives. I can tell you this: until you do, I'll make sure you don't leave this cell. You have a mighty fine life here. All of your needs are cared for. You have all the possessions you could desire. There's a price everyone pays, most of us happily, in grateful celebration of our mission. In return for all the *New Dawn* has done for you, we need your genetic code."

He stood up, placing his fedora back on his head. "Someday, you'll come to your senses and then you'll have to make it up to me. Whether that comes sooner or later, it's up to you. I have my whole life to wait."

Aries wanted to hit him with her balled fists until he hurt as much as her sore heart, but she stood mute and frozen as he left her cell, and the chrome wall solidified back in place.

…

The heat could drive any sane person delirious.

The sun beat down on Tiff, slowly microwaving the top of her head. When she ran a hand through her hair, it singed her fingers. With enough time in the sun, the blond spikes would bleach to white again, like they had five years ago. Tiff sipped from her water bottle and trekked ahead, following the coordinates on Reckon's life scanner, her boots slogging through loose sand.

She glanced behind her to check on the others. Loot dragged the packs of food and water behind him, making a winding trail in the dunes. Drifter followed the boy, keeping his laser cocked and ready to fire. He'd already fired at a few moving sand mounds to scare away whatever came at them. They were all armed. Her gun bumped hard against her pelvis as she walked, but she felt safer with the extra weight.

Reckon stumbled behind them, falling in the sand every few feet. Tiff worried about him the most. They still might need him to decode the map if Striker was unwilling to help.

"Reckon, keep up. I don't want to leave you behind."

He'd wrapped his head with strips of fabric from his bed sheets, reminding Tiff of the videos of mummies she'd seen from old Earth.

"Tell that to my legs. I'm being pulled to the ground."

"That's the gravity." Tiff could feel it as well in her burning muscles. "It's heavier here than on our ship or the space station."

"Yeah, it's real gravity." Loot's voice was full of awe. "Not some fake pull generated by a compressor."

"It feels horrid." Reckon stumbled again and pulled himself up with a face full of sand.

Loot grinned, his freckles stretching across the bridge of his nose. "I love it."

Tiff punched him in the shoulder. "Wait until I get you to Refuge."

"I hate to break up this loving family moment, but we've got a job to do." Drifter chewed his lower lip. He'd lost his gum during the crash and Tiff knew not having something to clench in his teeth made him anxious. Drifter tapped his fingers against his holster. "What do the coordinates say?"

Tiff squinted her eyes to make sure she read the device correctly. "There's a scattering of life-forms in this area, but more on the higher ground by the mountains. It's a few days' walk from here, but I think it's our best bet."

Drifter looked at Loot. "Will the rations hold out until then?"

Loot glanced down at the swollen backpacks. "They should."

"All right, Tiff. Lead us there."

As she crested the ridge, they emerged on a great plateau, surrounding a crater in the center. Tiff froze, scanning the ground. The red orange of the sand had been blown away to layers of deep brown and slate gray, as if the land had had a chunk bitten out.

"What the…?"

Drifter looked over her shoulder. "Looks like Striker's been busy."

"No, this isn't Striker's doing." Reckon huffed as he caught up and peered over the rim. "Those marks are made by machines, great mining drills. An excavation team worked here recently."

"That can't be possible. We're in the middle of nowhere."

"It's the only logical answer." Reckon dug in the ground, pulling out a frayed piece of metal. "Look here. See this symbol? It's from a colony ship."

Drifter stole the metal from his hands and smoothed his fingers over the indent of an ancient ocean-going vessel cutting through waves.

"You mean those high-up preachers that left our ancestors rotting on Earth?"

"Yup." Reckon kicked the sand with the toe of his boot, looking for more evidence.

Drifter pocketed the metal. Tiff wondered if he'd try to sell it at the station later. If they ever got back. A chill descended on her shoulders. Somehow she didn't think she'd ever see anyone on the space station again. She pushed the negative feeling away.

Her hunches usually came true, but she didn't have the same psychic abilities as her mother. Even now, the thought of her mother's ridiculous studio with its glowing beads and shiny relics made her sick. She never wanted to be like her, weak and vulnerable to her clients' whims to the extent she never told them the whole truth. Her brother had been her true role model, not her mother. Then her brother had grown reckless and delusional, too.

She looked back at Drifter. "Looks like Striker's gotten himself in way over his head."

Reckon fumbled with some of his devices, scanning the area. "If we're lucky, he let them be and didn't get involved."

Tiff's eyebrows rose. "Man, you don't know Striker at all, do you? He always wanted in on the action. Oh yeah." She threw a rock over the chasm in frustration. "He got involved. He probably got rich, too. He's probably not even here now."

"Come on." Drifter clutched her arm and yanked her forward. "Let's get moving. There's nothing left for us to take."

Tiff jerked her arm back and grabbed the life scanner out of Reckon's hands. Sure enough, the vast majority of life-forms populated the mountain ridge. She could see the peaks in the distance over the rolling dunes.

"You sure he's still here?" Reckon asked her under his breath. She wouldn't be surprised if he'd uncovered her mother's occupation. He seemed to think she would actually sense Striker's presence.

"Yeah, I'm sure." She hugged her shoulders as she walked on, skirting the scar in the desert sand. The longer she spent on Sahara 354, the more guilt piled on her for leaving him behind. It was as if the sun stared at her in judgment, branding her with the scarlet letter *B* for *Betrayer*.

Chapter Seventeen
What it Takes

"Way mad cool! This leg bone is as big as a table in the Omega dining hall."

Loot dropped the packs and ran up to a whitewashed bone twice his height, running his hands along the curve of an impossibly large rib cage. "What do you think this was?"

"I don't want to know." Tiff picked her way through the bones, careful not to brush one with her arm. The vibrations in the place reeked of death and it made her spine prickle.

"I think we should make camp for the night." Reckon's voice sounded weak behind Tiff's shoulder. She turned around and saw him sink to the ground, cradling a bottle of water.

Drifter gestured at the sky. "What night? This place has two suns, of all hellish things!"

Loot jumped into the jaws of a massive skull. "Yeah, my arms ache. Let's call it a day, Tiff."

"Every second we waste, Striker could get farther away." Tiff might as well have been pulling canisters of lead behind her instead of people. The entire journey was taking longer than she thought it should. A current of rising dread nudged her on, like time was the deciding factor in whether they got out of there alive.

"Where's he gonna go?" Drifter's exasperation showed on his

crooked-nosed face. "The man's stranded in this sand trap just like the rest of us."

"Fine." Tiff wiped sweat from her forehead. "We'll make camp. Let's get out of these bones first. I don't want some creature's empty eye socket staring at me while I sleep."

"One more mile," Drifter said. "That's it." He walked by her, stepping on the bones. He cracked a femur into splinters without a care. The sound rattled Tiff's teeth.

A hopeless sense of loss settled on her shoulders as she trespassed through the graveyard of a long-dead species. Her throat constricted, and she had trouble sucking in enough air. If these great beasts couldn't survive, then how would a five-foot, hundred-pound waif of a woman make it? Feeling as though she'd used up her own resources long ago, Tiff believed this race to paradise was her only hope. She couldn't go back to Outpost Omega—she couldn't live such a desperate life.

But who would help her? Tiff turned to Drifter, but the space pirate avoided her eyes and kept his distance. True to his name, his shifting nature couldn't possibly provide the support she needed to feel safe.

Tiff was relieved when they left the bones behind, and she walked on clean sand once again. An indent in the side of the mountain provided enough shelter to make camp. Tiff helped Drifter set up a perimeter fence with metal poles and connecting lasers. Loot volunteered to be the first at watch while they slept. He climbed an adjacent ridge and sat with his laser gun cocked.

While Reckon settled off to sleep, Tiff approached Drifter and sat beside him. A desert breeze caressed her sunburned cheeks. "Do you think we'll find him?"

Drifter ran a hand down his face, wiping away sweat. "How should I know? You're the freaking psychic. Shouldn't you be asking yourself?"

Tiff huffed air through her nose. "If you're gonna insult me, then I'll turn in for the night."

"Good." Drifter's gaze wandered out to the sand dunes.

Tiff wondered if he was in one of his weird, philosophical moods. That's when his hard edge really came out.

"You're bad news for me, girl. Your trouble is, you don't know what you want. First you wanted Striker. Then you abandoned him here, for me. When we got back to the station, all you could talk about was Striker, and now you're here, back in the desert, and you're trying to make amends with me? Shit, Tiff. Find out what you want already and be done with it. Stop wasting everyone's time."

His speech was the longest string of words he'd said since they'd left the space station. Drifter stood and walked away, leaving her alone on the ridge, still hurting from the truth of his words. He climbed down to their camp and unrolled his bedding. When he lay down, he turned his back to her.

The sun set in a massive blaze of firelight as the larger sun peeked over the horizon. Not wanting to go near Drifter, Tiff remained on the plateau. As she curled up to sleep, blocking the light with her torn jean coat, she thought about Drifter's statements. Even though she was the last woman on the planet, Drifter wouldn't have her back, and she didn't want him anyway. She'd used him all along.

He was wrong about her. She did know what she wanted. Tiff craved a life of continuity and safety. She wanted to know her man looked after her, no matter what, and planned their future together down to her last days with enough food, shelter, and water to survive. She'd concocted her tough-girl identity out of necessity, but that's not who she wanted to be. No man alive fulfilled her needs.

What she needed was a time machine. She'd watched all those scratchy, archival videos of old Earth. There was a golden era when women could stay home to raise their kids in pretty painted houses with small gardens and a family dog. She wanted such a life—not having to worry about fending off lusty men in the space station, or going hungry when the food processors broke down. If only she could travel back, if only Loot were her real son, playing catch with his father in the green grass.

Who would that father be?

The sound of laser fire interrupted her thoughts. Tiff sat up, her coat falling from her face as Loot's scream echoed off the mountain. Drifter was already up, reaching for his gun. He glanced over at her with a dark energy in his eyes. "Let the games begin."

Tiff fumbled for her laser gun and stood, then stumbled after Drifter. Reckon huddled underneath a small crevice in the rock face.

She had no time to admonish his cowardice.

Her breath heaved in and out as she crested the ridge, heart beating like a wild drum. She spotted Loot as he fired at a behemoth armored beast with crab claws for arms and a head full of antennae, twitching angrily. Although Tiff had never seen any animal, insect, or plant in person, to her it looked like a cross between a lobster and a centipede with a dandelion for a head. Its shell was the color of burnt orange, blending with the rippling sands.

The monster clacked its claws and Loot fell, dropping his gun. Drifter fired from the upper ridge, attracting its attention away from the boy.

"Loot!" Tiff yelled so hard she thought she'd spew out her lungs. "Over here!"

Loot scurried underneath the plethora of insect-like legs, grabbed his gun, and escaped as the monster turned its vengeance on Drifter.

Loot met her on the ridge. "It came out of nowhere!"

She pulled him off the ridge to hide behind a dune with her, grasping his arm so tightly, her fingernails poked through his coat.

"I'm sorry, Tiff. It just rose from the sand. I didn't see it coming."

"Let it go, Loot." Tiff felt tears brimming in her eyes. "You're okay now, and that's what matters."

"But Drifter—"

Tiff chanced a fleeting look over the dune. The beast was nearly as tall as the ridge, its front claws snapping only a few feet from Drifter's boots.

Drifter called over to them. "Fire your lasers! Drive it back!" The crab monster balanced on its hind legs, forcing Drifter to jump back as a claw grazed the ground by his feet.

"Stay behind me." Tiff unlocked the safety latch on her trigger and ran across the top of the dune. She fired at the beast, but the lasers only left darkened blotches on its armor. She changed the frequency, but still the blasts failed to penetrate the shell.

She spotted a black crevice underneath its arm and aimed, firing white light. Loot followed her and aimed pulses at the same spot. Together, their lasers weakened the joint and the creature fell back, clicking its mouthful of teeth, its front legs jittering.

"Drifter, fall back!"

He ran forward, shooting at the head sprouting with antennae. The monster retreated on its hind legs, claws swinging in front of its tube-like head in defense. Drifter leaped off the ridge and ran at it.

"Drifter, come back!" He was caught up in one of his rages, blind and deaf to reason. She'd seen it before. Once again, she had a decision to make. If she jumped off the ridge, Loot would follow, and no one would have a good shot at the creature.

They watched from the ridge as Drifter chased the monster. The blasts of laser fire tainted the air, and Tiff held onto Loot and waited. She lost sight of Drifter and the crab beast as they tumbled together down a dune in a slew of spindly legs.

Loot wiggled in her arms. "I want to go help him."

"You're not getting involved in his crazy suicide. Stay with me."

The firing ceased, and Tiff and Loot stood frozen in anticipation and fear. Smoke rose from behind the dune, and the air reeked of burnt flesh. She had a moment of regret.

Loot whispered in her arms. "Is he dead?"

A single black silhouette crested the ridge. In his arm, he held a part of the claw.

Loot cheered and hollered, throwing his gun up in the air. He jumped from the ridge, and Tiff raised her arm in salute, but inside she felt empty. Ashamed. She'd stayed on the ridge in safety instead of helping another person.

Tiff jumped down from the ridge as Loot ran to see the war trophy. Drifter seemed proud to show it off to the boy, but he never glanced in her direction.

She didn't blame him. Yet again, she'd put her life ahead of another man's, like she'd put her needs in front of Striker's five years ago.

A coward like she was didn't have what it took to love anyone unconditionally, to put her herself on the line.

Chapter Eighteen
Visitor

When Aries looked down, her hands were old, the skin thin and wrinkled like ancient silk. She wore two rings on her left hand: a silver wedding band and Barliss' diamond studded family heirloom. They felt heavy and loose on her bony fingers.

The carpet underneath her feet did little to dampen the sputtering engines of the *New Dawn*. The ship sailed along on its last leg in one final push to reach its destiny. She moved to the bubble-shaped, glass window, peering at a blue nebula surrounded by shimmering stars. Her reflection in the glass stared back at her in condemnation, a halo of gray wisps and sad, crinkled eyes. Her life was spent. She wouldn't live to reach the paradise planet. She'd never leave the ship.

The room seemed too small, and the chrome walls pressed in behind her, suffocating her with stale, recycled air. She pounded her fists on the glass. She wanted to burst out of the confines of her cell, let the vacuum of space rip her apart to free her soul. Several inches of thick glass muted her suffering and held her in.

A warning beep sounded and she whirled around to see the wall screen flash into color. Barliss stared back at her with wires running from his head like sprouting hair. His skin was blanched, pale as moonlight, and his cheeks sunken to the bone. If she were old, then he was older, a decade or more her senior. She recognized the commander's chair, attaching Barliss to the ship like a parasite. Her room had a single chair by the table, and one cup of bitter coffee, resting half drunk and untouched.

"My dear, is something wrong?"

"I'm trapped here, alone."

He spoke to her as if she were a half-wit. "Come now, we've talked of this before. You know I can't abandon my post. There's much work to be done if we're to keep our schedule. I am always with you, just the click of a button away."

A rising current of anger shook her hands and she felt as though she'd burst from the pressure. "No!" She pulled the metal chair from underneath the table and raised it above her head. "You can't keep me here!"

Barliss leaned sideways and spoke into an intercom. "She's off her meds. Medics to room ninety-eight, immediately!"

Aries slammed the legs of the chair into the wall screen, shattering the plastic and fragmenting Barliss' image. The pieces flew around her face. Some of specks cut her face and lodged in her hair. She bent down and picked up a large shard of glass the size of her forearm, as blood trickled down her cheeks.

The chrome wall behind her disappeared and medics poured in, circling her with caution like she was mad. Aries laughed bitterly. She was the only sane one of the bunch.

"Let me go."

"We can't do that, ma'am."

"I'm not supposed to be here. I was free."

They ignored her claims and stepped forward, using metal trays as shields. She lunged, but her bones were weak and her arm collapsed as the shard hit the metal. Gloved hands grabbed her arms and legs, pinning her down with impersonal, plastic skin. She screamed in pain as a nurse inserted a needle in her arm. The room around her blurred in a smear of bright light. She fell away inside herself, losing what remained of her identity or desires. She floated as an insignificant pebble in the grand scheme of the vast universe, a blink of essence in an endless place.

...

Aries woke with wide eyes. The monitor beside her beeped a rapid rhythm, the tempo of her escalated heart rate. She held up her arm and smoothed her fingers over the firm, young skin. Thank goodness she still had time on her side. The vision had only been a nightmare, of course. What medications raced through her veins?

She focused on the walls, trying to find the camera that spied on her like an evil eye. How many guards stood outside her door? With no sight panel, she could only guess. The nurse hadn't left anything sharp for her to use as a weapon, either. Still attached to the machines, Aries stood up and paced the room. She felt like a test mouse in a cage. Would they experiment with medications until she grew obedient? Would she end up like the old woman in her dream?

Aries tried to push the thought of never seeing Striker again from her mind. She denied the hopeless odds. There had to be some way to find out if he'd been captured. Although Barliss would never tell her, maybe she could find someone who would.

Aries halted abruptly in front of the touchscreen controlling the portal. The screen read blank gray. She pressed it several times. Nothing happened. They must have shut it off. Fiddling with the back of the panel, she wondered if she could rip it off the wall and rearrange the wires, possibly reactivating the controls. She glanced around the room but still couldn't find the camera. Perhaps if she blocked the entire panel with her body and leaned in close to the wall, she'd cover up her tinkering.

Her fingers probed tiny screws in the metal. Since she didn't have anything remotely like a screwdriver, she tried turning the screw with her fingernail. Her nail broke as the chrome vanished beside her. Jumping back, Aries put her hand behind her back.

"Trent?" A mix of emotions filled her, a surge of hope that she was finally seeing someone she knew, coupled with the fact it was her brother, the one who had bullied her into compliance all her life.

He nodded to someone she couldn't see outside the door and the chrome solidified behind him. "I've come to talk to you."

She ran up to him and held onto both his arms, whispering, "You've got to get me out of here."

Trent scowled and looked away as if her words disgusted him. He pulled away from her and sat on the stool across the room. "That choice is yours and yours alone. Your freedom rests in your own hands now."

His ambivalence shocked her and she shook her head. "Freedom? This is what you call freedom? Being married to a man I don't want? Performing a job I didn't choose?"

"It's the best life you could ever have." Trent held out his hand, offering it to her, but she wouldn't take it. "Look around you. We're surrounded by space in the middle of nowhere. Where else can you go?"

Aries thought of Striker and his plan to reacquire the map and fly to Refuge in an alien ship, but the whole story sounded like such a fantasy, her brother wouldn't believe her. He'd believe the doctors who said she'd become delusional, blurring fantasy with reality.

"You're lucky they found you alive."

Suddenly, Aries wondered why they'd sent him alone. "Where are Mom and Dad?"

Trent's voice was edged with anger. "They're not here. The authorities won't let them see you."

"Because they'd listen to me. They would sympathize."

Trent crossed his arms. "No. Because they think you're dangerous."

A rush of emotions flooded through her, free after all the years of holding her tongue. She'd cowered in his presence long enough.

"It's not that and you know it." Aries pointed an accusing finger at him. "They sent you because they thought you could convince me to agree to marry Barliss."

"They want me to try and talk some sense into you, yes."

"When the doctors found cancer in Grandfather's lungs, I saw you vote to forgo the treatment. I sat on the sofa and watched you circle the option in red ink. 'Let him die. His genetic code has been successfully passed to a new generation.' I remember the moment as clear as yesterday. You showed no sadness in your face, only a quiet and calm certainty. I wasn't old enough then to have my vote counted, so I kept my lips sealed, but I knew then where your loyalty lay."

"He'd done his job on the *New Dawn*. He was ready to pass on. We must use all resources to further the next generation. It's simple logic, not emotional ties."

Aries' voice rose. "What about compassion? You've always put the Guide above us, above Mom, Dad, everything."

"As I should. Look, you've brought a lot of pain and disgrace to our family. I can only hope you come to your senses and right the wrongs you've caused."

A door closed in her heart, shutting him out. Their differences in philosophy stretched so far they could never understand each other and she felt wrong to call him brother. "Good-bye, Trent. Give Mom and Dad my love."

Aries turned her back on him, every cell in her being wishing him to leave. She heard the rustle of his uniform as he rose from the seat and the sound of the door opening and closing. When she turned around, she was alone again. Trapped with her rebellious thoughts.

…

Barliss surveyed the team as they herded the giant elephantine beasts of Sahara 354 to wire cages at the back of the zootarium. His stomach churned, but it wasn't from the stench of three hundred chickens or pens choked with bleating goats. A growing sense of discontentment lurked underneath his military demeanor.

He was pleased with the outcome of the expedition and the success of his mission, but Aries' continued defiance of the doctors was making him feel more like a wet towel, twisted, wrung out and left hanging to dry. A man wearing a white lab coat directed the team as they backed each monstrous beast into confinement.

"Careful now, don't spook them!" His voice sounded eager. "Careful of the female's tentacles. They're very delicate." Their snorts joined the chorus of chicken clucks and goat grievances.

Once they closed the cages and locked them, the man gestured for his team to position large buckets of water near the front. Barliss moved to leave, out of time and out of patience. He had other concerns to deal with, but the head zoologist spotted him and waved, signaling for him to meet him in the adjoining room, free of the animal noises.

Barliss walked into a hundred-foot-tall atrium with pigeons flying overhead. Watching them made his tongue water with the thought of roasted wings. The man in the lab coat pushed through a wall of plastic separating the rooms and ran up to meet him. "I'm Doctor Cole. It's a pleasure to meet you, Lieutenant Barliss."

Barliss extended his hand. The man's reputation was unparalleled in the biological fields. It wouldn't hurt him to be on good terms with the doctor.

"I see you have your hands full, so let's keep it short, shall we?"

"Oh yes, rightly so." The doctor smoothed down the front of his coat. "I wanted to meet with you regarding a certain Aries Ryder."

Barliss stiffened. What had she done now? He balled up his fists and cooled a rising thread of anger. His voice was tight. "What of her?"

The zoologist smiled. "I may have a solution for you, so to speak."

Did word get around so quickly? Barliss felt his cheeks flush with embarrassment. "I have no need for help."

Doctor Cole put up a finger. "Hear me out."

Barliss gave a curt nod and looked around for potential eavesdroppers, but only two mottled pigeons looked on from the branches of a pear tree.

Doctor Cole stepped closer, his voice a low, conspiratorial whisper. "Before life-jobs were assigned, Aries Ryder requested biology. I turned her down for others with more optimal skill sets."

Barliss gave him a stern look. What did it matter to him? There was no sense in resurrecting the past.

The doctor cleared his throat. "What I'm getting at, sir, is we could make a bargain with her, assign her to a new job here in the zootarium. It may solve your obedience problem."

Barliss raised his hand to silence him. "No. No special rules for her." Although he wanted to punish Aries, not give her a reward, he quickly came up with a more logical reason. "Word will get out and everyone will want the more, shall we say, illustrious careers? There'd be no more cleaners, trash collectors, laundry supervisors. The Guide dictates it is more beneficial to have the most qualified, not the most enthusiastic."

"Yes, yes. I remember section ninety-three of the Guide. Do not think I forgot it."

"Then there's no question, is there?"

The doctor's face closed up. Perhaps he'd expected a reward in return, more resources directed to the bio team's management. "No, sir."

"Good. I appreciate your concern for Aries Ryder, but I'll deal with her myself."

"Of course." The doctor stepped away and bowed his head. "Nice to meet you, Lieutenant."

Barliss frowned. "Same here."

Doctor Cole left him in the atrium. Barliss stared at the pigeons as they flapped through the air, choosing perches in the farthest reaches of the atrium. Somehow they reminded him of Aries, beautiful creatures held in by glass, never to truly know what it was like to fly in the wind. Weren't they all like Aries? No human alive would get to see the *New Dawn* land on Paradise 21. He grew uncomfortably melancholy and pushed the thought away.

He should check on Aries' progress. Perhaps her brother had been able to change her mind. Barliss had offered him an excellent promotion as a reward. He stepped forward and his wrist beeped. At first Barliss thought it was some alarm, that he'd trespassed on the herbs cultivated by the foliage team, but his feet stood solidly on the plastic walkway. He brought his arm up and looked at his locator.

The devices were only meant as beacons to locate members of the crew. Messages were rarely sent and had to be approved by the higher in command. He stared at the tiny screen as letters flashed before his eyes, creating a full sentence.

May I request a private audience?

Barliss blinked to make sure he wasn't imagining the string of letters on his locator, but they were still there. He pressed a button on the side, identifying the sender. The device flashed a name: Commander Gearhardt.

Only the commander would have the power to alter the internal systems of the locators. It made perfect sense. What didn't line up was why he needed to speak to Barliss so soon after his return, and why the meeting was so clandestine. Barliss broke branches in his haste to get out of the atrium.

Chapter Nineteen
Fear

Striker peered over the ridge at the remnants of the raider den. Black smoke stained the clear blue sky, creating shadows as it rose from piles of ashes while the raiders gathered bodies and cremated them. More raiders picked through the desolation, some of them probably looting, while others roamed without direction, perhaps looking for lost family members. Striker felt a pang in his chest. Even the "lizard men," as Aries had called them, didn't deserve this kind of devastation.

There were too many raiders to win a fight against them, so he couldn't drag the processor right through their territory. Jumping down from the ridge, Striker skirted the den and searched for a discreet path around the refugees.

A body lay on the edge of the ridge. The raider's two-pronged tongue hung from an open mouth, which contained two small incisors that were as sharp as pins. Laser fire had blackened his midsection, and his scrawny leg bent at a strange angle.

Striker had never come this close to one besides the boy who'd chased the snake up so close to where he'd hidden with Aries. He pulled off its bone mask and looked into the blank stare of its dark eyes, wondering what thoughts had flitted behind them. The mask was carved with slits and tied with pieces of desert cowhide.

Striker held his breath from the smell of burnt tissue and pulled the crude coat from the creature's back. He tore off a strip of animal hide and shook it out, lizard scales glimmering as they fell into the sand. After wrapping it around his head, he tied the bone mask on as well. They did block the wind and sand, and hid a large portion of his face. He put the remainder of the lizard man's coat over his own black cloak. It didn't reach down to cover his black boots, and he had no way to fake a tail, but it might get him through. Consumed as they were by their colony's devastation, Striker doubted the raiders would be on the lookout for new victims. In any case, he didn't want to be confused with the humans who had brought the destruction down upon them.

Weaving his way in and out of the fallen tents, Striker worked toward the canyon where he and Aries had hidden the processor. He tried not to look at the bodies, because each one left a searing impression on his mind: a blackened arm reaching from a fallen tent, a cracked bone mask small enough for a child, an unraveled string of beads. He had to remind himself the people who'd created this mess had taken Aries, and the only way to get her back was to find the processor. Stepping over what must have been a raider's living area with broken clay pots, Striker avoided contact with the other wanderers.

Hissing erupted ahead of him. A fight had broken out, two raiders pushing at each other while others looked on. Striker walked around it, ducking through one of the only tents left standing.

A small raider with dull coloring bent over a pile of eggs, white and wet as the sides of someone's eyes. Was it a female? She licked the round tops with her tongue, flicking it in and out of her mouth to keep it moist. The vulnerability of the female with its eggs distracted Striker as he thought back to the eggs on his ship. In times of overwhelming destruction, every species struggles to protect its young, to survive. Feeling like an intruder, he tripped, knocking over a stand of clattering pots.

The female hissed, a long and drawn-out noise. Striker stepped back, but she ran at him, tail swinging behind her. Not wanting to fight her, he retreated until she pushed him through the front flaps, right into the middle of the dispute.

The two raiders engaged in the fight froze, and the onlookers turned their heads at incredible angles, by human standards. The female clicked her tongue and flicked her three-taloned hand at Striker in a rude gesture, as if to say he'd committed some blasphemous act by invading her egg tent.

The raiders stepped forward, closing in. He stumbled backward, but raiders surrounded him on all sides. They reached behind their backs and drew their spears. Striker put up both hands to show his peaceful intentions, but he'd forgotten he wore no gloves. As the crowd stared in shock at his tanned skin, he expected them to slaughter him right then and there and braced himself for a final fight, making fists with his fingers.

The raiders stared at his bare skin with wary eyes. One by one, they dropped their spears and scattered, running in all directions. The female disappeared back into the tent. Striker stood alone in the ring of sand made by the dueling raiders' claws.

For a moment, he felt a great sense of disgust for his own species. For all of recorded history, humans had forced their will on the natural world, exterminating other species and driving them to the far regions of old Earth. It was partly the reason he stood on this barren planet today. Perhaps humans were doomed to repeat history wherever they went. Perhaps the *New Dawn* would make a barren world out of a paradise.

He'd colonize Refuge, and he'd make his world different. Striker remembered the processor. Tearing the mask from his face, he ran toward the canyon at the far end of the colony. His heart beat faster with each leap he took. What if the *New Dawn*'s crew had found it? What if it wasn't there? When he entered the shallow cave, the pearly white shell of the alien construct peaked out in the shadows of the rock.

Striker leaned against it and caught his breath. He'd been here with Aries days ago, and she'd tried to tell him something, tried to open her heart. He wished now he hadn't shushed her. Her people had been closing in and he'd wanted to get her out of there. He'd thought there was no time for words, but now he kicked himself for not staying to hear her out. What would she have said?

Striker's determination hardened. He *would* see her again. He'd told the biggest lie of his life when he'd pushed Aries away and said he couldn't love her. The truth burned in his chest, waiting to be spoken.

She had to know.

The processor was too heavy for him to lift alone, and so he got behind it and pushed. His legs ached from chasing after the hovercrafts and traipsing across the sand dunes to get back to his own ship. He gritted his teeth against the pain and heaved. The processor slowly budged and he pushed it from the cave into the canyon, muscles burning in his arms.

It took him the entire day to drag it back to the alien ship. The duel suns rose and set on each horizon, casting pools of shadows between ridges and bathing the pristine white of the ship in red and orange light as he approached. The coral seemed to glisten stronger in the rays, as if the possibility of completeness tantalized its inner workings.

A rising sense of anticipation overtook him, and his heart beat faster as he dragged the processor to the prow. Five years of work, and now he'd know if it had all been for naught, if he'd be able to get Aries back, if he'd be able to repay the alien race by bringing their eggs to Refuge.

Striker dusted the sand off the processor with the stolen raider coat and inserted it into an indent in the side of the hull, the place where he thought it had broken off. He prayed under his breath as the processor slid into place. The coral fused together, reconnecting with the mother ship. He smoothed his fingers over the melded crack. The entire white shell glowed brighter and brighter until the blue light obliterated the red-orange rays of the suns. His skin prickled with anticipation as he rode a tidal wave of emotions all overwhelming him at once. If the outer shell had that much energy, he couldn't imagine what it was like inside. Collecting himself, he jumped onto the ship, tracing the hieroglyphs to open the hatch.

...

The monster's claw tasted better than anything Tiff had ever eaten. She shoved it in her mouth and chewed, enjoying the sensation of her teeth puncturing the flesh. She ate until her belly felt round and she grew sleepy in the arid heat.

Drifter turned another portion of meat over the fire and smiled. "Not bad, huh?" His beady eyes had that arrogant look that drove her crazy and she turned away, spitting out a piece of shell. She wasn't about to give him the satisfaction of agreeing with him.

A piece of meat hung from Loot's chin and he sucked it in with a grin. "It's so different than our recycled food back at the station." Drifter handed him another spit from the fire.

Tiff turned toward the horizon. "When are we going to head out?"

The feeling of time slipping away came back to her in a wash, and a sharp anxiety made her dizzy all at once. Maybe she'd just eaten too much, or maybe Striker slipped farther away every minute they wasted. Tiff wondered if he knew they'd landed. Would he run from them or greet them with weapons? She couldn't bear to imagine what he thought of her.

"Give us time to digest our food, will ya?" Reckon chugged water from a bottle and Tiff made a mental note not to touch that one once he put it down. Her eyes wandered to a black cloud rising behind the next mountain.

"Over there! I see smoke."

"Where?" Loot ran to the edge of the ridge. Tiff glanced at Drifter, but he gave her a suspicious look through his oily hair and rotated another chunk of the monster claw.

"She's right." Loot pointed to the horizon. "It's coming from the canyon between those two mountains. Well, that's where we oughtta go, you think?" Loot looked at Tiff with eagerness in his eyes. His optimism pulled at her heart, but the place beyond the ridge exuded negative vibes.

Reckon shuddered and wiped his face. "I don't know. Seems to me, we should stay clear of anything smoking."

"Wrong." Drifter's voice had an edge of finality to it, like he'd cast the deciding vote. "I say we pack up and see what's over there."

Tiff closed her eyes. Something about being on the planet and feeling the gravity, the wind and the sun, and tasting real food, made her body charge with an acute feeling of being alive. She allowed the wind to carry her thoughts, feeling the ground's pull underneath her feet and the sun's rays at her back. She sensed Striker's presence near, like the shadow of an old friend. Tugging on the strand of thought, she pushed the boundaries holding it back. She saw a flash of black fabric, a whitewashed shell, and the curve of a strong-boned cheek.

"He's been there." She blurted without a thought as to how her companions would react. She opened her eyes and saw them all staring at her. She'd have to be convincing if they were to believe her. Her voice hardened. "His presence is fading. We must leave now."

Drifter kicked sand on the fire and reached for his laser gun. He clicked the safety switch off and nodded in the direction of the smoke. "Let's go."

Tiff stared at Drifter. "That's it? No questions, no complaining?"

Drifter jerked his head and flung back his hair. It used to make her skin hot with desire, but now that move just annoyed her. "You don't think I've ever suspected you have the same sixth sense as your mom?"

Surprised by his faith in her, Tiff's heart opened a little, but then closed back up. "You always called her a crazy bitch."

He raised an eyebrow. "I didn't mean her fortune-telling."

It took them most of the day to reach the canyon, skirting the mountainside and stepping over fallen rocks. Patches of scraggly shrubs poked through the jagged terrain with prickles the size of needles. Tiff and Loot scouted for the safest path, since they had the best balance. As they took the lead, Drifter kept his distance, shuffling behind them and whispering with Reckon.

Loot walked beside her as they slid down an incline of pebbles. "Why did you abandon Striker here, anyway?"

"You know, it was so long ago I don't even remember why, exactly. Kind of like when it's been so long, you forget to be mad at the person you're supposed to be mad at."

Tiff dusted her knees off and continued, looking back to make sure Drifter was far enough away he couldn't hear. "Striker had crazy dreams of finding a paradise planet and relocating all of Outpost Omega. When he found Refuge, I wondered why he didn't just want to be there with me. The two of us, alone, together. If he brought everyone else along, it would just end up like another ruined old Earth: wars, pollution, overpopulation, you know. You've heard the stories."

"Yeah, I heard 'em." Loot kicked stray rocks and hit the cactus five meters ahead of them, causing a spider-mouse to scurry for shelter. "Still, it's really good of him to try to save everyone like that. I mean, what a hero."

The more they talked about it, the angrier she got, resurrecting her old demons. "He loved his ideals more than he loved me, and I hated him for it. If it came down to it, he would have left me for his greater cause."

"I'll never leave you. Even though you do act like my mom." Loot punched her shoulder and she smiled, ruffling his hair. The one good thing she'd done in her life was take him in. She hoped it made up for everything else.

They crested the ridge as the plumes of smoke grew on the horizon. The ruins of a primitive civilization stretched before them in piles of blackened soot.

"Cool, it's a lizard man." Loot scurried down the ridge to where a body lay burnt in the middle.

"Don't touch it." Tiff ran to keep up with him, her fingers staying on the grip of her gun. "We don't know if the thing is diseased or venomous."

Over her shoulder she heard Drifter call out, "I'll cover you from the ridge."

"Don't shoot anything." Tiff yelled back to him, "It may be Striker."

"Wouldn't want to hurt a hair on his head now, would we?"

"Not if you want to get off this planet, we don't."

As Loot bent over the strange, reptilian face, Tiff kept her distance and cocked her laser, peering through the debris for any signs of a live lizard creature.

Reckon caught up to them. When she turned to him, she saw fear in his eyes. His voice cracked on his words. "I thought they were colonists, not marauders."

Tiff shrugged. "The lizard men must have posed some kind of threat or stolen something very valuable to them." Although her explanation seemed logical, the carnage made Tiff uneasy.

Drifter finished sweeping the area, tucked his laser into its holster, and slid down the incline. "Well, these lizard people sure as hell pissed the colonists off."

"I'll say." Loot covered a body with a piece of hide from a fallen tent. "Where is everyone?"

"Dead." Reckon had unholstered his gun and held it in shaky

hands. "Or they ran away."

"Let's hope so." Tiff gestured in front of her. "Whoever these colonists are, let's pray they're long gone by now. Come on. Search the area. Look for any signs of Striker."

As she picked her way among the ruins, Tiff had a sinking feeling that Striker had moved on.

"Looks like we missed the party." Drifter threw a piece of burnt hide over his shoulder and kicked some broken tools in the debris. "There's no sign of him, psychic girl."

Reckon sat on a rock and wiped the sweat from his red forehead. "Yeah. Anything that happened here is long done."

Loot walked to her side and put a hand on her shoulder. He spoke under his breath, "Don't worry. We'll find him."

Tiff squeezed back tears as anger and frustration balled up like two fists inside her. She should be the one comforting the boy, but the finality of the dead colony only made her feel like a failure. She yelled a curse through gritted teeth and kicked a rock across the ruins so hard it left a dent in the metal sole of her boot.

"You stay here." Loot handed her an almost empty water bottle. "I'll make camp, 'kay?"

She couldn't bring herself to answer him with her usual "Okay." Hope seeped away from Tiff, like someone had cut a vital vein in her arm and let her blood flow out. Her body went limp and she gave in to the doubt lurking in her heart. She'd had a true vision when she'd felt like she'd never see the space station again. They were on a wild goose chase, marooned on this forsaken planet for the rest of their lives.

As Tiff looked for something to rip apart, she heard Drifter shout with a voice full of awe. "Oh man! Look at that!"

She raised her head, dreading whatever vile creation came at them next. No giant crab spider descended from above. Instead, blue light filled the sky, like an aurora borealis shining from somewhere in the distance.

"What do you suppose it is?" Loot stopped hammering a perimeter laser in the sand to shield his gaze.

"Can't be electromagnetic or weather-related." Reckon squinted his eyes. "Something on the ground is projecting it."

"Don't make camp." Tiff reached out and clamped her hand on Loot's arm. Her voice was desperate, but she couldn't control it. Her anguish had bounced back to hope and her body filled with bubbles of anxiety. "We're going over there."

Chapter Twenty
Reunion

The hallway leading to the commander's flight seat lay as empty as the vortex to a black hole. Barliss hesitated, wondering where the attendants had run off to. They weren't supposed to leave the commander alone at any moment. Barliss buzzed the panel, requesting entry to the control deck, since his lieutenant's status didn't grant him clearance. After stating his name, the doors parted and disappeared into the walls. He straightened his uniform, took a deep breath and stepped in. Cool, conditioned air blew out, ruffling his hair. The tangy scent of chemicals tickled his nose. Wires sprouted from the man in the great chair in the center of the room like flowers from a vase, spreading up to connect to the ship's systems and controls. Tubes holding gallons of pale liquids reflected the fluorescent lights surrounding the armrests of the chair.

"Good Evening, Lieutenant." The pilot's seat rotated to face him and the commander's moon-white face wrinkled into a thin smile. He looked like a stick man in his firmly pressed uniform, the cotton still creased in perfect folds as if he never bent down.

Barliss bowed, looking down at his boots. He scolded himself for not polishing the scuffs before walking in. He felt like he trespassed in the commander's sterile, pristine accommodations, tramping in with all kinds of germs and dirt. "Commander Gearhardt."

"I'm sorry you have to see me like this." The commander gestured to the wires protruding from his head like metal dreadlocks. "I'm getting older and it's harder for me to disconnect. The risks are not worth the pretense."

Barliss had no idea how old the commander was, but the man had been ancient even when Barliss had run around as a boy with plastic laser guns. One of the tubes bubbled and he tried not to stare as the liquid traveled down a clear hose and into the commander's arm. "I understand."

"The disadvantages are well worth the service. I have seen many years beyond my countrymen, experienced several generations of life, and, best of all, served the Guide most honorably."

"You have, sir." Barliss' mind ticked away, wondering why the commander explained his duties to a lowly officer of the *New Dawn*. Was he dying? Barliss had thought the man was immortal. "Surely you'll live to see the ship reach Paradise 21."

"Dear Barliss," the commander waved him closer. "My body is wasting away. Each month, these preservatives have less of an effect." One gray-white eyebrow twitched up. "Which is why I've sent my attendants away and summoned you here."

Barliss stood within arm's reach, and yet the commander waved him closer still. He complied with awkward steps, careful not to crunch a wire or tube with his sand-crusted boots. No matter how many times he washed them, the red-orange grit wouldn't go away. He stood so close, he could see the pink inflammation of the commander's skin around each wire as it chaffed his head.

"Anything I can do to serve you, Commander." Barliss tried to steady his voice, but he stumbled on each word.

The commander's eyes shone bright with intensity. "I want you to follow in my footsteps and lead the *New Dawn* on its final push to Paradise 21."

Shock hit Barliss, stinging him all over with numbness. The old man sat up in his chair expectantly, the wires pulled taut behind him.

"Sir?" Barliss questioned if he'd heard the commander correctly.

"Of course, you won't have to plug in until you're fully trained and even then you can disconnect to live your life as any normal man.

It's only in your later years you'll be confined like me. There's no pain, only a sense of greater meaning, a responsibility of purpose. It's a big decision, one that will affect the rest of your life and lengthen it by threefold." The commander raised his hand and waved it across the main sight panel as if he conducted the stars.

Barliss' voice turned husky with wonderment. "I don't know what to say. It's a tremendous honor. There are many more officers above me that—"

"I've already chosen you. All you need to do is accept."

The moment was surreal. Barliss felt like he was floating, unable to feel his feet touch the floor. The main control deck swirled around him, wires dancing around the commander like snakes on a Medusa's head. Doubt seeped in, tainting a moment that should have been blissful. The extent of his unworthiness overwhelmed him, spreading like a disease through his mind.

The commander peered into his eyes so deeply, Barliss thought the old man stared at his soul. Fearing what the commander might see, Barliss stepped back.

"I know you have doubts about your abilities, Lieutenant. I've seen the evil devils manifest all along. Yet you persevered where many others have failed, fighting your insecurities, challenging the confines of your own genetic code."

He placed a paper-light hand on Barliss' shoulder and pulled him close. Barliss found himself oddly steadied. "I look at you and I see someone who will beat the odds, someone who has sacrificed everything for his station, someone who will make the right decisions when the time comes." The old man's weak breath fell on Barliss' cheek like the flutter of a butterfly's wings. "I believe in you, even if you don't fully believe in yourself."

A door opened in Barliss' inner heart. He'd locked it long ago when his father had frowned in disappointment at his poor test scores in emotional intelligence. His parents had created him with the promise of all the best genes, and yet he'd come out lacking, and the old man had never let him live it down. He'd earned every small victory without anyone's support and had worked his way up the chain of command by his own political savvy. Now the most important person in all humanity offered him the dream he'd always wanted.

Licking his dry lips, something changed inside him. His fragile slew of insecurities turned to a hardened edge of resolution. Barliss grasped the commander's hand in his own and shook it lightly.

The commander gazed back at him with expectation, weariness wrinkling around his bright eyes.

This time Barliss didn't cringe or flounder. He stood up, tall as a man newly knighted. "I accept."

...

Striker opened the hatch and stepped onto the platform of the elevator. Strange cooing noises, like whistles on the wind, surrounded him as he descended into the belly of the ship. The coral closed over his head.

Were the gentle tones birdcalls? Striker knew no desert buzzard could find its way into the elevator shaft. The platform hit the bottom, and the door opened to the main corridor. The sounds came through an internal speaker, resonating all over the ship.

The dead aliens spoke to him. He looked around the walls with wonder. They must have recorded their voices into the mainframe. The pattern of sounds repeated, like an ongoing message. He wished he'd found a phonetic guide.

Bright sapphire light illuminated the once-dim corridors. Feeling as though he walked through an entirely different ship, he headed for the main shaft to the central control room, where Aries had found him soldering a broken leg on one of the high stools. The screens on the walls teemed with symbols and sky charts of systems he'd never seen before as the ship rebooted and came alive. Although Striker had no linguistic skills, he could break through code, and if he figured out the patterns in the symbols, he could learn to fly the ship.

Excitement flashed through him and his hands shook as the blue light pulsed around him, casting the controls in a dreamy indigo glow. Striker chanced pressing a panel, and a blueprint of the ship appeared on the main screen. Symbols flashed around it, probably reporting diagnostic evaluations, but one area of the ship lit up brighter than the others. Striker drew his finger across the screen and pressed on the spot catching his eye. The blueprint enlarged that particular region and he recognized the egg hatchery down in the belly.

Was it a warning? Striker left the control room and descended into the lower level, jumping two and three steps at a time, afraid the egg chambers might open. Since they'd lasted this long, he didn't want to be the cause of their destruction. He needed to be sure he'd secured their contents before taking off.

Mist flowed around his feet as he opened the door to the egg chamber and stumbled in, pressing his hot hands against the cool glass. The eggs sat exactly where he'd left them, eternally suspended in airtight containers and fog. Wiping a crust of glimmering specks from the glass, he pressed his forehead against the clear space to peer into the closest chamber.

The egg glowed in the dim light like a tiny, stolen moon. As the ship awakened around him, the light brightened and air circulated on the other side of the glass. Tiny dust particles swirled up around the base like shimmering flies. The egg twitched, a slight teetering off center and back again, and Striker pushed his face closer, his breath blooming in foggy spurts on the glass, and waited, watching for another movement.

"Come on," he whispered under his breath, expecting the shell to crack and a feathery arm to reach out. Nothing happened. The egg lay as still as a fossil. Maybe he'd imagined the movement. He sighed, running his fingers through the wave of hair that always fell just above his eyes and tried to absorb all of the changes taking place around him. If it had moved, then his hope that some of the eggs were still alive was justified.

He brushed dust off the glass of another specimen as a new litany of cooing noises erupted on the speakers. This time the sounds were more persistent, more closely spaced, with a heightened tone. A screen flashed on in the egg chamber and Striker turned to face it.

It was another blueprint of the ship, only this time the lighted area centered on the top, near the communications tower. A blue light flashed around the hatch.

Could it be someone trying to get in? The warning coos made Striker's blood bubble with anxiety and he left the egg room, leaping up the stairs to meet the intruders. As he reached the elevator, the platform rose and he jumped, grabbing a handhold. He pulled himself up as it climbed to the surface. If danger waited above, he'd have only his fists for defense. His metal rod was still in the control room.

The blazing desert sun cracked through as the hatch opened and Striker emerged from the ship and stepped off the platform. Four people stood beneath him in the sand, but his eyes focused on one as dark emotions seized his heart. He'd thought he'd never see her again, but there she was. The pain she'd caused came back, fresh and sharp.

"Tiff. What are you doing here?"

"Striker." Her voice caught in her throat like a cough. His revulsion at seeing her must have come across because she looked away and breathed deeply before taking a step closer.

"Hold it now." Drifter caught her arm and raised a laser gun at him. Striker knew then why they'd decided to pay a visit.

"The map." Striker shot Tiff another nasty stare. "You've come back for me because you found the map."

"That's right." Drifter cocked his gun and stared through the site. "You're going to tell us how to break the code. We'd like to have your ship, too." The lanky man spit on the ground, and his lips turned into a self-satisfied grin.

Not only had these lowlifes abandoned him here, but now they'd come back to use him and steal his ship, all five years of his hard work. He wished he had an arsenal of laser guns, but blasting them with all that power still wouldn't ease the sense of injustice and betrayal in his heart. Striker considered how long it would take for the hatch to close before the platform reached the belly of the ship. They'd probably all be able to jump down with him, and he didn't want them wrecking his only hope to get Aries back.

Striker stared Drifter down as coolly as he'd once stared down Aries' colonial officer. To his surprise, the oldest member of the group, a scraggly-haired man, held up his own gun, turning on Drifter.

"Put down your gun, Drifter, or I'll blow a hole in your gut," the old man said.

"Reckon?" Drifter seemed more angry than worried. "What are you doing?"

"Choosing sides." The old man looked up at Striker and flashed a black-toothed grin. "Your pop's hired me for ya, Striker. I'm on your side. I've got the map. Brought it to you."

Drifter moved to fire, but Tiff pointed her gun at his head. "Put the gun down."

"Tiff?"

"I've chosen my side as well, and you're not on it." She gestured to the younger boy, and he raised his gun against Drifter as well, although not as boldly as the others. She raised her thin eyebrows. "Mutiny. It's three against one. Even if you shoot one of us, the others will kill you."

Drifter swore and put his gun down. "Well, aren't you the fickle ones." He shook his head at Tiff. "Miss Opportunist here has just chosen her man."

Tiff spoke to the boy. "Loot, take away Drifter's gun and tie up his hands." When she looked at Striker, there was a glimmer of pleading in her gaze. "We need your help. Our ship is wrecked and we can't decode the map."

"Wait a minute now." Striker felt as though his head had been struck with lightning and all the dust from the past had been stirred up to clog his eyes. Emotions swirled round and he couldn't separate the good from the bad. If his father had sent the old man they called Reckon, then he had a duty to make sure at least one of the pirates had a way back to the station. The boy looked young and innocent, but the thought of helping Tiff and Drifter after they'd abandoned him made no sense. "You think you can come back and I'll help you out?"

Tiff looked away as if he'd hurt her and Striker wanted to shout at her until she woke up to the fact she'd hurt him. Not the other way around. She'd always thought about herself, a single-minded, egocentric point of view.

She looked at him with a steely gaze. "We're asking nice, and we're the ones with the laser guns, remember?"

As much as his hate ran deep for Tiff, his love for Aries was greater. As he looked down at them, an idea flashed through his mind. Aries was his goal. He needed help to get her back. Striker looked into the easterly wind to where the *New Dawn* had disappeared.

He crossed his arms. "Let's make a deal. Those colonists have stolen someone from me, and I'm going to do whatever it takes to get her back. You help me rescue her, and I'll fly you all out of this hellhole and to Refuge. My word on it."

"What?" Drifter asked. "Go after the same colonists who murdered all those lizard men and baked their homes? No way. No way are we going up against them. Not for some woman."

Striker knew they had no choice. He called their bluff. "Then there's no deal. That's where I'm headed, and I'm not going to crack that map open and go to Refuge without her. You might as well kill me now and be done with it. Before you do, keep in mind I'm the only one that can fly this alien ship and decode the coordinates. Don't worry, though, you'll have a lovely life here on this rock. I should know."

They stood before his sarcastic wrath, squirming in indecision. Tiff's face soured as if she'd swallowed poison. The boy's eyes darted back and forth from Tiff to Reckon, and the old man held his gun as though it were his lifeline. Drifter glowered.

"What do you say, guys?" Tiff's voice came out weak. She looked as though she struggled to hold herself together. Striker knew her well enough to read through her broken façade. Something about his speech had thrown her. Was she jealous at his plan to go after a woman? Or just afraid of the colonists?

The boy looked up to Striker and gave him a nod. "I say we go. We owe it to him if he's going to fly us home."

Reckon nodded as well. "I've already chosen my side."

Tiff cringed like a cornered desert rat.

Drifter tried to weasel his way in. "Don't do it, Tiff. He'll kill us all for some woman. Come back to me and we can sail away together on that ship."

"No." Tiff shook her head. Her words were tense through gritted teeth. "None of you can fly it and none of you can decode that map." She looked back to Striker. "I'm with you. Let's go."

That was it. No further apology for marooning him here. Then again, Striker hadn't expected one. Tiff had never been good at apologies.

Chapter Twenty-one
Stolen Heart

"Now, Aries, tell me again about this mysterious man on Sahara 354."

The psychologist raised her pen above a clipboard and studied Aries like she was a specimen in a lab experiment. The doctor, with her puffy hair styled in the old-woman fashion of her parents' generation, reminded Aries of Mrs. Tanker, one of her classroom teachers who had erased her drawings of plants and animals on her lap screen. Aries exhaled slowly. She'd already explained three different times with three different doctors, and yet this woman persisted, trying to catch any inconsistencies in her memory. "He's a space pirate. His crew exiled him there five years ago."

"On Sahara 354?"

"Yes, Doctor Pern."

The tight-lipped woman scribbled something down and peered through her red-rimmed glasses. "Tell me, how could he have beaten the *New Dawn* halfway across the galaxy? You know as well as I do we left those not fortunate enough to be chosen for the *New Dawn* behind three hundred years ago."

"He found a wormhole and jumped through space." Aries knew how crazy she sounded, but talking about Striker was all she had left and the only way she'd find out any information as to his whereabouts.

"I see. None of the search and rescue teams reported finding a human of any kind."

Aries scrunched up her bed sheet in each fist and her voice rose. "That's because Astor Barliss deleted it from the records and told his men to keep their mouths shut."

The doctor put her pen down and leaned forward. "You mean to tell me a highly respected lieutenant lied and covered up evidence in his reports?" Her eyes dared Aries to challenge her.

Aries sat back and crossed her arms. "Yes."

The doctor shook her head and stood up, jotting something else down on the clipboard. "I'm going to put you on another medication. Let's start with Clozaril."

"Will it get rid of my bad dreams?"

Doctor Pern peered over the rim of her glasses in a cold stare. "No, it's for hallucinations. It's the most effective antipsychotic available aboard the *New Dawn* and in short supply, mind you. Of course, we'll have to monitor you for symptoms of agranulocytosis—"

"Please." Aries stood up from the bed. "I don't need any more drugs. I need to get out of here. Please, you've got to believe me."

The doctor ignored her and pressed the door panel. As the metal disappeared, she gave Aries one last look filled with pity. "You're very sick, my dear. The only way for you to secure your release is to prove to us you're cured of your delusions."

The woman disappeared with a swirl of white fabric. Aries slumped on her bed, heaving a sigh of frustration. Her emotions toward Striker ran so deeply, they were rooted in her heart. She couldn't deny them as much as she couldn't deny his existence to anyone. Even though she remained adamant with the doctors, her hope of seeing him again diminished with every day that passed. A dark, dreary urge to waste away in the cell threatened her resolution. The only thing she held onto was the fact Striker was real. By giving up her freedom, she may have saved him from Barliss' wrath.

Aries pressed her forehead against the wall and closed her eyes, feeling the rumble of the engines underneath her as the *New Dawn* coursed through space, taking her farther away from the man she loved.

A new certainty dawned on her. If Barliss had killed Striker, he would have used that to break her. He would have shown her the evidence and forced her to face the fact that Striker was gone. But Barliss hadn't mentioned him.

Maybe Striker was still out there somewhere, still alive.

…

Tiff gazed up at her former lover. He stood on the alien ship like some demigod on his chariot, the wind whipping his dark hair across the strong cheekbones of his suntanned face. When she'd first seen him again, his presence had stopped her breath. She couldn't believe she'd left such a gorgeous man behind.

Of course, learning about his mission to recover another woman stung like a scorpion's tail right through the middle of her heart. When he looked at her, all she saw was the hate she had put there.

His voice was hard and gritty. "Listen up. If you're coming with me, then you have to accept me as your captain. Drifter, Tiff and you, what's your name?"

"Loot, sir."

"Okay, Loot, as well. Start digging up as much of the ship as possible. We need to clear the engines and the wings first. Reckon, I'd like to talk to you down in the hatch."

"Yes, sir." He nodded, wispy hair blowing around in the breeze. "Captain, sir."

Tiff averted her eyes as Reckon passed her with a pleased smirk plastered on his face. Taking out her frustration on the nearest target, she yanked Drifter forward by his shirt collar. "Come on. You heard the man. Let's get started."

She cast one last, melancholy look in Striker's direction. He didn't seem to notice her. Clasping Reckon on the back, the two of them descended into the ship's belly and the hatch closed with a final snap. She wanted to be there under Striker's arm instead of Reckon, but he'd left her in the desert heat, about to haul sand up to her waist.

"I'm not helping anyone get anywhere." Drifter whipped his head back to fling his long hair out of his eyes, since his hands were still tied behind his back. "Go ahead, Tiff. Go help your new man."

Tiff reached her breaking point. Using her grip on his shirt, she threw him down in the sand. "Fine. I'm not untying you."

She took a swig from a bottle of water and waved Loot over. The boy smoothed his hands over the helm of the starship in awe.

"Loot." Her voice came out weak and she hated herself for being so vulnerable. She hated Striker for loving another woman, and she hated Drifter for convincing her to follow him five years ago. Loot ignored her, entranced by Striker's new digs. She wondered if she'd lose him, too.

Tiff dug her hands into the sand around the ship. They had no tools, so she used her arms, pushing sand back. As she looked down the length of the hull, the enormity of the job overwhelmed her. A mound of sand covered the bottom half of the ship and she couldn't tell to what length the hull ran underground.

Tiff decided to focus on one spot above the right wing. Sweat dribbled down the indent in her back. She pushed heaps of sand off the wing. Loot waded through the sand and joined her, shoveling with a piece of metal he'd pulled from his backpack. His presence calmed her. Maybe she hadn't lost everything, after all.

"As good a guy as he looks, I know you better than to think you're gonna follow him into the colonists' clutches." He huffed, throwing a handful of sand over his shoulder. His voice came down to a whisper. "What's the plan, Tiff?"

She shot a glance back, but Drifter was too busy sleeping in the shade of the hulk to pay attention to anything. She leaned in close, wiping sand from her cheeks. Like the heap of sand burying the ship, her plan seemed enormous and impossible. She had to take it step by step.

"I'm going to get Striker back. Convince him he doesn't need to go after this other woman. Then we all go home, free."

She expected Loot to support her, but instead the boy shook his head.

Tiff paused, knee-deep in sand, and clapped her hands together to free the grit working its way into the cracks in her skin. "What is it?"

He bit his lip as though he wondered whether or not to tell her.

"Come on, Loot. You know you can tell me anything and I'm not gonna get mad. I'm not like Drifter. I won't hold it against you."

Loot sighed. "It doesn't look like it's gonna go that way. That man's determined. I saw it in his eyes. Whoever this woman is, she's stolen his heart."

"And his common sense." A gust of wind shot sand into her mouth and eyes and she coughed and spat. "Don't you think I can win him over?"

The boy shrugged. "I just don't want you to get hurt."

"I'm a pirate. Someone stole something from me, and I'm gonna steal him back."

…

Striker studied the old pirate as they descended on the platform into the alien ship.

The years hadn't been kind to the man. Sand, wind, and sun had beaten his wrinkled face, and he looked in severe need of a bath and a dentist. Offering him a canteen of water, Striker reminded himself this old fogey had ridden in with his mutinous crew. He couldn't be trusted.

Still, Striker allowed the man time to drink before questioning him. "How do you know my father?"

Reckon nodded as if he asked a fair question and wiped dribbling water from his whiskered chin. "I'll tell it to you straight. Drifter hired me to find and decode your map. I'm a coder by profession, like you and your father, and I needed the money." He quirked an eyebrow and gave him a lopsided grin, showing a scattering of holes between his molars. "Times are tough, and I've run out of golden teeth. When I found out about Refuge, I wanted a spot there. You see, I'd like to retire to somewhere, shall we say, with a nice view?"

He chuckled and nudged Striker with his shoulder before his expression grew somber. "Outpost Omega hasn't gotten any better in the five years you've been on vacation." His breath whistled between his good teeth. "It's gotten worse."

"That, I can believe." Striker raised his eyebrows and said no more, giving Reckon a cue to keep on talking.

The old man cleared his throat. "So there I was, flying to Sahara 354, working on some way to crack the map, when a nanodrive pops out of my tool box." His eyes focused on Striker's, boring into him more than he'd like. "It was a message from your father."

He pulled a shiny object out of his front pocket and offered it to

Striker. "You can watch it, if you'd like."

Striker slipped the nanodrive into his pocket. Maybe later, after he got the ship to fly, he'd verify it—after he helped himself to one of his new crew's nanodrive readers. Right now, images of his father would only distract him from the mission. Between Drifter and Tiff and Aries, he had enough on his mind. "What did he say?"

"If I helped you and brought you back, you'd take me to Refuge. Your father gave his word."

"I'll keep to it."

The door to the corridor whished open and Striker watched Reckon's eyes bulge as the inside of the ship lit up his crumpled face.

"You say you're a coder?" Striker put his arm around the old man's bony shoulders. "Boy, do I have something to show you."

They walked to the main controls, where strange symbols flashed on the wall screens like old Earth's Las Vegas at night. Reckon walked up to the nearest set of writings, and his gaze flitted back and forth. He muttered a curse under his breath as he took it all in.

Striker clapped him on the shoulder. "Wanna help?"

"That's like showing a pirate an unmanned vessel and asking him if he wants to strip it for parts." Reckon winked. "You betcha."

The old man's presence lifted a weight from Striker's shoulders and the mission's impossibility didn't loom as big. He wasn't alone any longer. His own father had sent Outpost Omega's second-greatest coder along for the ride. If there were a way to fly the ship and get Aries back, the two of them would find it. Smiling, he showed Reckon his scribbles on a piece of old metal. "This is what I've got so far."

They worked well into the next sunrise, assigning different symbols with numbers and plugging them in. The work took Striker's mind off worrying about Aries and being disgusted with Tiff. He enjoyed immersing himself in the language of his lifework.

After inputting a series of numbers and letters, they sat back, watching the screens fluctuate. The symbols flashed until one particular design emerged. Each screen came to rest with the same scattering of icons. A flashing cue came up on the main panel, and Reckon looked at Striker. "I believe the ship is asking you to engage."

Striker stood up and walked toward the control panel as if he'd met his destiny. A single panel pulsed with blue light. He hesitated, finger hesitating over the hieroglyph.

"Go on. Push it." Reckon's voice was an encouraging plea behind him.

Striker breathed deeply and traced the symbol. A sound, low and deep like an ancient beast awakening, rumbled beneath them, gaining force until it stirred in Striker's chest. A diagram of the ship came up, glowing indigo light where two giant cylinders rested in the back.

"The engines!" Striker shouted, feeling hope surge within him. "We've done it!"

Chapter Twenty-two
Escape

Coffins, ejected from the *New Dawn*'s hull, soared into the void of space like fallen dominos in a twisted game of fate. Aries watched the spewed corpses drift away as workers in oxygen masks and lab coats placed her own withered and frail body into a metal box. Impossibly plush cushions pressed in on her and she couldn't wiggle her arms free. She opened her mouth to shout at the workers, but they ignored her pleas and closed the lid on her casket, silencing her screams.

Had they made the coffins airtight? Would her body explode from the lack of pressure in a second or would she run out of oxygen in minutes? Aries held her breath as the conveyor belt took her from the pressurized chamber to the exit door at the rear of the *New Dawn*.

Red lights flashed in warning as the room depressurized and a whish of air ejected her into space. She watched through a small, clear window in the casket as the ceiling changed from white tubes to stars. A sense of weightlessness came over her as the metal coffin flipped over and over in space. Finally, she was free. The *New Dawn* grew smaller in each view as the casket rotated. The levels of lighted walkways and gravity simulator rings around the torpedo-shaped frame looked like a child's toy.

She released her breath. At first it was a relief, but slowly, as she choked on the remnants of air left, the sides pressed in and her world went black. She tried to open her eyelids, but they stuck like glued velvet over her eyes. She opened her mouth to scream, but she had no air left to make a sound. Deaf and blind, she ceased to exist.

…

Aries coughed as she awoke. She'd kicked her sheets off the bed. Sweat seeped through her white tank top. As she adjusted from one hell to the next, she realized something in the room had changed. The stool near the writing table had been moved across the room. Someone had visited while she'd suffered another drug-induced sleep.

Sitting up, she saw a single red rose with a mini-screen beside it on the metal table near the door. Instantly, she thought of Barliss. Would the man never stop playing the game? It wasn't for her benefit. He maintained this façade for the rest of the Lifers.

As she rose from the bed, fighting dizziness, she felt like some miscast actress in a tragic play, assigned a role she never wanted and didn't fit. Sighing, Aries picked up the mini-screen. She clicked the monitor on, recognizing her mother's stilted handwriting as she read her own name.

Aries,
We always wanted what was best for you. Get well.
Love, Mom and Dad.

The formal and concise message didn't sound like her parents at all. Still, she recognized the same writing that had neatly penned her name on her textbooks growing up. Was the cryptic message all they allowed her mother to write? Or was she too afraid to divulge more?

Aries studied the rose. Of course, it was a copy, an imitation. The last rose bush had died hundreds of years ago on old Earth. She remembered a picture in her history book of mourning crowds around its last, ravaged leaves. Her mother knew Aries had torn the picture out and taped it to her bedside. Maybe she was trying to tell her something.

Biting her lip, Aries looked down at the rose. The satin petals were oddly square, as if its maker didn't truly know the curve of a rosebud. She picked it up and held it before her, twirling it around in her fingertips as a blur of red.

Something fell from the petals, clinking on the floor like a chip of metal. Aries' first thought went to the video cameras. She cast a glance around the room. She didn't want to draw attention to the gift. Placing the rose back on the table, she sat on the bed and scanned the floor for the item while feigning sleepiness.

A glint of silver caught her eye in the corner near the door. Aries walked over and covered it with her bare foot. Next, she shuffled back to the bed and pulled up the covers. Using her toes, she grabbed the object and brought it underneath the bed sheets. Kicking it up to her hand, she held a tiny circuit board: a key to opening her cell door.

Her parents really did wish the best for her if they'd smuggled in a way for her to escape. A wave of love for them overcame her.

Barliss hadn't given her a new locator. She didn't know if his negligence was due to the fact he'd locked her up, or that she knew how to disengage the beacon. Whatever the case, he wouldn't be able to find her easily. Although he'd probably assigned guards to watch over the escape pods, she could hide for days or even months in the inner workings of the ship without being found. That would give her enough time to plan another escape.

Aries forced herself to calm the storm of anxiety rising inside her. She had to think clearly. Third shift would be the easiest time, since most officers and Lifers slept. She looked around for any indication of the time, but the nurses left the florescent lights on all the time. How long ago had Doctor Pern visited? An hour ago or an entire day? The medication blurred reality. She struggled to string her memories together in a cohesive timeline.

Impatience bubbled up inside her. The longer she waited, the more chance they'd find the penny-sized circuit board. She yearned to find out what had happened to Striker. What if every second counted?

Aries got out of bed, walked to the door panel, and inserted the key. Strange electronic noises fizzled in the main panel as the circuit unloaded a virus. Numbers flashed on the screen and the metal melted away. Taking the stool as a weapon, she peered into the corridor.

"Hey!" One guard jumped up from a desk by the door. Aries lunged, swinging the legs of the stool at his groin. He backed up, too startled to move in time to deflect the blow. She hit him and he went down in a crumpled heap.

She turned to see another guard pressing the touchscreen on the wall. Before she could get to him, a siren sounded in a high-pitched wail.

"Stop where you are." He held up his laser. Aries threw the stool at him and sprinted down the corridor without looking back. She ducked as she heard him fire and felt blasts whizz past her, but she managed to turn the corner before he got a clear shot.

The alarm rang in her ears, loud enough to wake someone from a coma. Soon, guards would pour into the surrounding corridors. Aries could already hear men shouting. She kicked in a vent screen where the wall met the floor, her bare toes stinging with pain, and wiggled inside. She heard the guard's boots stomping and reached for the screen, her fingers scrambling around the edges. She replaced the metal grating as the guard turned the corner. His boots ran by her as her fingers disappeared between the ridges. She refastened the edges of the screen into the wall.

Two three-by-three-foot air shafts branched out from the central vent where she hid. One would take her into the air duct cleaning system, and the other would spiral up to the central humidifier and oxygen conversion tanks located above the forest's bio-dome. She'd learned this in her first ship schematic class. Thanking her teacher for making her memorize every detail, Aries scooted into the shaft that led to the bio-dome.

She could hide in the tanks for days without being detected. All she needed was a stash of food and water. Aries pulled herself up to the first junction. Here, she could lie flat and pull herself forward on her elbows. She huffed her way through miles of pipeline, licking condensation puddles along the way.

She reached an end unit used for utility purposes. She had a ways to go before the bio-dome, but her pace slowed and her stomach rumbled, so she curled up to rest. Aries remembered Striker's lizard bake and smiled. She'd eat it now. Nostalgia came over her and she sniffed back tears. She missed him more than anything.

Lying in the cold shaft, she wondered if he had given up on her.

. . .

"The first input connection will be the most painful." Dr. Pern brushed the back of Barliss' neck with a wet swab as he lay, facedown, on the operating table. Her cold fingers made his skin prickle with goosebumps, and he felt like a chicken waiting to get its head chopped off. A cold sweat broke out down his back underneath the skimpy hospital gown, and the hairs on his bare legs stood up.

His voice came out weaker than he intended. "The commander said it would be painless."

"Once the initial procedure is done, yes."

Barliss tightened his palms into fists and suppressed an urge to spring up and run out of the operating room. Initial connection was the first physical step in the process, and he'd already signed the papers accepting the position. He couldn't back down because of a small procedure with a drill. It'd happened sooner than he'd expected, but the commander had ordered the connection done immediately. Barliss could understand his reasons. The old man must be eager to set his replacement up before he wasted completely away. The *New Dawn* couldn't fly without a brain behind the helm.

"You'll experience a brief sense of displacement while the ship attaches to your consciousness. Your mind may wander into memories of your life. When you wake, you'll be connected to the mainframe. Your state of consciousness will be forever heightened." Doctor Pern's voice sliced through him. He shivered. He could feel her hovering above him like an angel, or a reaper, come to claim his soul. "Put him under."

An assistant injected a needle into his arm without hesitation. She pulled the tip out, and the initial sting receded. Her voice was calmer than Doctor Pern's and had a kind ring to it. "Count down from ten."

He only got to seven.

...

Barliss opened his eyes and saw Gerald's flabby face leaning over him, wearing the ship's former workout jumpsuits. "You had quite a fall. Are you all right?"

"I guess so." Barliss looked down the length of his body and wiggled his toes inside his sneakers. He wore his orange jogging jumpsuit with the *New Dawn* symbol on the right shoulder. Gerald gave him a hand towel to wipe the sweat from his face.

"Let's call it a day. I hear they're opening the last case of wheat beer in the lieutenants' quarters. Care to let me in?"

"Sure." Barliss brightened with the thought of drinking. He needed a reward for attempting the impossible workout regime dictated by the Guide. At least a number of higher-ups had seen him running long enough to make an impression. He had a reputation to build.

Gerald pulled him up to his feet with a heave and they both stared as a group of young ladies entered the track at the opposite end.

"Would you look at that? Mrs. Macy's gym class. All the graduating pretty women destined for computer-designated mates." Gerald sighed. "If only we got to choose."

Barliss scanned the crowd with mild interest until his eyes fell on a head of blazing auburn locks like a miniature sunset in a barren land. A perfect heart-shaped face turned in his direction with eyes flecked blue like cosmic dust. He'd never seen such a beauty in all his life. As the young women jogged around the track, he watched her progress, wondering how he'd never seen her before.

"Hey, speaking of which, why haven't you been set up with anyone yet? You're ten years older than me."

Barliss shrugged, although he'd been dodging the system for years now, lengthening his bachelorhood by bribing the computer analysts. "Guess they haven't found one for me."

"Those girls will be up for their assignments soon. Imagine the lucky guys…"

As Gerald drooled on the track, Barliss watched the beauty smile at her blond-haired friend. The two ladies broke away from the crowd and ran with athletic grace, their slim legs propelling them forward like gazelles.

Barliss decided he'd make another trip to the computer mainframe. Maybe Gerald was right. It was about time he was paired off, and he had the exact woman in mind. All he had to do was come up with something special to tempt the analysts, something stowed away in the archives of old Earth, like a pack of cigarettes or a bottle of Jack Daniel's.

An alarm sounded in his ears and Barliss looked around the track for an emergency, but the other runners kept their pace as if they didn't hear it. Gerald smirked and rubbed his hands together, perhaps contemplating his future mate, and the pair of women giggled, pushing each other off the track.

Barliss' memory faded as the alarm grew louder. Something was wrong on the *New Dawn* and needed his complete attention. He sighed, unwilling to give up this last vision of Aries running free.

Chapter Twenty-three
Ascension

"Reckon, check on the excavation of the ship and get the others. We're taking off!"

Striker smoothed his hands over the controls, his emotions surging. This ship would take him to Aries. He'd see her again and set her free. Together, they'd reach Refuge.

He grabbed her locator and punched in the coordinates of the *New Dawn*. A sky chart came up and Striker decoded the symbols as fast as his mind could tick. Estimated travel time was forty-eight hours. Striker's eyes widened with hope. That was it. The alien ship could reach the *New Dawn*'s position in a mere two days.

Tiff, Drifter and Loot walked in, followed by Reckon holding his laser at their backs. Drifter hunched over, lurking like a ghost waiting to strike. Tiff and Loot were covered with sand, crusted over from head to foot as if the desert gods had dipped them in batter and breaded them whole.

"'Bout time you came to get us." Tiff's hard-edged voice reminded Striker of a knife lunge.

He ignored her and looked to Reckon. "How's it look out there?"

"They managed to uncover most of the engines. Enough, I'd say, for takeoff." The old man's voice bubbled with eagerness.

"Good, because we're getting off this sandy rock." Using the tip of a wire, Striker traced another set of hieroglyphs on a giant crystal touchpad and the rumble of the engines heightened. Tiff and Loot's work impressed him, but he wasn't ready to make nice with the woman who'd betrayed him. The boy, however, had never done him harm. He glanced over at the kid. "You may want to find a secure seat."

"Do you know what you're doing, Striker? Or are you going to get us all blown up?" Drifter leaned on the wall like it was his ship and Reckon held up his laser in warning. He licked his cracked lips. Striker figured his former first mate was too proud to ask for some water.

Striker waved the old man back. "I've got it, Reckon. Thanks."

He turned to Drifter. "This is your only chance of getting off this desert hell. I'd think you'd be thankful and have a little faith. But no one is forcing you to come along. You could make a nice life here, build a sand castle, find some lizard pets."

Drifter grinned in a menacing stretch of his lips. "Let's leave the desert nomad reputation to you."

The engines rumbled like primordial thunder, revving up. Striker pulled back on the main controls. The ship tilted, everyone swaying backward as the engines blew out the sand around the ship. "Don't push it too far," Reckon advised. "We can go back out and keep digging."

Tiff jutted her chin out. "Speak for yourself, old man. I'm not going back out there."

"There's no need to." Striker trusted the analytics. The ship told him he had enough clearance, so he fired the engines harder. "We can break free. I know it."

As the hull emerged from the ground, the ship jerked forward with the force behind the thrusters. Striker fell back into the captain's chair, and the rest of them fell on their butts on the floor. Regaining his balance, Striker pulled the main lever forward, leveling out the ship as it hovered in midair.

"Last chance if anyone's changed their mind." Striker looked around the control deck, but no one so much as twitched a finger.

"I didn't think so."

He drew his finger along the screen, plotting a direct course toward the *New Dawn*. The ship responded to his request by computing a clear path into orbit. Once the coordinates were set, Striker pressed a fingernail into the panel to engage, and the ship shook, rattling his bones. Striker looked back to a series of frightened faces, some hiding it better than others. They'd each found a seat along the back of the control deck in a massive indent in the coral. He settled into the white half-bubble of the captain's chair. "Hold on."

The main screen retracted on both sides, giving way to a glass-like sight panel. Striker stood up as the desert scene spread out before him, the red sun burning his eyes.

"Way cool!" Loot's voice was wispy with awe. Striker couldn't help but agree with him as he squinted against the glare.

A light flashed on the controls and Striker had to focus to decode the symbol below it. He scratched a circle with the wire tip, and the ship arched up to meet the new trajectory. Orange sand turned into endless blue sky. Striker engaged the thrusters and the ship took off, cutting through the atmosphere. The force pushed him back into the chair, and he wondered how much pressure the hull could stand after all those years of disuse.

The blue sky gave way to a star-studded backdrop of space. After the ship broke free of the planet's gravity, the shaking subsided and it cruised smoothly. Triumphant cries erupted behind him as Tiff and the boy jumped out of their seats. Striker focused on Reckon. The old man winked, giving him a thumbs-up.

"Where are we going, anyway?" Drifter slid out of his seat, dusting off his pants. Although he didn't seem impressed, Striker bet his life the ascent into space on the alien craft made his old nemesis wish he knew the correct hieroglyphs to take it for a spin himself.

"We're going directly to the colony ship."

A chorus of protest erupted behind him. Tiff batted her fist in the air. "You're going to get us all killed."

At the same time, Drifter threw back his head in frustration. "Without a plan?"

Loot stood up. "How are five of us going to beat a whole shipload of them?"

Striker looked out of the sight panel, his eyes scanning over a purple-pinkish galaxy cluster as the ship took them farther from Sahara 354 and closer to the *New Dawn*. He'd come up with a plan. He always did.

"We've got two days to figure it out."

...

Aries woke with a raw hunger gnawing at her stomach walls. She'd seized her only opportunity to escape, which had forced her to flee without planning her next meal, or anything else for that matter. Now she squirmed on the floor of an air duct, holding her growling midsection in her arms.

She needed to find the air duct leading to the food supplies. Retracing her steps, she thought back to which direction she'd turned and where she'd climbed. It had seemed so clear when she started, but now the air ducts were a maze in her mind, and her head ached, thinking about directions. The medication had made her delusional. Now, as it wore off, she was left with the reality of the situation. She was lost.

Fighting off dizziness, Aries looked around. She could climb down the ladder to the workroom below, but she'd chance being seen. Aries weighed her options. She could be lost in the air ducts for days. She shivered with the thought of that. She might even die of starvation in the inner workings of the *New Dawn*. No one would find her until she'd decomposed. At least it was better than being shot out into space in an airtight coffin.

Aries listened for sounds of footsteps or voices but couldn't hear anything. Only the dim emergency lights cast the shaft in a red glow. Her stomach gurgled, the sound echoing in the small chamber, and she took it as a cue. Climbing down the ladder, she found herself in a workroom with pipes running across the ceiling and a table of containers storing various plumbing tools. A map of the air duct system was pinned on the wall.

She figured out her position on the map, calculating the distance to the nearest food source. Her best bet were a pair of storage units located on the deck above her, twenty meters away. If those were empty, she'd have to sneak into the bio-dome and raid the crops. That was the riskiest option, because workers would be watering and pruning.

Aries tore the map off the pin and folded it up, stuffing it under her arm. She found an unused light stick on the counter and cracked it in half, illuminating the room in a green glow. At least she wouldn't be crawling around in the dark anymore. She climbed back into the air duct and elbowed her way forward to the storage chambers.

She reached the junction above the storerooms, feeling lightheaded from lack of water. Aries backed up and kicked the metal under her feet until the grating fell, stirring up dust from the room below. A mildew scent wafted up. She covered her mouth. Not a promising sign for food.

She lowered herself, landing on her feet. Holding up the green light stick, she examined the contents of the room. A long hallway led into darkness, lined with boxes and shelves on each side. The dust lay as thick as carpeting and it tickled Aries' nose, making her stifle a sneeze. She held one arm across her nose and mouth and stepped toward the first plastic container lying underneath a swash of stars and stripes.

Although the *New Dawn* had its own emblem of a sailing ship, Aries recognized the pattern from her textbooks as an old American flag. Why would they have such a thing onboard? Maybe they kept artifacts from old Earth here. Aries had never heard of physical items in the archives. She'd assumed when they'd left the planet, they'd also left everything behind.

She removed the cotton fabric and snapped open the container. Crumbling frames stood up on end and she pushed the first one back, staring at a pastoral landscape with, what was their name? Yes, she remembered: horses pulling a carriage. The next picture was a man in a white wig holding an unfurling document that read: *The Declaration of Independence*. A third picture showed a young woman with a white turban wrapped around her head, a pearl earring peeking out from her ear.

"Paintings." Her breath blew dust into the air. "From old Earth."

She closed the container. There would be nothing to eat in that storage chamber and she had to press on if she were to find sustenance to keep going, but curiosity tugged at her. Her stomach could wait a few more moments.

Aries walked through the maze of shelves, holding up her light to illuminate the shady objects. An old violin with droopy strings lay in a box next to pages of crumbling sheet music, preserved in plastic. She looked further down the shelf and jumped back as a porcelain doll with a cracked face stared back at her with glassy eyes through the clear lid of a container. Miniature carved men-at-arms lay scattered over an ivory chessboard.

Then came the jars. Rows and rows of clear liquid, secured in the walls by rubber clasps, held what could only be specimens from long-dead species on old Earth. Aries said their names as she passed, running her fingers along the glass.

"Ceratophryinae, known as a horned frog."

Beady eyes popped out from a bulging throat and bumpy skin. The green and brown markings were strikingly beautiful and she picked up the jar to see the patterns more clearly in the green glow of the light stick. She turned the jar around in her hand, the frog rolling around inside before placing it back on the shelf.

"Thamnophis elegans terrestris, known as a coast garter snake."

The slender body spiraled up in the clear liquid as if it would strike if she opened the jar. Next she picked up a hairy-legged tarantula, suspended in an eternal striking pose, and a furry Eastern gray squirrel, its tail curling behind it. They were bigger in life than she'd assumed by the pictures, but more beautiful and tame than anything she'd encountered on Sahara 354. Old Earth must have been quite a place.

A wave of melancholy washed over her as she stared at the last remnants of a slew of extinct species, victims of the blight of humankind. She wondered what their lives would have been like, and hers, too, if she'd lived with them in their original habitat. She glimpsed something red behind a jar of beetles. Aries reached back and brought out a container holding a real rose from the gardens of old Earth, preserved in formaldehyde. She squeezed her palm over the lid and heaved until her knuckles turned white, opening the jar. A sickly sweet scent permeated the room. Reaching down in the liquid, she picked it up, the soft petals melting in her fingertips. She'd never thought she'd get to see, let alone feel, a real one.

She heard a too-familiar beep behind her. Someone stood on the other side of the door, punching in an entry sequence. Quickly closing up the jar, she rushed to the air duct, dragging a plastic container underneath in order to climb back up. She hid the broken ceiling panel behind some old boxes and pulled herself up as the door opened and the fluorescent lights blinked on.

Aries peered down from the shadows, hiding her glow stick underneath her shirt. An old man in a janitor's uniform carried a vacuum on his back. Aries rolled her eyes. It would be her luck, the one time they cleaned the storage chamber, she was hiding in it. He switched the vacuum on, the machine buzzing as a cloud of dust scattered. At least the sound would cover her escape.

Aries didn't stay to see if he noticed her footprints, the missing ceiling panel, or the misplaced jar with the rose. Instead, she squirmed as fast as she could toward the air ducts leading to the bio-dome. Anxiety outweighed her hunger, but she knew it would come back in full force once her adrenaline settled. Her light stick dimmed and her fingers shook, her mind flooding with dizziness.

Damn those medicines. Food. She needed food, and she needed it fast.

Chapter Twenty-four
Good Old Times

Tiff dug through her backpack like a beggar salvaging newly dumped trash for scraps. Most of her items were covered in sand and scratched up from the journey. Her favorite water bottle was cracked and her last case of makeup had broken in half, the black eyeliner leaking all over her change of clothes. She had a moment of panic before she found her sonic microplayer nestled beneath her hooded sweatshirt. Thank goodness she'd stuffed it in before they left their ruined ship.

"We're on an alien ship going into battle with fundamentalist psychos and you bring out your sonic microplayer?" Drifter's tone stank of bitterness. His hands were tied behind his back, so all he could do was taunt her with words. It made fury boil inside her.

"I need it to relax." Tiff pressed tried to turn it on, but the energy cell must have died. Nothing happened. "Damn." Why wasn't anything going her way?

"Guess you'll have to suffer like the rest of us." Drifter's dry, cracked lips twisted in a sardonic smirk. He looked so dastardly, Tiff wanted to poke his eyes out so he could never make fun of her again. What had she seen in him? She was revolted at the memory of her lips touching his.

The feeling she'd never see Outpost Omega again rushed back to her and she had to steady herself against the sleek white wall. If she was never going to see it again, it could only mean one of two things: she would succeed in finding Refuge, or she would die. A shiver crossed her shoulders. Somehow she didn't think she'd ever see Refuge. Tiff gritted her teeth and dug deep inside herself to find courage. No, she was going to make things happen her way and steal the reins of fate. She had no other choice but to fight for a better life.

Tiff ignored Drifter's leers and walked over to Reckon, who sat in front of multiple screens typing in code on two different panels. "You have to help me connect this to the ship's power source."

"Can't." Reckon didn't even glance at her. His eyes were stuck to the trail of numbers like a hunter stalking a deer. "I have to help Striker find a way onto the colony ship. We're all supposed to be thinking of a plan, remember?"

She used the sweetest voice she could muster and placed a delicate hand on his shoulder, her fingertips brushing his stubbly cheek. "Please, Reckon. This is important to me."

It worked. His face softened and his fingers stopped twitching. He glanced at her hand on his shoulder and then looked into her eyes. "All right." The old man turned around, peering into the corridor.

"Striker's not here. He said he needed to check on something in the belly of the ship."

Reckon seemed satisfied with her explanation. "Fine. Let me see it." Tiff gave Reckon the iPod. He turned it over, running his finger along the input device.

"If you could connect it to the ship's power source…"

Reckon quirked an eyebrow. "I'll try my best."

"Hey, Reckon, what does this ship run on, anyway?" Loot had woken up in the middle of their conversation. He'd been asleep for most of the journey. Tiff was relieved he had finally gotten some rest.

"Solar power coupled with a form of nuclear I've never seen."

"Wow. No wonder the ship goes so fast." Loot sat up and ran his fingers through his hair. "The hull's been soaking up desert heat for centuries."

Meanwhile, Reckon walked over and touched a panel in the wall. A drawer of cables opened up out of nowhere. Tiff gave him a questioning look, feeling her eyes widen.

"Striker's been nice enough to show me around." The old man grinned. "Now let's see. This should do." He found a cable with frayed wires on one end and twisted the wires just right before sticking it into the sonic microplayer.

A techno beat blared through the ship's intercom system, bouncing deep in the bottom of her gut. Everyone covered their ears.

Tiff smiled, turning the music down a few notches and thanked Reckon with a kiss on his cheek. She head banged to the beat, mouthing the refrain.

"What are you trying to do, make us all deaf?" Drifter yelled from across the room.

"No." Tiff gave him one of her practiced scornful looks, reserved for scoundrels and ex-boyfriends. He was both. "I'm getting us outta here."

The familiar music calmed her down, but she'd lied about her motives. She had a secret plan.

Striker appeared in the doorway, shaking his head. "What's all that racket?"

"Tiff's living it up." Drifter jerked his chin in her direction like an ultimate tattletale.

Tiff resisted the urge to smile. She'd finally grabbed Striker's attention. She plunked herself down in front of him and gazed into his smoldering gray-green eyes. "I need to talk to you."

"Well, turn that music down and come on." Striker gestured for her to accompany him down the corridor.

Tiff complied, softening the music before following him into the corridor.

She saw him clench his lower jaw as he turned to face her, arms crossed. "What do you want?"

Tiff tilted her head. "Don't you recognize it?"

"What?" She saw his mouth sour as recognition hit. It was their song. The song that had been playing when she'd first jumped onto his ship deck and asked to join the crew. As he registered it, the lead singer's voice oozed out the refrain in soft, velvety tones: "I'll see your sparkling green eyes in paradise."

Emotions passed through his features: confusion, pain. "Why are you playing it?"

She moved toward him. He towered over her and she had to crane her head to look into his eyes. "Because it brings back good memories, happier times."

Striker stepped back and crossed his arms, preventing her from slipping into his embrace. "What if I don't want to remember? What if I've moved on?"

Tiff ignored his question, even though it sliced her heart with a knife of regret. "We were so good together once. You and I." She ran her finger down the length of his arm. "I'm glad to see you."

He shifted uncomfortably. He'd backed into the wall, and he couldn't back up any farther.

She moved to caress his shoulder. "You know, I'm the one that insisted we go back for you. I'm the one who wanted to set things right."

"There is no 'setting things right,' Tiff." Striker grabbed her hand. "When you left me here, our relationship ended. You killed it. There's no way to resuscitate something's that been dead for five years, even if I wanted to."

Tiff's hand gripped his, squeezing hard. Even though he held her hand to keep her at bay, she shivered at his touch. "I've missed you so much."

"You've missed the map, that's what you've missed."

Tiff balked, her hand going limp. Is that really what he thought of her? She did feel love for him, but now, because of her actions, he'd never believe her.

Bitterness stung her heart. She only had one last card to play. "You don't have to do this, you know."

He raised an eyebrow. "Do what?"

"Risk our lives for some girl you barely know."

Anger flashed in his features. She'd miscalculated.

"Aries is not just some girl. She doesn't deserve to be locked up in that ship."

Tiff's voice hardened. Hearing her name was like putting a brick wall up between them. "Striker, forget about her. We could be together again, you and me."

"Yeah. I need that as much as another stab in the back." Striker pushed by her and grumbled, "I've got more important things to do."

Tiff's world shattered, like some pretty façade she'd been building on glass. She was losing him, so she clenched on tight, grasping his arm. How could a prissy, colonial snob be better than she was?

"What does she have that I don't have?"

He whirled around and crowded into her personal space, forcing her to slink back against the wall. "I'll tell you what. Aries put her life on the line for me. She gave up her freedom for mine."

Tiff loosened her grip on his arm. It wasn't what she'd expected to hear.

"Yeah, you look surprised? Self-sacrifice is a concept you know nothing about." He put up an incriminating finger and pressed it into her chest. "I'll tell you what you are: you're just another desperate pirate, putting yourself above everyone else. You left me to die here and only came back when you *needed* something from me."

He yanked his arm back, breaking free from her. Tiff felt the last of her hope die. Some mistakes couldn't be taken back. Like her brother's misjudgment of his ship's engine capacity. *Ka-boom.*

"Aries is a better person than you'll ever be."

Striker's words hit a dissonant chord inside her. He was right. She was a selfish, conniving bitch. Having Striker say it made it all that much more true. Her chest burned and Tiff thought she'd explode into tears, but Reckon bolted into the corridor at that moment.

"Sorry to intrude, Captain, sir."

Striker exhaled. "It's all right. You're not interrupting anything. What's up?"

"You've got to see this. I've been playing around in the ship's functions and you're never going to believe what these bird people came up with. It may be the one thing that can get us on that speeding colony ship."

"Show me." Striker's voice gained energy with what Tiff heard as hope.

They raced to the control room and Tiff followed, too curious to stay away. Reckon positioned himself in the captain's chair and brought up the main sight panel. Stars blurred as they sped through space.

"I'm going to need a stationary position near another object for the demonstration." He looked at Striker for approval.

"Okay, if you think it's worth it, then by all means, I'll slow it down."

Striker pulled on a few levers and the engines calmed. He looked at the readings. "There's a small asteroid over here."

"Excellent. Park it within a mile of the asteroid's surface." Reckon used three wire tips to paint figures across the panels like he was creating a masterpiece with light pens. "I've been playing around with the functions for awhile now, and I found a device that simulates two high pressure points and connects them, creating a corridor of atmosphere that can withstand the vacuum of space."

"Say that again." Striker leaned forward.

"It can connect two objects in space and create a walkway, so to speak, in which to travel between them. Meaning, we could connect to the *New Dawn* and walk through space to knock on their door." He smiled at his joke. "Are you watching?"

Of course Striker was, Tiff thought bitterly. They all were. She couldn't keep her eyes off the sight panel. A spot of light flickered on the surface of the asteroid. A blue laser shot from the hull of the ship to connect to the asteroid. When the laser dispersed, a clear, cylindrical tube coalesced, distorting the space around it in a ripple of light.

"That's it?"

"Yeppers." Reckon sat back, obviously pleased.

"You're certain we can walk across it?"

"We'll have to test it out, of course. The farther apart you stretch it, the less stable it becomes, so someone's going to have to stay aboard to adjust the speed to match the *New Dawn*'s."

"Good work. Looks like you've earned your place on the ship to Refuge and then some." Striker turned to look at the old man. "I owe you one."

Reckon winked. "All in a good day's work, Captain."

Tiff's anger reached an ugly head, like a pimple filled with puss waiting to pop. She wanted to throw a wrench in their fuzzy, warm thoughts of accomplishment and comradeship. She hated the thought of Striker with Aries. If she was miserable, then he should be, too. "That's all fine and dandy, but how are we going to get onto their ship?

It's not like they'll open the hatch for us to come in."

Striker shrugged. "I'll decode the door."

She narrowed her eyes. "How do we locate her on a ship the size of a small city? By the looks of what they did to those lizard men, they're not going to hand her over."

Striker's eyes burned and his face hardened. "Then we fight."

Chapter Twenty-five
Transformation

Barliss awoke with a colossal headache. He lay in a hospital bed in his T-shirt and boxers. He moved to sit up, but a tug on the back of his head stopped him from rising. Reaching behind his head, he felt a wire running from an input hole just below his hairline to a panel in the wall.

"Look who's up!" The nurse who'd administered his anesthesia before the procedure straightened the white sheets covering his legs. Usually a subordinate talking to him in that way would annoy him, but Barliss had no urge to put her in her place.

"How do you feel?"

Not like himself. Barliss' thoughts whirled. Images of Aries running, Gerald's round face drooling over young women and, finally, the drill careening toward his head swirled in his mind. The procedure was finished. He was connected to the mainframe.

He felt another presence looming in his thoughts, making the synapses in his brain fire at an accelerated rate. A higher intelligence presided over his consciousness, calming his surge of panic. "I'm fine."

"Good. As you can probably guess, the procedure was successful. Dr. Pern will be in soon to talk with you about initial communication." She wrapped a plastic pad around his arm and checked his blood pressure.

Barliss closed his eyes. He stood on the banks of a vast ocean of information waiting to pour into his thoughts and overwhelm him. Each gigabyte of knowledge humanity had accumulated over the years was stored in the ship's archives, including every word of the Guide. The commander's gentle voice entered his thoughts like a guardian angel, goading him on. *Take your time, Barliss. Have a look around.*

Barliss sensed every person onboard, every click of a door panel and every order processed through central command. He craved the success of the *New Dawn*'s mission now more than ever and could feel the dual engines working in overdrive, thanks to the new stores of lithium, propelling the ship forward.

The ship was an organism, each person a different cell. As he surfed the vast sea of knowledge and life, he sensed an anomaly in one area, a pinprick of a sore in the organism's systems. Barliss nudged toward the incongruity, seeking it out as one would prod a wound. A string of numbers emerged, flashing behind his eyes in a warning. The ship talked to him in a series of code. *Emergency breach in sector eight alpha.*

Barliss tensed. That was Aries' room.

"Lieutenant, I need to take your temperature."

"No. I don't have time. I must get on the main deck immediately."

He pulled at the wire and a sharp pain zapped his neck. His body tensed as if someone had hit him with a stun gun and he fell back on the bed.

"You can't remove it, Lieutenant." The nurse sounded like she'd told a toddler he couldn't fly. She smoothed his hair. "It's connected to the nerves in your brain."

"How am I going to walk around and do my job?" Images of the commander came to mind, always riding in his hoverchair. Barliss fought a rising sense of terror. The commander's voice resonated in his thoughts, *Patience, dear Barliss. We have teams dispatched to find her. The escape pods are disabled. There is nowhere for her to go. You must focus on the central directive.*

Whether it was the commander, or the ship itself, a presence in his brain reached out to him, soothing his nerves and steadying his climbing heart rate. The nurse reached over and pulled out a box the size of a wallet. "You can plug the wire into this. It stays charged for up to three months."

She reached behind his head. "May I?"

"Yes."

She unplugged the wire from the wall and re-plugged it back into the box. For a moment he experienced a sense of enormous loss and displacement before reconnecting.

"There. Now you can move about the room."

"Where's my uniform? I need to attend to an urgent matter."

"Dr. Pern is arriving shortly."

Barliss would have snapped at her before, but now he remained calm, his voice even and controlled. "I understand your concern, but this is an order from high command. Bring me a change of clothes immediately."

Looking like she'd just swallowed a large pill, the nurse hurried to a panel in the wall and pressed the touchscreen. The chrome dissolved above her head, revealing a shelf with his uniform and other belongings. She picked up his things and placed them on the foot of the bed. "Here you go, Lieutenant. Or should I say, Commander-in-Training?" She bowed and left him.

Barliss dressed in his uniform, careful not to detach the wire from the box. He didn't want that awful feeling of displacement to come over him again. The computer mainframe instructed him to remain in the hospital and begin training with Dr. Pern, but Barliss overrode it and looked at the door. It dematerialized without Barliss needing to do something as mundane as pressing a panel. He walked into the corridor in search of his runaway bride.

...

Aries bent over a vent shaft, watching figures patrolling the fields in the bio-dome through a grating. Every time one white lab-coated figure walked farther away, another came closer. Her instinct told her to stay in the air shaft, but her stomach felt like it was eating itself.

Juicy tomatoes poked out from the greenery and she imagined herself sinking her teeth into one of them. Even Striker's stories of recycled food sounded appetizing.

Another wave of nostalgia washed over her. Her stint on Sahara 354 had been dangerous and exhausting, but it was also the best time she'd ever had in her life. If she could have anything in the world, she'd live with Striker in that desert for the rest of their lives. It didn't even matter now if the alien ship ever worked or if she got to see Paradise 21. Her paradise was with him.

Aries sniffed, wiping tears from her cheeks impatiently. Honestly, how was she ever going to find out if Striker was aboard if she kept sniveling like a lovesick teenager? She straightened up and watched as two of the lab-coated figures left the fields, leaving only three patrolling the corn crops.

Aries had already unscrewed the grating. She moved it aside in the air shaft, held her breath, and jumped. She landed in the compost heaps in the back, the same place where she'd hidden with Tria so many years ago. Ducking underneath discarded branches, she made her way to the tomato patch.

The smell of the fresh vegetables tantalized her tongue. Aries plucked a ripened tomato and bit into it, letting the juice run down the sides of her face. She'd never been so hungry. How long had she been navigating the air shafts? Two days? Three?

Five tomatoes later, her stomach lurched and she sat down on the soil. She should have thought out a more balanced diet and snuck around to the pear trees. That prickly feeling she got right before she vomited came over her. "Oh God, no. Not now."

Aries held her head and counted her breaths. "One, two, three: breathe in. Four, five, six: breathe out." She tried to think of calming images, but Barliss' stern face kept coming back to her, making her want to vomit even more.

She held onto her stomach and thought of Striker. Aries pictured herself sleeping next to him under the shade of the tarp in the desert and the way his hair fell across his forehead. She'd wanted to reach out and kiss him, but he'd pulled away. Now she wished she had, despite his reluctance. The surge of nausea passed, leaving her with melancholy instead.

"Hey, you over there!"

What she hadn't been doing, was watching out for vegetable pruners.

Aries scrambled up and darted toward the air shaft. She heard voices behind her.

"What did you see?"

"I saw a woman stealing tomatoes."

"Over there. She's running toward the compost heaps."

Aries had no way to jump back to the air shaft. Blinded by the food, she hadn't thought of escape. Her only hope was the cornfield. The golden stems reached high enough to cover her head. She zigzagged through the vegetable patches.

Two biologists ran at her, one from the left and one from the right. Aries leaped into the long husks and pushed through three rows before crouching down. She heard their steps crunching through the dry husks on the soil.

Crawling on all fours, she sneaked to the far end, where a giant greenhouse towered over the golden husks. Hearing their steps behind her in the cornfield, she dashed for the door to the greenhouse. Thankfully, they'd left it unlocked. From her escapades with Tria, she knew it had another door on the opposite side, leading to the upper decks.

She ducked underneath tables of Petri dishes, expecting the Lifers to come crashing through the door after her. A computer blinked on and off in sleep mode in the far corner, luring her over. Aries chanced a glance out the smoky windows of the greenhouse and saw no one coming.

The computer held the information Aries needed. Tria had taught her how to hack into information files in the mainframe. She could search for Striker in the prisoner cells or in Barliss' confidential rescue reports. Peering again through the foggy glass, she saw the cornhusks shift as the biologists searched for her. She could spare one minute.

Aries touched the screen. The computer flashed on. Growth reports popped up, along with seasonal statistics and crop yields. Aries pulled up a different window and typed in Striker's name, along with prisoner and confidential.

Please redefine the parameters of your search.

Damn. Aries stared at the screen in frustration. Did this mean the search crews didn't find him? That he was still on Sahara 354? She tried again, typing in a secret clearance code Tria had taught her years ago. Again, nothing. Maybe the code was obsolete.

Suddenly the screen blinked of its own accord, turning green, then a fuzzy blue. She'd never seen a computer do anything like that. Perhaps the monitor was burning out.

A face emerged from the static: a long, straight nose, hard-edged cheeks, and a mold of bright hair. Barliss. If he wasn't so dangerous and controlling he would have been handsome, galactically gorgeous. A hard knot tightened in her stomach. Was he their screensaver?

His eyes blinked and stared at her. Aries backed away from the screen.

"He's not on this ship, Aries."

That was definitely Barliss' voice, but it sounded different, calmer, with less gruffness. His eyes had a strange, faraway look in them, almost glazed over as if he'd watched the main sight panel for too long. His change in demeanor scared her more than the fact he stared at her through pixels.

"Barliss?"

"Yes."

Aries looked over her shoulder, but besides the tiny sprouts poking through the soil beds, she was alone in the greenhouse.

"What are you doing on the computer screen?"

He smiled, his lips curling like two thick earthworms, a gesture he'd never done in her presence. "There is a lot I need to tell you. Please, stay where you are."

Aries stared in shock, utterly stupefied. She felt her mouth drop open.

"I'll be right there to get you."

There was only one explanation for his consciousness streaming through the main computers. Barliss was connected to the ship like the commander. Her nightmarish vision of him sitting at the helm of the *New Dawn* came true.

"I'm not staying anywhere!"

She yanked the screen off the desk. It crashed to the floor, shattering with electrical sparks. The biologists shouted from the cornfield.

Aries bolted through the opposite door, running from at least three white-coated biologists. The image of Barliss' pixilated face burned in her retinas. He was more powerful than ever, and she didn't stand a chance.

Chapter Twenty-six
Second Repo

Striker programmed the lasers, adjusting each setting to stun. Innocent people shouldn't have to die, even if they were crazed colonists on the *New Dawn*. The population of humanity dwindled, and killing each other would only lead to further decimation. All he wanted was Aries and a free getaway.

As Striker began recharging the energy cell of each laser, Loot appeared as a shadow in the doorway. The boy's face was somber, his body tense, like a wound toy waiting to spring. "Can I come in?"

"Sure." Striker gestured with a tilt of his head, since his hands were busy. "You can help me prepare the weapons."

Loot walked to the other side of the table and Striker handed him a rag. "Wipe off as much sand as possible. Pay special attention to the creases around the triggers." Striker forced a smile. "We wouldn't want it jamming on us at the wrong moment, now would we?"

"No, sir."

He eyed the boy as Loot picked up a laser, wondering how he'd gotten mixed up with Drifter and Tiff. "Did you come from the orphanage on Outpost Omega?"

"That's where my first memories were. I ran away when I grew large enough to fend for myself. Tiff found me and took me in."

Loot's wiry body barely filled his shirt and breeches and his eyes looked almost feral in the blue light. Striker wondered where the boy's parents had run off to. Outpost Omega brimmed with orphans, most of them dying before they reached adulthood. Loot was fortunate. It didn't sound like Tiff to take anyone in, but maybe she'd grown up a little. Maybe he'd judged her too harshly.

"You're lucky Tiff took you in."

"I know you don't like her, sir. But she's got a lot of good in her. It's just hidden underneath all that spite."

"It's too late for me and Tiff, son. But I wish you and her the best. You both can come with me to Refuge. I'm going to invite everyone at Outpost Omega. No one should have to live a life like yours, not even pirates."

"You really are a hero." Loot looked up to him, making Striker smile.

"Nah. I'm just another man looking for a better world."

"I hope you find it, sir. I hope we all do."

Striker squeezed the boy's shoulder before checking on another laser. "You can stay on the ship with Reckon. He'll look after you while I'm on the *New Dawn*."

"That's why I came to talk to you, sir." The boy raised his head to meet Striker's gaze. "I'm going with you."

Loot's determination pained Striker's heart. He shook his head. "It's too dangerous. You're much better off staying on the ship with Reckon. You can help him keep the pace steady as he maintains the corridor."

"I'm old enough to make my own decision, Captain." The boy's voice hardened. "I want to help you. One man can't take on a whole colony ship."

Striker put his laser down and studied Loot. At that age, every boy felt invincible. He didn't want Loot learning of his mortality the hard way. "It's a dangerous mission. You'd be risking your life."

Loot snapped back the laser in a smooth motion. It was recharged, ready to fire. "I know how to work these." His eyes challenged him. "I've done it before."

"The boy's right," Reckon chimed in behind them. He'd been so quiet, Striker had forgotten he was there. "Striker, you can't go in alone.

You can't trust Drifter. He'd shoot you in the back if he had the chance."

"I don't like the idea of putting the boy in danger."

"Please, sir." Loot stepped forward. "I've dreamed of a mission like this all my life. I'm curious about these colonists and I want to see the inside of their ship."

Striker ran his fingers along the barrel of the laser. Loot reminded him of himself as a boy, eager for adventure and ready to change the world. "All right. Stay close to me at all times."

"Yes, sir." A smile flickered across his face. "I won't let you down."

The screen beeped, and Striker turned to the sight panel. A glint of silver winked at them from the corner of the display.

Reckon looked up from his simulations. "What is it?"

Adrenaline rushed through Striker's body. "Loot, round up the others and bring them to the main deck." He wanted to jump at the sight panel and soar through space toward the silver speck. "It's the *New Dawn*."

Reckon's eyes opened wide. "Wow, there really is a *New Dawn*. Can you imagine? An entire city flying through space." He turned to Striker. "Fly behind it. You'll need to get within one mile of its hull for the corridor to work."

Striker took his place in the captain's seat. As he navigated the ship closer, he saw the *New Dawn* for the first time. The cylindrical tube was made of the same metal as its surface vessels had been, but it was also surrounded by rotating gravity rings. The *New Dawn* was twenty times the size of the alien craft, and he felt like a guppy swimming alongside a shark. As his ship came up behind the *New Dawn*, he searched for an entrance point along the rear of the hull.

"Will they see us trailing them?" Reckon's voice faltered.

"I doubt they're focused on what's behind them." Striker winked and found an entry point on the lower left side. "Over there." He pointed to a door hatch as the details of the *New Dawn* came into view. "It's a loading dock. Set your coordinates."

"Yes, sir." Reckon's fingers flew over the panels, the wires he held touching all the right symbols. "I'm creating the first of the pressure points."

Striker stifled a surge of impatience. Aries would still be there in the next five minutes and even fifteen. He had to keep his composure if he was to save her. "How long will it take?"

Reckon shook his head. "Not long."

Tiff and Drifter emerged on the main deck, bickering like children left alone for too long. Drifter was the loudest. "You're just a skanky pirate wench who—freakin' quasars! That's the colony ship?"

"Tie him to the pedestal in the back of the deck, Loot," Striker said. "He's staying here with Reckon."

As Loot secured Drifter to the ship, Striker said under his breath, "Reckon, can you handle him while we're gone?"

"If he's tied up, yes." Reckon nodded. "I'll be fine."

A light reflected off the *New Dawn*'s hull as Reckon used the alien technology to create the corridor in space. "I've attached it to our upper hatch." On the main sight panel, a stream of white light illuminated the walkway. "It's ready."

Striker threw a laser to Loot and gave him a nod. "Let's go."

He moved to the door, but a small hand grasped his arm. "I'm coming, too."

Tiff sounded desperate. Striker didn't know if it were for the boy's safety or his own. He didn't care.

"No, you're not. Stay here. Watch over Drifter."

"Like hell I will." She dug her nails into his arm. He could see the resolve in the hard set of her jaw.

"Tiff, let me go."

She held on tight. "You can trust me, Striker. I owe it to you to help after—after—that Sahara thing."

It was as much of an apology as he'd ever get. He couldn't deny her this request. Even if he left without her, she'd follow him.

"Okay." He gestured to the lasers. "Take as many as you can carry."

He gave Reckon a nod and left without another backward glance. The most important rescue mission of his life stood before him. He'd stolen a lot of things as a pirate. Never another human being, but how hard could it be?

"You sure you trust this alien technology?" Tiff crossed her arms. Although she tried to look tough, Striker could see a glimmer of fear in her eyes.

"Reckon's been testing it the whole way here." They reached the platform, and he traced the familiar pattern on the wall.

"What if it doesn't work?"

Striker had the same growing doubt, but he squashed it immediately. This was the only way to get Aries back. "Everything else onboard has worked. Reckon's a coding genius."

They stepped on the platform. The hieroglyphics pulsed around him, and he traced the geometric patterns.

"Here we go." The platform rose. Striker checked his handheld scanner. "It's registering atmospheric conditions on the other side." The hatch opened slowly above their heads, revealing a glimmering, star-speckled sky.

Loot released his breath as if he'd been holding it the whole trip up. "We're not dead." The boy's voice resonated like they were in a tunnel, but it felt like they stood in the center of the universe, the stars stretching out at their fingertips.

Striker put a reassuring hand on his shoulder. "Nope. We're not."

"Way cool to the max."

Without the corridor, they'd be sucked out into space, but now they stood atop the ship in a bubble of pressurized air as it kept pace with the *New Dawn*. The view was quite a sight, infinite space without a thick layer of metal or glass in between him and the vast unknown. As he glanced up at the *New Dawn*, his dreamy thoughts fizzled out. There was a mission to accomplish. Aries was trapped somewhere inside.

Striker looked back at Tiff and Loot. "We're going to have to jump."

"You're kidding, right? Jump onto what? There's only space for millions of miles around." Tiff clung to the hatch as if she'd blow away. Striker didn't even feel a hint of a breeze. The chamber was secure.

"I'll go first." As he jumped, Tiff and Loot screamed behind him. He didn't fall very far. His boots hit an invisible barrier and he stood on open space, feeling like he was a god walking on thin air.

"Monstrously awesome!" Loot's voice was hoarse with awe. The boy followed him and leaped onto the corridor, throwing his arms out to keep his balance. Tiff slid down the side of the alien ship slowly, testing the boundaries. Once her feet touched the bottom of the barrier, Striker turned toward the *New Dawn*.

"Let's go."

They followed him, walking through space on an invisible runway to the outer hull of the *New Dawn*. Striker found the panel for the loading dock and got to work decoding the door.

Tiff shifted from foot to foot, as if she were afraid to step too long in one spot. "Let's hope Reckon can keep this thing in place."

"It'll hold. Just get ready," Striker said, keeping his head down over the panel.

Tiff adjusted the shoulder straps for her lasers. "I'm always ready."

Striker punched in the code sequence. The door beeped once and opened. "Easy as pie."

It reminded Striker of his own ship bay. This place glowed brighter than Outpost Omega, as if everything had been preserved from the old Earth days, brand spanking new. The loading dock seemed empty, but red warning lights flashed inside.

"You've set off the alarm," Tiff spat as they jumped inside and ducked behind a storage bin.

Striker ran a hand over his hair. "That's impossible. I decoded it and turned it off." He checked the panel on the inside of the door and punched in a few sequences. "No. This alarm was going off before we got here."

He read the information flashing on the tiny screen. "It's a code red, section eight alpha: prisoner escapee. They have no idea we're onboard."

...

Every computer and wall panel Aries passed flickered on, streaming Barliss' face. She couldn't get away from him and the search teams were closing in. His voice resonated on the intercom. "Aries, there's nowhere to hide."

If he thought she'd go back into that prison cell of a room, he was wrong. Aries ran through an empty lab, knocking vials of seeds to the ground. If only she could get to the escape pods.

She tripped on a garden hose and skidded on her elbows across the floor, banging her head. Pain erupted behind her forehead and zapped her courage. Who was she kidding? The *New Dawn* had traveled so far from Sahara 354, she'd need a whole other spaceship to go back, not some rickety escape pod.

The computer on the table above her head booted up, and she picked herself up again, ducking underneath the desk before the familiar image could solidify. Barliss had her cornered. He was right: there was nowhere to hide. Curled up into a fetal position under the desk, she heard footsteps run past. It would only be a matter of minutes before they found her.

Aries held her breath, her heart thumping so hard she could feel it in her throat.

"The lieutenant said the trail ends here."

"Yeah, it looks like she's been here." She heard the man kick a vial across the floor and watched it settle just beyond her nose.

"Been here and gone."

"Jeez, you'd think she was a ghost."

"Come on. Let's keep going. There are three more greenhouses to sweep."

The two men left and Aries released her breath.

She'd fooled them, but Barliss had closed in on her location and search crews trapped her from both directions. An overwhelming urge to cry erupted in her chest, but she swallowed it back down.

No. She'd run no longer. This was no way to live her life.

Aries stood up. Fear had been a constant companion all her life, eroding each day into silent worries and controlling each decision she made. This day, her fear would cease.

Aries strode swiftly to the computer and banged on the keypad, bringing the screen to life.

"Barliss, I know you're in there."

His face appeared through the static. He didn't wait for the edges to solidify before speaking.

"Yes, Aries."

"I'm ready to talk to you. You know where I am. Come alone and I won't run."

Before he could respond, she took a step back, brought her knee up nearly to her chin and kicked out, hard, at the monitor. The heel of her boot shattered the screen.

Chapter Twenty-seven
Battle in the Bio-dome

"How in all the universe are we going to find her?" Tiff peered over a supply container, her laser cocked and ready to fire. Loot crept across the other side of the loading bay, scouting.

"I'm working on that." Striker glared at her and resumed hacking into the computer's systems. The clearance codes were tiresome but easy enough to figure out. Striker conducted a file search and found Aries' name on the prisoner cells. "Here she is: sector eight alpha, cell fifty-seven."

"Great." Tiff's voice was less than enthusiastic. "Let's go get her and get the hell outta here."

Striker read through the information. "It's not that simple." A rush of pride burned in his chest as he searched for her. "It appears *she's* the prisoner that's escaped."

"Shit." Tiff's face soured even more. "She'll be even harder to find, and we won't be the only ones looking for her."

Striker gained access to the progress of the search teams. "They haven't found her yet. The last sighting was near the bio-dome."

A laser fired across the loading dock, hitting the chrome above their heads. Striker and Tiff ducked and turned around.

"Oh no. Loot." Tiff moved to run after him.

Striker held her back. "We can't help him if we're both dead. This way." He gestured around the back of the loading dock where the machinery sat, unused.

"If anything's happened to him…" Tiff hissed.

They heard scuffling and hid behind a mammoth vehicle, its wheels taller than they were, combined. Striker pressed his back against the rubber tire, thinking of a plan.

"It's all right. You can come out now." Loot's voice rang out and Striker's chest heaved with relief.

"Told you I could take care of myself." The boy dragged an unconscious man behind him and dumped him at Striker's feet. "I caught him just before he alerted anyone."

Striker smiled, impressed. "Good work, Loot."

The boy shrugged, but Striker could tell he valued the compliment, because his mouth quirked in a smile despite his effort to appear casual. "Come on, sir. I've found a maintenance shaft leading to the upper decks."

Tiff ruffled Loot's hair. "If anyone can work their way through the air shafts, it's Loot." She looked back at Striker as the boy led the way.

Striker still had trouble reconciling the selfish Tiff he knew with the one who was so protective of a child.

Loot brought them to the base of a ladder at least twenty decks high. Loot jumped up and started to climbed as nimbly as a monkey. He called down, "Which deck is the bio-dome?"

"Deck fifteen." Striker waited as Tiff began the climb, then he followed, concentrating only on the rung in front of him, and on Aries. His skin burned as he thought of seeing her again.

"Are we almost there?" Tiff panted.

Loot looked down at both of them and shook his head. "That leaves us thirteen more decks to climb."

"Ugh." Tiff quickened her pace and Striker followed. For her this was a chore, a means to get to Refuge, but for him, this mission was his destiny.

"Striker, can you find the door entry code?" Loot asked, as they reached the right deck.

"Sure." He pulled himself up on the landing and immediately went to work on what he did best: decoding. In moments, the door dematerialized and a strange smell wafted into the maintenance shaft. It was an earthy tang, like the soil on Sahara 354, but with a pungent humidity Striker had never experienced before.

"What is it?" Tiff's pixie nostrils flared and her face scrunched up.

"Trees." Striker peered into the deck. "It's a forest."

They stepped from the metal maintenance shaft into an ocean of green.

"Whoa." Loot whispered, brushing a fern out of his way. "It's like a real forest from before the destruction of old Earth."

"Leave it to the colonists to take everything that matters with them." Tiff ran her hand over a leaf. "Leaving us with nothing."

"Come on." Striker picked his way through the squishy soil. "I see a break in the trees. This way."

At the edge of the forest, they faced an expanse of crops, gardens and greenhouses. The artificial light replicated old Earth sunbeams, shining down over the massive terrarium which teemed with life— including human life. Striker could hear men's voices.

"Let's get a better view." Striker gestured toward the trees. He climbed one, while Tiff and Loot each climbed into the ones beside him. From his vantage point, he took in the situation at a glance. Humans in white lab coats combed the fields like ants and patrolled the gardens down every row.

"Obviously, she's not here." Tiff crouched on a branch of the adjacent tree. "They would have found her by now."

"Just wait."

Tiff's lips thinned. "We're sitting targets, and this bio-dome is swarming with colonists."

Only half-listening to her complaints, Striker spotted the same henchman who'd threatened to blow his legs off on Sahara 354. The man strode across the main walkway and turned toward the greenhouses. Uniformed people followed in his wake, but he waved them back as he got closer to the greenhouses. All the people in white lab coats had stopped searching, and now stood in place like pieces on a chessboard, waiting for giant fingers to move them around.

Striker put a finger to his lips to signal Tiff for silence. "Something's going on down below."

...

Aries watched from the foggy glass of the greenhouse as Barliss waved his attendants away. She was relieved he'd respected her enough to listen to her request. He'd meet her one on one.

The glass door swung open as he stepped in. He closed it behind him, blocking out everyone in the bio-dome and leaving them alone.

"Aries."

"Barliss."

His eyes had the same glazed look she'd noticed on the screen, like a part of his consciousness was lost in another world. A single wire ran from his neck to an inner pocket in his primly pressed uniform. His skin was paler than when she'd last seen him, his expression placid.

"I want my freedom," Aries said.

"I know." Barliss stepped toward her. "I know everything."

"You don't know me. You never have understood me."

"I know every pill you swallow. I know how many minutes you've slept."

"That's impossible." The thought made her squirm inside.

"I'm part of the *New Dawn* now, Aries. I'm the Commander-In-Training."

Aries was horrified, but underneath her revulsion, she wasn't surprised.

"You've always craved status, but it's a hollow pursuit. When will you learn that the people around you aren't toys to push around?"

"Oh yes, they are." Barliss waved his long fingers. "And now I have the power to watch their every move, to run this ship how it should be run, with me standing at the helm."

"But you won't be standing at all, don't you see?" Aries couldn't help but try to help this man, even though he'd tortured her. "You're going to end up all alone in a hoverchair, kept alive by chemicals and wires in your veins."

"It's wonderful, Aries, being united with the mainframe. It's a whole world of interconnection, an entire universe of knowledge at my fingertips. Won't you share it with me?" He reached his hand out, strong fingers waiting to grasp her wrist.

"No." The word came out of her mouth like the shot of a laser. His eyes grew sharper, like she'd tugged a part of him back to reality. "I want to go back to Sahara 354. I need a transport vessel to get there."

Barliss pursed his thick lips as his hand snapped back to his side. He nodded as if he'd expected such a reaction. His voice took on a lecturing tone, "The *New Dawn*'s mission is to preserve humanity and deliver our genetic code in all the possible variations to another world, where we can live with abundant resources, free of contamination."

He spread his arms, "You are an integral part of the *New Dawn* and its cargo. As the commander-in-training, I must protect the mission objective. Therefore, I cannot let you go."

"The *New Dawn*'s computers can't account for everything that makes a relationship a success." Striker's features flashed in her memory. "A human being is so much more than just genetic code. Whatever computer you're connected to is tragically flawed if it put the two of us together."

A flicker of doubt crossed his features and Aries wondered if she'd hit the answer to everything right on the head. She pressed further. "You can't tell me the *New Dawn* knows the right path for all of us, if it paired you and me."

Barliss' face screwed up as if he fought an internal battle. He jolted his head like he had water stuck in his ear and touched the wire at the back of his neck. "You're right."

Aries almost choked on her own spit. Had she hear him correctly?

Barliss slumped forward. "The mainframe won't allow me to deceive. The computer didn't put us together. I did."

"What?" The truth hit her hard in the gut and she stepped back.

Barliss' voice returned to its calm, even cadence. "I saw you running one day on the track and I had to have you. I manipulated the system. You were supposed to be paired with a lower officer—Langston, if you care to know. I changed it. I changed the future, our future, and when I did, I mixed everything up. All I've been doing is trying to put it back together again."

Barliss' flat, factual confession was flattering in a sick, screwed-up kind of way. Aries thought about Langston and their rivalry in mechanics class. Would she have been happy with him? Would she have stayed on the *New Dawn*? Emotions swirled through her, and she rode their currents like a ship in the pull of a black hole. She thought of her parents, of Trent and Tria, of her erased animal pictures and her stifled dreams. She thought of Striker's stories of old Earth and Outpost Omega, and all the suffering the *New Dawn* had left behind. Her place in the universe became clear in her mind, like the threads of a tapestry all weaving together to form her true path.

"It doesn't matter who I was paired with. The computer wouldn't have been right."

Barliss smiled, showing perfect, straight teeth. "Good, now you're listening. I'm telling you, I understand the desire to have choices. I'm still human, after all. And I choose you."

"Yes, but the other person has to choose you back, Barliss." She stared him down, understanding full well how rejection felt. "You're not my choice."

A vein in his neck began to throb. He took in a deep breath and continued. "I'm going to be the ultimate power on this ship. You cannot choose anyone better."

"You have no control over me. My place is with the pirates, the people the *New Dawn* left behind."

Barliss jerked his head a bit, and spoke through gritted teeth. "You are a Lifer. Your place is here."

"I choose to leave." She shouted, proud to say it. "And I choose Striker, the man I left behind on Sahara 354."

"You choose a pirate over me? The inferior product of two inferior genetic codes over me? One of the chosen, the up-and-coming leader?"

Apparently, Barliss' rage was too much for the computer mainframe to quell. He took a quick intake of breath and his face turned pink, then red. He charged at her and she turned to run, but he gripped her arm, pulling her against his chest. Aries kicked at his legs and clawed at his face, but he wouldn't let her go.

"You're mine." His spittle hit her face.

She felt his hands around her neck. She tried to wrench herself free, but his fingers clamped against her skin, squeezing tight. Black splotches erupted in front of her eyes. She couldn't get any air in. Her lungs burned. It was the same feeling as her nightmare in the coffin. In a panic, Aries reached up and pulled on the wire behind his neck, yanking it right out of his head.

Barliss screamed, a rippling wail cutting through the air. He released her and she fell to the floor. Gasping for breath, Aries grabbed at the laser holster near his hip and yanked out the gun.

Outside the greenhouse, the white lab-coated figures ran toward them. Before they could reach her, lasers erupted from the forest, keeping them at bay. Someone on the *New Dawn* was on her side. Her parents? They'd helped her, but she couldn't imagine them overtly defying the Guide. Her mother had never touched a weapon in her life.

But Aries had. She kept it aimed at Barliss, but she didn't need to fire. He staggered back and fell to his the knees. His face slackened as if she'd just unplugged his consciousness. Aries grabbed him and held the laser gun to his head. He could be her ticket out, her human shield.

He slumped against her and she struggled with his weight. She couldn't hold him up. Using him as a way out would never work. Instead, she decided to put her faith in the mystery snipers in the forest. Leaving Barliss on the floor, she opened the glass door and stepped into chaos.

...

When the Lifer had entered the greenhouse, Striker had caught a glimpse of Aries. Someone had gone down in the greenhouse, and judging by the way the workers had started rushing toward the glass structure, it hadn't been Aries. He and Tiff and Loot had opened fire, keeping everyone out of the greenhouse.

A second later, Aries bolted from the greenhouse holding a laser.

"There she is!" Striker pointed from the trees as blasts erupted over his head, raining bark and leaves.

"Keep firing!" He nodded to Loot and Tiff. "Divert their attention from the greenhouse." Aries was running in the opposite direction of the trees. If she disappeared to another deck, he'd never find her. He had to get her attention.

"Aries! Over here."

She looked like she'd heard him, because her head perked up and she darted to the cornfields.

A surge of colonists ran after her, blocking her from reaching the tree line. Striker yelled across the fire to Loot and Tiff, "I'm going down there. Cover me."

Loot nodded. He aimed at a man scurrying up the incline and brought him down with one shot. Striker was glad he'd set the lasers to stun. Otherwise, twenty men would be dead now by Loot's hand alone.

Tiff shot him a glaring look. "It's too dangerous. Stay up here."

Striker looked across the bio-dome. The colonists were closing in on Aries, even as she tried to zigzag across the fields. Lasers fired all around her. One sent an explosion of corn by her head. She went down and didn't come back up again.

Striker's heart stopped. "I'm going down there, and I need you to go with me. Distract them to the right while I go to the left, where she fell."

Tiff nodded curtly. "Loot, cover us."

Striker dropped out of the tree and headed to the cornfield. She followed close behind. They hid behind a storage shed just beyond the fields.

"She went down over—"

"Striker, look out!"

A man emerged from the fields, cocked his gun. Striker froze. The blast sparked from the laser point.

"No!" Tiff screamed and Striker felt her clutch onto him. She looked into his eyes as the laser hit her in the back.

"Tiff!"

Her face loosened in what looked like relief. Striker fired, taking the sniper out. Tiff collapsed, so he dragged her to the back of the shed. Not wanting to look, Striker turned her over. The laser had fired a true shot and not a stun. Tiff's back was blackened and steaming. Her small mouth tightened in pain.

"We're even now, you hear?" She whispered and her eyelids flickered.

"Tiff, don't go! Stay conscious. You're gonna be all right." Striker shook her, but her body went limp and the color drained from her face. Her blood slickened his fingers.

"You were the one I always loved." She muttered under her breath, mostly to herself. "Too bad I realized it too late."

"Tiff!" Loot screamed from trees. Striker looked away to signal him down, and when his eyes came back to Tiff, her breathing had stopped. He lifted her eyelid, and her eye rolled like a marble, staring at nothing.

She wasn't supposed to die for him. A great sense of loss hit him in his gut. Tiff was just proving herself to be a good person. She'd done this to prove he'd judged her too harshly, to make them even. She'd succeeded. Looking into her blank eyes, he finally forgave her.

Loot ran up beside him and cradled Tiff in his arms. "Go," he yelled at Striker through his tears. "Go get Aries."

Without Loot's laser shots to slow them down, the colonists were closing in quickly.

"She's dead, Loot." Striker grabbed the boy's shoulder. "Come with me."

"No." He pulled away from Striker and knelt by her side, running a hand through her hair. "I won't leave her."

The men were a stone's throw away, relentlessly zeroing in on the shed. Their blasts tore into the wood, raining splinters. Striker knew they couldn't drag Tiff's body away in time. "You have to leave her and come with me."

"No. Go without me. Go!" He swiped Striker's hand away.

Behind them, Aries screamed. Striker's head whirled in the direction of her voice. She was still alive and conscious!

"Go help Aries," Loot shouted, "or Tiff's death will be for nothing! You can still make it out. I'll hold them back."

Striker moved to grab Loot, and the boy turned his gun on him. "I'll shoot." The wild look in his eyes told him he meant it. Striker yelled in anger and ducked as Loot shot a warning beyond his head.

He sprinted into the cornstalks to find Aries.

Chapter Twenty-eight
Mutiny

Reckon whistled a tune as he maintained the corridor in space, matching the *New Dawn*'s changes in speed by a tenth of a millisecond. His nimble fingertips danced over the panels of blue light, casting shadows on the walls. He felt like he'd stolen the power of the gods.

"I didn't think I'd ever see technology this advanced. In fact, since I've been alive—which has been too many years to say, mind you—mankind's advances have stopped altogether and dare I say, even reverted back. Ain't that right, Drifter?"

Silence, and then a strange clang followed his speech.

"Drifter?" Reckon turned around. Drifter had disappeared. His bindings lay unraveled on the floor.

"Shit." After clicking on the autopilot, Reckon locked the controls with a quick code. His eyes scanned the table. Striker had left him two lasers, and both were gone. "Just my luck."

He wished he'd come up with some sort of intercom to alert Striker, but he bet the man had other worries on his mind right now. Keeping an eye on Drifter was up to him, and he owed it to Striker. He'd grown fond of the man, another coder like himself, and a decent trader, a pirate that kept his own code of honor. He had to find Drifter before he stole the ship and killed the only man in his way: him.

Reckon slipped into the corridor, peeking down both sides, when a sudden, crushing blow to his skull knocked him to the floor, smashing his cheek into the cold deck. Pain seared behind his eyes. Stunned, it took him a few moments to compute what had happened before he squirmed around.

Drifter towered over him, holding a laser in each hand. "Shut it down."

Jeezum crow.

How was he going to overtake an armed man? Reckon edged back on his elbows, buying time to think. His head ached and he felt a warm trickle on his forehead. He wiped it with the back of his hand and saw blood. "Shut what down?"

"You know what." The gun rattled as Drifter shook it at him. "We're getting outta here."

"What about Striker, Loot and Tiff?"

"I have no need for them anymore." Drifter's eyes narrowed to two slits, reminding Reckon of a picture of a demon he had in his comic books growing up. There was no loyalty, no compassion.

"You weren't ever going to take me to Refuge, were you? You would have killed me once we decoded the map."

"Does it matter now?"

Striker's father had been right. Reckon was glad he'd chosen his side—for all the good it did him at the moment.

"You can fly the ship, and I bet you can decode that map if given… proper motivation." Drifter aimed the laser right between the old man's eyes. "Let's go."

Reckon's knees shook as he got to his feet. What was Drifter's weakness? He was more physically fit and would win a fight even without the two lasers in his hands. Drifter was an excellent opportunist, sizing up each situation and finding a way to come out on top. This was such a time. Drifter jerked his head back toward the control room, and Reckon stumbled forward, catching himself against the wall.

Drifter didn't have knowledge of the ship and how it worked, so he needed Reckon. For now, Drifter wasn't going to kill him. Acid burned in Reckon's stomach as he realized he had to run. Drifter would do anything to get him to work the ship, even if it meant torture.

He had another idea altogether.

The lasers Striker had left behind were the heavier ones, and they weighed Drifter down. Reckon bolted toward the hatch, his feet slipping on the slick floor.

Drifter called after him, "There's nowhere to run, old man."

Reckon had a lead as he rounded the corner and pressed the panel for the hatch. Instead of stepping on the platform, he sent it up empty and hid behind the corner, hoping Drifter would take the bait.

Reckon heard Drifter running, lasers thumping against his legs. The old man squeezed his eyes shut, holding his breath.

Drifter cursed and kicked the wall. "What in the hell's he gonna do up there?"

Seconds ticked by as the hatch opened and closed again and the platform came back down. The trickle of blood from Reckon's forehead progressed into a stream, but Reckon held himself motionless.

The familiar sound of boots stepping on the platform echoed down the corridor. Once Reckon heard the coral walls shift as the platform rose, he chanced a peek around the corner. Drifter had taken the ruse. He headed up to the corridor in space.

Reckon could have locked the hatch, but that would leave Drifter standing there with two lasers, waiting for Striker and the others to emerge from the *New Dawn*. There was only one way to protect all of them, and it shocked him almost into inaction—but not quite.

Reckon hobbled back toward the control panel. The platform would take two minutes to rise before the hatch opened. There was only one way to go, and once Drifter realized Reckon wasn't out there, he'd rush back down.

All the different scenarios rattled around in Reckon's mind as he reached the control room. What if Drifter had already headed back down? What if he'd never gone up in the first place? He glanced at the main sight panel and blew out a quick breath of relief. Drifter stood on the space corridor, looking into the void for signs of Reckon.

"Well, I ain't out there now, am I?" Reckon pressed the code to unlock the controls and the panels glowed brighter, enticing him, egging him on. Drifter turned and stared into the main sight panel, locking eyes with the old man. Reckon's fingers moved to the controls and Drifter's eyes widened. Reckon finished his code and stared him down. His old fingers hovered over the final command.

Could he do it? Could he send Drifter into space? Reckon hesitated and Drifter bellowed, raising each laser toward the glass.

If Drifter fired, he'd kill them all. The sight panel might not be designed to withstand a sustained laser blast. If he penetrated the glass, not only would Reckon be sucked into space, but the others would be left with no way to escape. Reckon hardened his nerves and pressed the panel in. It felt like a mere click of a key but it was way more than that. The corridor flickered out of existence. In one millisecond, Drifter was gone.

…

Stalks whipped in Aries' face as she darted through the cornfields, lunging in the direction of the ridge. Once she heard Striker call out her name, her heart raced on overdrive. Escape wasn't enough. She needed to be with him.

Striker must have been taken captive, just as she'd suspected. And he'd escaped his cell, just as she had. There he stood, waving his arms like a beacon in a storm. *Take that Dr. Pern. Hallucination, my ass.*

Firing Barliss' weapon at two white-coated biologists, Aries ducked and ran across three rows of cornstalks. Corn erupted over her head and she lunged and ducked, hiding. The firing continued in a steady stream. Damn it, she'd missed. She beat the ground with her fist in frustration. She was a lousy aim, and they stood between her and the tree line.

The stalks rustled behind her. She crouched down in the irrigation ditch, aiming her laser. The figure dashed between two rows, revealing a smear of black instead of white. Aries lowered her gun and stumbled forward, feeling a tingle of excitement run down her back. It had to be him.

"Striker, over here." She shouted only loud enough that anyone in the ten-foot perimeter could hear. Footsteps crunched the dried stalks on the ground. The husks parted and a person in an officer's uniform emerged, holding his gun.

"Langston." She should have known he'd find her. He'd tested higher in everything than she and Tria combined. Capturing her would be an excellent star on his resume.

"Hands up."

She stared at his perfect square of cut hair, his perfectly creased pants, and the complete control set in his jaw. He was another Barliss, complying with the system, eager to gain power. She hated him for it. If she didn't put her hands up, he'd shoot, stunning her to the ground.

Aries' hands rose slowly as she gauged his reaction time.

"You always were trouble waiting to happen. Both you and Tria."

Langston continued, undeterred, a smile working its way into the corners of his mouth. "I saw that glimmer of rebellion in your eyes, even when you hid it from Trent. I knew the day would come where I could capitalize on your indiscretions."

He waved his laser. "Drop the gun."

Aries only had one chance. She ducked to the side, bringing her arm down and cocked the gun to fire. As she moved, Langston moved as well, his body fluid. She heard the buzz of laser fire before her finger could get around the trigger.

She'd lost. Aries glanced down, expecting her body to jerk when the shot hit her, but nothing came. Langston crumpled to the ground instead, and Aries looked up in shock to see Striker standing there, holding a laser with a steaming barrel.

Relief flowed through her, washing away the anger and hate. Underneath it all lay something much more profound, a reason to push on through all the chaos.

"Striker." She relished his name on her tongue. "You're okay."

"Aries."

She ran into his arms and squeezed her body against his. She buried her nose in his shoulder, breathing in his scent as her arms wrapped around his neck. He was solid under her touch, his skin burning hot as he wrapped his arms around her waist, holding her close so they pressed together as one.

"I thought you were still on Sahara 354. I've been trying to get back to you. I didn't know you were on the *New Dawn* this whole time."

"I wasn't. I got the ship working. I had to—I had to come for you," he said.

She tilted her head back to look into his eyes.

The gray-green misted over like the bio-dome's meadow during an artificial rain. "You shouldn't have given yourself up for me, Aries. Don't do anything like that again."

"I couldn't stand to see them kill you. Even if I couldn't be with you, at least I'd know you were safe, you were alive."

"I'm alive. Now let's get the hell out of here."

Shots fired around them like fireworks, breaking the stalks in half and sprinkling bits of corn in her hair. Aries didn't know how long it would take for Barliss to plug himself back into the mainframe.

"Someone's firing at the Lifers! Did you bring others?"

"Pirates. One is dead. The other wants to stay."

Aries glanced through the cornstalks. White coats still moved in every direction.

"He wants to stay?" It was a thought Aries couldn't comprehend.

A burst of fire exploded a shed on the far side of the cornfield, and the colonists shouted and raced toward the commotion. Striker brought her head down with his, ducking underneath the shots. "That's him. He's buying us time."

She knew it was hopeless, but they had to try. "We have to go back for him. He risked his life for me."

Striker shook his head and gripped her arm so she couldn't run. "We can't. If we go back now, we'll all be caught. Besides, he doesn't want to leave her body. He told me to get you out of here."

All at once, Aries understood. Two people had given their lives for her. One, a woman, was already dead. As the laser fire ripped through the air, the weight of the knowledge hardened her resolve.

"Then let's do what he said. Come on." Taking Striker's hand, Aries led him out of the corn crops on the side adjacent to the laboratory. In the sterile room, lab experiments bubbled on metal tabletops and miniature greenhouses protected the most precious of their seeds. Aries sealed the door and locked it.

"Aries, there's no way out of here."

"We're going through the ventilator shafts. Come on."

She picked up a seedling dispenser and banged on the grating with the handle until the bolts loosened. "Find something to climb on."

Striker pushed over a soil container and jumped on top. She leaped up beside him and he hoisted her up. Gripping the metal, she pulled herself up the rest of the way. Once she wiggled herself in, she reached down to help him.

"It's a little cramped, don't you think?" Striker raised an eyebrow.

Aries gave him an apologetic look. All she ever felt was confined, confined in the cell, confined in the shafts, confined in the *New Dawn* itself. Striker was the only proof of a world where people were free, but to get back there, she'd need to confine him as well. "Sorry, but this is our only way out."

He clasped both her hands in his and squeezed. "I'll be fine."

They crawled on their stomachs past a few junctions and away from the noise of the battle, before Aries felt it was safe to take a break. So far, no one followed. The pirate that had stayed behind had done his job well. Aries gave him a silent thanks, wishing she'd get a chance to meet him, knowing he'd never see the outside of the ship again if they let him live.

"Ready to move, Striker? The escape pods are down this way."

He put a hand on her boot to stop her. "We don't need them. The alien ship has a version of an escape pod you're not gonna believe. Take me to the loading dock, the last one on the right side underneath the wing."

Aries paused. That's where they ejected the coffins into space. She cringed, thinking about her nightmare. It was the last place she wanted to visit. It was also the last place the colonists would look for them. By now, guards would be swarming over the escape pods like bees in a honeycomb.

"It's not my favorite place, but all right."

Striker grabbed her ankle and squeezed. She turned to look at him over her shoulder and he winked. "It will be your favorite place, now."

Aries climbed through the vents until her sleeves tore and her elbows rubbed raw. Striker kept her spirits up, talking to her the whole way. "I'm going to christen her the *SP Nautilus*. *SP* for Space Pirate, and *Nautilus*, you know, like the shell."

"Very clever. Are you taking applications for your crew?"

"Well, I do need a beautiful biologist."

"Beautiful, huh?"

"That's one of the prerequisites."

Aries wanted to press him further, but the maintenance shaft ended just above a utility room. "This is it."

"How do you know someone isn't down there?"

"I don't." She backed up enough to kick the chrome panel with her heel. It clattered on the floor below them. Aries braced herself for someone to yell for help or reach up and grab her, but nothing happened. She stuck her head down and saw an empty room. "Nobody here. Come on."

They jumped down. Striker gently slid his fingers in between hers as she pressed the touchscreen and the chrome dematerialized. Red warning lights flashed, but the corridor lay empty. Perhaps the Lifers had been told to stay in their rooms until the guards found her. She laughed at the thought: crazy Aries Ryder, running around with a laser like a madwoman. She'd be the next bedtime story before the moms tucked their little ones into their sleep pods. She only hoped it had a happy ending.

"Over here." Aries led him to an elevator and pressed the touchscreen. They waited anxiously as the elevator rose and the chrome dematerialized. They stepped in it and relief spread through her as the chrome materialized. The elevator descended swiftly, but slowed three decks down.

"Oh no, someone's getting on."

Striker winked at her. "Leave this to me."

The elevator door dematerialized, and a boy holding his mother's hand appeared. Striker waved at him, but when the child saw their lasers, he dropped a small toy ship, a miniature of the *New Dawn*, and little figures tumbled out. His mother pulled him against her and backed away.

"Sorry, ma'am. This one's taken." Striker gave her his most enchanting smile and pressed the touchscreen for the door to close. Mother and child stared with slackened faces as the metal re-materialized.

Aries let go of her breath. "Do you think they'll alert the authorities?" Her anxiety piled up miles high like the garbage dumps on old Earth.

"Doesn't matter. Just a few more floors and we'll be outta here."

Aries hoped he was right. Every floor they passed made her heart beat faster. All it took was one stray laser, and Striker would be taken away from her again.

They reached the bottom floor and the door opened to an empty loading dock. Aries tried not to look at the coffins stacked up in rows against the wall, or the giant machines that reached up to pull them down. A memory of a *New Dawn* flag folded onto her grandfather's coffin came back to her, but she pushed it away. She wouldn't suffer the same fate. In moments she'd be free.

Striker ran across the loading dock to the exterior door. "Let's see how Reckon's doing."

The air lock opened and Aries shouted in protest, expecting the vacuum of space to suck all the air out, and her along with it. She grabbed the nearest metal railing and braced herself, but nothing happened.

"The old man's done good." Striker looked back. Shouts echoed down the corridors and he winced. "Come on. The first step is a doozy."

Taking his hand, Aries followed Striker onto the walkway in space. He let go of her hand almost immediately to turn back to the ship. The guards had been close. Striker quickly entered the code to close the door. "It won't keep them out for long. Let's go!"

They ran across the black void of space, stars streaking by. Aries recognized the white hull of the alien ship as it coasted behind the *New Dawn*.

As they neared the alien ship, the hatch opened as if someone had been waiting for them. Aries and Striker jumped onto the platform. The moment the hatch closed, Striker shouted, "We're in! Close the corridor. *Now.*"

Aries heard a scratchy old voice talk back through the intercom. "What about the others?"

"Tiff is dead, and Loot wanted to stay."

Silence on the other end. Striker sprinted ahead and Aries followed. When she reached the main control room, she saw a grizzled old man sitting in the pilot's chair. "Where's Drifter?" Striker asked him.

The old man pointed to a bloody cut on his forehead. "Mutiny. I trapped him in the corridor and—" The old man could barely say the next words. "And sent him off into space."

Striker put a hand on his shoulder. "You did the right thing. Now, let's go."

"You got it." The old man scratched a shape in the panel, and the corridor disappeared. Striker took the main control seat and the old man grasped Aries' hand, leading her to the indents in the coral in the back of the room.

Striker gave her a reassuring smile before turning back to the controls. "Hold on. I'm dropping speed."

In an instant, the *New Dawn* was gone.

Aries stared at the main sight panel, disbelieving. Had she truly escaped this time? So many emotions whirled around in her head. She thought of Barliss lying on the floor, the wire sticking out of his neck, of Trent running on the treadmill, of her parents sitting in their congregation pew. She'd never see any of them again. She could only stare speechlessly at the clear space on the main sight panel.

The old man held out his hand. "You must be Aries. Now I know why Striker went back for you." He chuckled under his breath. "I'm Reckon."

She held his gnarled fingers in her own. "Thank you for saving me, Reckon. I'm sorry about your friends."

His eyes flickered at the mention of the other pirates, and he dropped his head. Aries could tell Striker overheard their conversation because his head tilted sideways and his profile showed rigid and dark.

Reckon's voice was almost a whimper, "What will happen to Loot?"

Aries shook her head and squeezed his hand. "I don't know."

Chapter Twenty-nine
A New Life

Tiff floated, white wisps of clouds swirling around her, dissipating at her touch. A gust whipped her up and she soared above a vast, white-crested ocean, riding the currents of a purposeful wind. Greenery sprawled on the horizon in a lush green thicket, bringing tears to her eyes. The waves broke against rock-strewn shores and beaches of golden sand. She twirled, reaching for the tree tops. Her fingers closed on air.

Was this the afterlife? Tiff called out for her brother, grandmother and Loot, but no one answered her pleas. She was the only soul in a vast, timeless place, full of beauty, but empty at its core. Finally looking at paradise, she'd never felt so alone.

Moments in her life flitted through her mind: her mother sitting at her ridiculous crystal ball, telling a fortune that would never come true; her brother banging a metal plate on his ship, glancing up and sticking out his tongue; the first time she saw Loot, sleeping in a ball in the heat compressor above their ship; Striker running a hand through his jet black hair as he studied a particular code late at night. It had been such a tormented life, full of suffering and want, but with moments of kindness and love sprinkled throughout. Despite all of the pain, she didn't want it to end.

The sun peeked out behind a cloud and she turned herself over to find warmth in the rays. The light was so bright it seared her vision, blotting out the other colors of the paradise world. She shut her eyes, but the light penetrated through her lids, beckoning her closer. Tiff struggled against it, squeezing her eyes shut and clawing at the sky, but the light only grew stronger, blocking out every memory she conjured, every thought she grasped.

Tiff gasped in a long breath of sterilized air and woke up. A heart monitor beeped by her side. She lay in a real bed with sheets as white and thin as paper. Tubes stuck out of her arms. Panic sent a jolt through her. She tugged on the IVs, but each intravenous tube was taped with thick white bandaging to her skin.

"Ma'am, you need to calm down." An older woman with red-rimmed glasses and puffy hair walked to her bedside.

She shot up, feeling pain jolt up her back. "Where am I? Where's Loot?"

"The boy is fine. He's resting in an adjoining room. You need to lie down." The woman pushed her back onto the pillows. "You were hit with a laser in the back."

The searing pain of her skin burning and melding to her cotton sweatshirt came back to her and she wilted inside. She could still see Striker's eyes, full of sadness and pity, but no hint of love.

"I should be dead."

"Yes. If you were anywhere else in the universe, then you would be." The woman pointed her nose in the air. "I've applied advanced techniques of skin regeneration and restarted your heart. Believe me, it was easy. I've had a lot of practice keeping a 356-year-old man alive."

Her bragging was all gibberish to Tiff. "Where am I? Who are you?"

"My dear, I'm Dr. Pern. You're my patient on the *New Dawn*."

...

Aries placed her hands against the frosty glass and wiped away the glimmering dust. The egg sat upright, a speckled specimen of a unique alien form of life. She wished she could extract it from the container, but she feared the being inside would die before they reached Refuge. No, it was better to leave it and take it out when the environment was more stable. If only she had something, anything to do other than wait.

"Pretty neat, huh?"

Aries pulled away as if caught stealing a look at the secret digital archives on the *New Dawn*. Reckon ambled down the row of egg containers, a ragtag fogey in an ethereal hatchery of blue light. "I could hardly believe it when I first saw them, too."

"It's funny. I always wanted to be a biologist, and now here I am, carrying the last hope of an entire species with me." She shook her head. "I have a hard time believing it's true."

"Does Striker know you like biology?"

With the mention of Striker, Aries' mouth slammed shut. She took a long breath. "I haven't had much of a chance to talk to him these days."

Reckon gave her a sidelong glance and then flicked his eyes back to the eggs. "Too busy flying his ship, huh?"

Even though Striker had been cold to her the last few days, she still found a need to protect him from criticism. "He mourns for those that were lost. It was all for me to be free."

"Hey now, missy." Reckon's voice grew authoritative. "No one should be forced to carry out someone else's dream. Those colonists have it all wrong. Striker couldn't bear the thought of them forcing you to live out your life in a prison. You have too much of a free spirit in your heart. That's why he likes you so much." Reckon put a hand on her shoulder. "Striker's a good man. A lot has happened to him in the last few days. Don't worry. He'll come around."

Reckon reminded her of her grandfather. He had the same wrinkles around his eyes and bushy brows. "Thanks, Reckon."

"No problem."

The intercom clicked on and Striker's voice echoed in the hatchery. "All hands on deck. We're coming up on Outpost Omega."

Aries followed Reckon up to the main deck, leaping two steps at a time. Anxiety and excitement simmered in her veins. She'd read so much about the space station in the yellowed pages of her history books, without any hope that she'd ever see it with her own eyes. The physics of the wormhole made it possible for her to span the journey of three lifetimes on the *New Dawn*.

The scene before her looked just like the textbook's pictures. A ring of pillars with a shining flame of light at its core connected bubbles of millions of tiny lights. Eight cities, each one as large as the *New Dawn*, twinkled in space. It had been built as a communications station for all of the colony ships, a way for them to stay in contact as they fled Earth with the last hope of the human race.

"It's breathtaking." Aries walked up to the main sight panel as Striker maneuvered the ship to a loading dock on the far side of the closest bubble city.

"And dangerous." Striker warned her with a flash of his eyes. "We're all going to stay together, right?"

"Yes, sir." Reckon gave him a salute.

"You still got the map?"

Reckon pulled out his backpack and rummaged through it. He pulled out a square metal object that reminded Aries of a Rubik's Cube. "Got it right here."

"What about you, Aries?" Aries thought Striker's voice had a more tender ring to it when he spoke to her than when he spoke to Reckon, but maybe that was just her own wishful thinking. He'd said he couldn't love again, yet so many of his actions told her otherwise.

"I'm fine. I'll stick by you and Reckon."

"Good."

The ship hovered over a peninsula jutting out into space. Closer up, Aries could see grooves in the metal, where ships had taken off and landed for centuries. The paint had worn away, and the plates protecting the loading dock were warped at the corners. Pockmarks and holes where small meteors had pierced the metal made the runway look like Swiss cheese. Crude patches of scrap metal were bolted to the façade like roofs of a shantytown. It had been beautiful from a distance, but up close, the space station was literally falling apart.

"Can you activate the door code? Omega's never seen a ship like this before." Reckon secured his pack to his back and adjusted the straps.

"I think so." Striker's fingers flicked over the panels and the blue light pulsed at his fingertips. "I need to find a way to match the frequency with this alien ship."

Striker's hands were strong and tan. Aires wanted to reach out and hold them. Now was not the time. She still didn't know how he'd react. After the deaths of his crew, every instinct she had felt inappropriate.

"Got it."

The door opened and he maneuvered the ship into a loading dock. Giant clasps rose up from the floor and secured the wings in place. The door closed behind them and they waited as the chamber pressurized and filled with breathable air.

Striker turned to Aries and smiled. For the first time since the rescue mission, she saw a hint of the man she'd met in the desert. "Welcome to my home."

Chapter Thirty
Propositions

Tiff's bandages covering her back itched so much she wanted to rip them off. She feared what lay underneath. Had her skin really been regenerated? Would it look the same? She tugged on the bandage close to her neck to have a peek. The door dematerialized and she whipped her hand back, hiding it under the covers. Dr. Pern would have a fit if she caught her tampering with her work.

It wasn't Dr. Pern coming to check in on her. Loot stood in the doorway with a goofy smile on his face and warmth in his eyes.

"Tiff!" He ran to the side of her bed and put his arms around her, his head resting on her chest. "I thought I'd lost you."

"I'm right here. It's okay."

"They wouldn't let me see you until you were better. They said you were unconscious for three days."

"Three days?" Had it really been that long? Ever since that strange dream, she'd felt out of touch with reality. Seeing Loot grounded her. She smoothed over his hair, trying to control the tears spilling down her cheeks. "Dr. Pern told me you stayed behind even after the others left me for dead."

Loot nodded. "I couldn't leave you."

The others could. She thought back to the battle scene. Striker must have thought she was dead to leave her. Indeed, she had been dead. Dr. Pern had brought her back. Apparently, even with her lying dead, saving Aries had remained Striker's priority. She pushed the thought away because it hurt too much. "Are the colonists treating you all right?"

Loot's eyes brightened. "Oh yeah. They bring me real food, like tomatoes and bananas, and what do they call it? Those little red bubble things? Oh yeah, grapes."

"They haven't charged you with any crimes?"

Loot shook his head. "Nope. Guess they think I'm just a boy. Not able to make decisions for myself."

Tiff exhaled in relief. "Where are you staying?"

"Right beside your room."

"Is it nice?"

"Compared to Outpost Omega?" Loot ogled the room. "Duh! Yeah."

"Good." At least these space colonists took care of him. Tiff relaxed some, allowing her body to rest. Her muscles ached, and she hadn't yet gotten up to walk around.

"Hey, I know you're recovering and all, but you have to get out there, Tiff. They have everything anyone could ever want. Workout rooms, entertainment decks, even animals like goats and pigs. I don't know why that woman left it behind."

"From what Reckon heard from Striker, she didn't like who they told her to marry."

Loot shrugged. "Small price to pay if you ask me. I'd marry the ugliest old snaggle-toothed hag just to live here."

"Loot!" Tiff sounded angry, but she laughed. He laughed, too, and they sat in silence for a while, enjoying each other's company. Tiff wondered if they really were dead and in some kind of heaven together. The throbbing in her back told her otherwise. No, this was real and she and Loot were together, happy and safe. She wanted the moment to last forever.

"There's a real nice man that's been showing me around. He says he wants to talk to you. He's waiting outside. Will you see him?"

"Who is he?"

Loot shrugged, "Don't know. Someone high up in the command.

He's got a wire coming out of his neck, which weirded me out at first, but he's been real nice, telling me about the history of the *New Dawn*, asking me questions about where I came from."

A nervous thread pulled at Tiff's psychic senses, but she pushed it away. If this man were kind to Loot, then she owed it to him to meet him. "All right. Send him in."

"The doctor lady says you'll be healthy enough to walk in a week or so, then I'll show you around, 'kay?"

"Okay."

She let Loot go after one more hug. He walked into the corridor. An older man in a uniform paused in the doorway. "May I come in?"

"Yes." Tiff tried to sit up without pulling too hard on all of the tubes in her arm. She had no idea how to treat this man, a colonist, one of the people who supposedly attacked the lizard men, killing them all. He seemed civil enough and even a bit nervous.

"Allow me to introduce myself. My name is Astor Barliss, and I'm the next commander of the *New Dawn*."

Tiff's stomach sank. The next commander? Here, to meet her? Boy, she must be in deep trouble. He extended his hand and she gripped it with a firm shake. "I'm Tiff."

"As Loot has told me, yes."

"Thank you for being kind to him. After all we've done, I don't understand why your people are helping us."

He nodded, adjusting the wire behind his neck before speaking. "Our goal here on the *New Dawn* is to preserve human DNA until we reach Paradise 21, where mankind can once more flourish. We've lost two able-bodied women this year, before their genetic codes were passed on. One died during an attempted escape, and your friends stole one of our colonists."

"They're not my friends." Tiff crossed her arms and narrowed her eyes, hoping to appear tough, so he wouldn't see the hurt underneath. "They left Loot and me here to die."

"I know." He patted her hand with long, strong-looking fingers. His eyes grew foggy. "I know what it's like to be left behind. Anger turns to resentment, and then the sadness weighs in." He paused, then focused back on her. "That's why I have a proposition to present."

Tiff opened her mouth to decline, but he waved her back. "Hear me out first."

He sat on a stool by her bed, his shoulders slumping as if a million regrets chained him to the floor. Although he was a commander, to Tiff he looked like a broken man who'd gone to hell and back again.

Oddly enough, she felt drawn to him. With his perfect hair, straight edged jaw, and wide chest, he reminded her of the husband in the old 1950s movies, the one that came home in a suit and tie, tired every night after work. She found the resemblance oddly comforting.

"I've made many mistakes as a lieutenant, and I don't wish to make them again as a commander. I know what's it like to force people, and I know the consequences of those actions. So, I'm not going to force you to do anything. I'm only presenting an opportunity, should you want it."

Tiff leaned forward. He had her interest piqued. "Everyone should get a second chance." In her case, a third or fourth, but she didn't want to mention that. "Okay, let's hear it."

"A month from now, the *New Dawn* will pass by another planet like Sahara 354: Sahara 413. I can set you up with an escape pod, and you and the boy can make your way to a new world."

He locked eyes with her, his eyebrows raised. "You have another choice as well. You can stay with us here on the *New Dawn* and replace the two colonists we've lost. We've tested both you and the boy and found unique strands of genetic code separating you from anyone here onboard. You have recessive traits long lost to us in our gene pool, and we'd value your contribution to our mission. You'd have all of the necessities of life, along with some luxuries as well. We'd take care of you and Loot into your old age. The *New Dawn* would be your home. We only ask that you and Loot each be assigned an appropriate mate to further the genes of our race."

His offer whirled around in her head and Tiff clutched the sides of the bed to steady herself. She already knew Loot's answer, and she'd long known what she wanted as well: a safe home, a father for Loot, and a life free of suffering. One question remained. "Who would my mate be?"

"I was hoping you'd ask."

Barliss reached into his back pocket and pulled out a diamond ring.

...

The inside of Space Central stank like a toilet that couldn't be flushed. Aries gagged and coughed, covering her nose with her sleeve. The smell only grew stronger as they walked through the corridor that connected the loading dock to one of the main bubble cities.

Striker gave her an apologetic smile. "I'm sorry. I forgot about the stench. I should have warned you."

"That's okay," her voice was strained as she struggled to breathe through the fabric. She was aware of the lasers she carried, one on each side, for protection. "I just can't believe people live like this."

Reckon snickered. "Darlin', you ain't seen nothing yet. Just try not to look like a newbie, okay?"

People lay in heaps on the walkway, covered by scraps of clothing and tattered plastic wrap. They stared at Aries with dark, hungry eyes and she stared back, her mouth hanging open.

"Don't look at them." Striker guided her away by the arm and whispered into her ear. "It only encourages them to beg."

"What do they beg for?"

"Food, water, anything they can eat."

"My goodness. Everyone had an equal share on the *New Dawn* and we grew enough food to feed us all. In fact, most of the colonists packed on the pounds. The problem was too much food, not too little."

Striker laughed. "You're not in Kansas anymore."

Aries had no idea what that meant, but she looked forward to learning everything Striker knew.

They rounded a bend where a gang of young teens lurked in the shadows. The boldest one, a boy with a filigree of tattoos on his face, kicked a light ball with the spikes on the toes of his boots. His hood, designed like a cobra's head, glittered in an oily sheen as he stepped forward. He gave their lasers one look and backed away. As he turned, Aries caught a glimpse of his eyes, cold and wild like a lion waiting to pounce.

"Don't worry." Striker squeezed Aries' arm. He must have felt her tensing up. "No one's going to bother us. Not while you're with me."

The city sprawled before them, a shantytown of metal buildings and walkways, suspended in space with bubble glass and stars on all sides. It reminded Aries of the snow globe she'd had in her room on the *New Dawn*. Passed down through generations of her family, her mother had told her it was where her ancestors came from, a city on old Earth once called New York. She would imagine casting herself inside it, living in a time long past. Little white sparkles of fake snow had danced around the tall buildings when she shook it.

The only sparkles in this city lay outside the glass walls. The stars created a glimmering backdrop, but were also a sobering reminder of the nothingness surrounding them on all sides. Dim lamps lit the walkways like tiny fireflies in an ocean of black.

Aries felt a chill run down her body and hugged her arms to her chest. "It's so dark, so cold."

Striker put an arm around her. "In Outpost Omega, there's no day, only night."

Vendors clogged the main streets, selling what Aries could only see as trash. The first stall she passed had broken eyeglasses, each pair more shattered and bent than the last. The next stall, run by an elderly woman with a scar the size of a kitchen knife down her face, displayed dolls' heads with no bodies. Some of the porcelain faces were scratched where the eyes had been plucked out. On the other side of the street, a young man sold bins of nails and screws of all sizes. He leered at her with rotten, blackened teeth.

"Does anyone here produce new goods?" Aries asked Striker in a whisper, careful not to offend any of the merchants.

"We ran out of resources decades ago. Now we recycle anything and everything we can find."

They turned down an alley and entered a building through the back door, climbing up a series of rusted metal stairways until they reached the floor Striker wanted. His pace quickened as he neared the end of the hallway. He buzzed the door button as soon as he reached it.

He spoke into the intercom. "Dad, it's me, Striker."

Silence. Aries heard a shout from outside. Someone didn't like the price they offered for a merchant's goods. Striker didn't seem to notice. His face fell with worry. "I hope I didn't come too late."

Ignoring the commotion outside, Aries put a hand on Striker's shoulder, "Wait. Give it time."

Moments later, the door dematerialized and an old man stepped out. He had sharp, bright, emerald eyes like his son, a distinguished streak of gray on either side of his temples, and a curved nose like an eagle's beak. In every way he resembled a retired ship commander, toughened by life and time.

"Son."

Aries watched as Striker's dad embraced him, touched by their obvious happiness. How long ago had Striker said his crew marooned him? Five years. That was a long time to be missing. Of course, she would never see her own parents again. At least she knew they'd wanted her to be happy.

"Reckon did his job, Dad." Striker let go of his father and turned to pull the old man forward.

Reckon waved the accolades away. "Nah. I did nothing special."

Striker's father extended his hand. "I am forever grateful to you. I'll keep my promise. You have a ticket to Refuge."

Striker's father turned to Aries. "Who, may I ask, is this?"

Striker put his arm around her and squeezed her shoulders gently. "This is Aries. She helped me find a way off Sahara 354." He looked down at her with such intensity, she felt her cheeks grow hot even in the chill of Outpost Omega. "She saved my life."

"Aries, nice to meet you." His father wrapped his arms around her and hugged her like she was his own daughter. He looked at her and Reckon. "Thank you both for reuniting me with my son."

Aries smiled. "It's an honor to meet you, sir."

"They know me around here as Decoder, but you can call me James. Come in, come in." He gestured for them to follow him into the small room. A single window looking out to space hung over stacked containers of reprocessed food. A metal table had all sorts of puzzles with codes, little cubes resembling Striker's map. A single picture hung on the metal wall, illuminated by the only lamp. His father was depicted in it, years younger, with a woman that had a thin nose and flowing auburn hair.

James noticed her studying the picture. "That is Lisa Galen the third, my wife."

Striker scratched his head, annoyed. He pulled up a stool and cleared a spot on the metal table to rest his arms. "Dad, we don't have time for reminiscing. I'm going to post the coordinates of Refuge on the main channel of the pirate radio. Everyone who lives here will be welcome to start a new life. As for all of us, we're going to the orphanage. We're gonna pack the ship up as tight as possible with every child needing a home."

His father smiled, wrinkles crinkling around his bright eyes. "Following in the footsteps of Captain James Wilfred the first." He raised an eyebrow. "Our ancestor would be proud."

"Will you come with us?"

His father's eyes scanned the room with watery melancholy, resting on the picture. "I wish your mother were alive to see this. She'd want me to go with you." He wiped his face. "This is where we lived our lives together. I can't leave her memory behind."

Striker's face hardened, but he seemed unsurprised. Aries wondered if they fought constantly about the old memories. In any other situation, she'd keep her opinion to herself, but she cared so much for Striker, she had to say something.

"Sir, you can take her memory with you. We'll need help with the rebuilding process and we sure could use your advice."

Striker turned away and pressed the door panel. "It's hopeless, Aries. Don't waste your time." He stormed off into the hallway.

The moment was slipping away, and Striker's small family threatened to tear at the seams. Aries did everything she could to hold it together. She grasped both of James' hands in her own and looked into his eyes. "Please."

"You remind me so much of her," Striker's father whispered. "I can see why Striker thinks you're special."

Aries felt her cheeks redden. She had no idea he'd seen anything between them.

He pulled his hands away and turned back to his small cell. Under his breath he muttered, "Yes, I'll go."

He looked at Reckon. "Go get Striker. He'll need time to cool off. I'll make you all a decent meal."

...

The orphanage hid in a back corner of the space station behind heaps of trash. Aries followed Striker as he led her, along with his father and Reckon, through a path in between mounds of wreckage. Wires poked out of garbage bags like dead snakes, and broken glass twinkled like fallen stars through the litter. Aries had to watch where she put her foot down with every step. The desolation overwhelmed her. Even Sahara 354 had been better than this.

She heard a rustling above her, and a cracked tin can bounced down the side of the heap. A small boy disappeared into the cockpit of an old scout ship. His eyes peered back at her through the busted windshield.

"There are kids hiding in the trash."

"Scavengers," Striker explained. "The orphanage sends them out to search for items they can use."

"Horrible." Aries covered her mouth in shock.

James came up behind her and put a hand on her shoulder. "Now they'll have a better life."

Ramshackle doors held together by rusted bolts screeched open and an old woman with hair like a rat's nest peered out. "What do ya want?"

Striker stepped forward. "We'd like to adopt."

While children hollered and cried in the background, the old woman studied them warily. Cataracts clouded one of her eyes. Using her good eye, she focused on their clothes and their lasers. Aries felt her stare like the rays of one of Sahara 354's suns. Behind her, Reckon blew his nose and Striker's father stood perfectly still, arms crossed.

"What for?" the woman finally asked. "People drop kids off here. No one takes 'em out."

"We do." Aries stepped forward, thinking as a woman, she'd be the best spokesperson for the group. "We can give them a better home than anyone here."

Striker brought out a cube and clicked it open. Aries leaned forward to watch as the panels parted and the insides ticked. Light flickered from a lens, projecting a movie on the outer chrome wall of the orphanage. Star systems whizzed by, followed by nebulous clouds and cosmic dust. A sun, surrounded by three planets, came into focus. The view plunged toward a small moon orbiting one of the planets.

Underneath a thick atmosphere of puffy clouds lay a miniature paradise, filled with blue and green.

Striker clicked off the image. "I call it Refuge. I've sent the coordinates to everyone here at the station. I'd like to start a new colony, and I'll need volunteers to help build a city."

"My kids ain't slave labor."

"They won't be. There will be schools as soon as we line up teachers. There will be food. Water. Fresh air."

The old woman huffed and scrunched up her face like a raisin. Aries bit her lip. What if she didn't believe them? What if she kept all the children here to live in the garbage? Striker just might take them by force.

Trailing the tattered shawls she wore, the old woman disappeared back into the darkness of the orphanage and Striker's shoulders slumped.

Reckon shouted from behind them, "Stupid old hag, doesn't know what's good for her."

Suddenly, the children's cries ceased. The doors screeched and parted again, revealing rows of beds with children of all ages huddled in groups of three and four. The old woman reemerged in the threshold and jabbed a thumb behind her. "Which one do you want to take with ya?"

Striker smiled, the first unreserved smile Aries had seen since they'd left the *New Dawn*. "All of them."

Chapter Thirty-one
Broken Shells

Aries belted the last of the orphans into her seat on the ship, a girl with round, blue eyes, who clutched a doll with no head. Aries felt an urge to walk back to the stand in the street and buy a porcelain head to match, but Outpost Omega verged on social collapse. The sooner they left, the safer they'd all be.

"You stay here, okay? We're going to take you home."

The girl nodded her head, dirty curls bobbing up and down, and settled into the seat.

"I'll stay with them, young lady."

Aries turned. Striker's father leaned on the threshold with a pack of recycled food in each hand. Sadness tinged the corners of his eyes, but hope dwelt there as well.

"You sure?" Aries didn't want to make him babysit children that weren't his when he hadn't seen his son in over five years.

He nodded. "Go see Striker. You two need to talk."

Aries smoothed the little girl's hair and kissed her cheek before rising to confront yet another problem. All she wanted to do was avoid the fact she'd caused Striker's grief.

"He's too busy preparing for launch, and he's still mourning the loss of two crew members. It's not the right time."

"It's the perfect time. He needs to get over it to get on with his life."

Striker's father gave her a look that said he'd known his son all his life and knew what worked best for him. Aries pursed her lips, considering his request. Perhaps he did know best.

"Okay. You may be right. Guess I'll find out."

He squeezed Aries' shoulder encouragingly as she passed. "If anyone knows what to say to snap him out of it, you do."

"Let's hope so."

Aries found Striker in the ship's belly, looking over the eggs. He looked more vulnerable than they did, his shell already cracked.

"You did it. You're going to get to set them free."

Striker's gaze snapped up from the glass casings. He half-smiled at Aries. "At least they'll have a chance."

Aries walked beside him. His hand rested protectively on the glass and she put her hand over his. "Thank you for coming back for me. I know it came at a high cost."

Striker looked away. "If only I could have saved Loot and Tiff as well."

Aries took in a deep breath and collected her thoughts. She'd been through so much. Traveling to hell and back again had taught her that making choices was an integral part of life. "All I ever wanted was freedom of choice, to choose my husband, my job, my destiny. Loot and Tiff chose theirs. Reckon told me they asked to come with you onto the *New Dawn*, and you said Loot wanted to stay on the *New Dawn*. You can't beat yourself up over their choices. You can only make your own."

Striker nodded. "I know you're right. Logically I know it. I just needed to hear someone else say it." His gaze came back to her. "What about you, Aries? Did you get what you wanted? What are you going to choose next?"

She locked eyes with his, her gaze unwavering. "I choose to take care of the children we've adopted and to watch over an alien race's eggs. I choose to live my life on Refuge. Most of all, I choose you."

She waited for his response, her face only inches away from his, her hand growing hot as it rested on his. Striker's eyes were so bright, they reminded her of the forests of old Earth. She held her breath as he leaned down and whispered, "Aries, I choose you, too."

She closed the distance, putting her other hand on his cheek and pulling his head down to meet hers. All of those days apart from him melted away. As she wrapped her arms around his neck, she felt as though all of the pieces of her life fit together. She'd found her true destiny.

...

"There it is!"

A sphere of green and blue filled the main sight panel like an embodiment of hope. Aries heart fluttered. She'd have to get used to experiencing happiness. Every time the buoyant feeling hit her, it encompassed her whole being with such fierce elation, she felt dizzy.

"Now, let's find a landing spot." Striker's fingers glided over the panels as he directed the *SP Nautilus* toward Refuge. Reckon sat in the coral indent by his side. "How about here? It looks long enough."

Striker looked down at the coordinates and brought up the location on the main screen. A stretch of grassland with bell-shaped flowers and tiny, whizzing insects came up. Aries couldn't believe they flew so close to paradise.

"Big enough, yes. It's going to be bumpy." Striker turned his head to look at Aries.

Aries thought back to her first landing in the escape pod. So much had changed since then. She'd been a ball of nerves, filled with desperation, anxiety and resentment. Now she was about to do the job she'd always wanted, living on a paradise planet she thought she'd never see, side by side with the man she loved. Her heart swelled so full of ecstasy, she thought it would fly out of her mouth and burst like a balloon in the air. She wanted to rush over and kiss every part of his face. Instead, she gave him a sly smile. "Go ahead. I've had worse landings."

The nose of the ship dived and she felt her stomach lurch, her last meal with the reprocessed food in James' room coming back to haunt her. Holding on to the slick white coral seat, she hoped all of the orphans were buckled in where she'd left them five minutes ago. At least Striker's dad had volunteered to watch over them.

Reckon looked like he wore a mask. The force pulled back his weathered skin and his cheeks wrinkled up on either side of his face. "So, Striker, have you ever landed this thing?"

"On a planet with gravity? No."

"Great."

As they laughed, Aries caught Striker's gaze. He mouthed the words, "I love you."

The ship pitched downward. It shook so hard Aries feared the coral would shatter, but all she could think about were Striker's words. She couldn't believe he'd chosen that particular moment to tell her his true feelings.

Her stomach flipped and her heart pounded as the ship broke free of the atmosphere and soared above green treetops and glistening blue expanses. The engines slowed, and the buzz in her ears lessened as Striker ran the wire tips along the panels to angle the wings. They rode into a wind so strong it roared like a tempest around them, the wings pushing against the gusts to slow the ship down.

"Here it is. The fields are in sight!" Reckon shouted.

"I got it. I got it." Striker reversed the engines.

"Can't you slow it down any more?" Reckon's voice shook.

"Nope. This is how we have to go."

The land came up faster than Aries thought it would, and she braced herself for impact.

Everything in the main control deck rattled like the ship was falling apart around them. Aries held on so tight her fingers lost color and went numb. The bottom of the ship hit and the vessel toppled over, sand and grass collecting on the sight panel as it plowed into a hill.

The force threw everyone forward into the makeshift seatbelts they'd fashioned out of the laser gun straps. The leather pressed against Aries' chest, squeezing the air out of her lungs.

Silence stung her ears. She couldn't tell if the loud noises of the landing had damaged her hearing, or if nothing made a sound. She felt like a rag in one of the tumbler machines on the *New Dawn*, tossed around at high speed. Her insides bubbled and she fought back dizziness. A moan cut through the silence and she saw Reckon squirming out from behind the strap of his chair.

Aries pulled herself up and rushed to his side, worried that he'd broken his old, frail bones. "Are you okay?"

Reckon winced as he touched his side. "A little bruised, but I think

I'm okay."

Striker's chair lay empty, his seatbelt ripped in two pieces.

"Where's Striker?" Aries looked around and saw his boots sticking out from behind the controls. "Striker!" She threw herself across the deck. He lay on his back, his eyes closed.

She ran her hands through his hair and along his body, searching for a wound, but couldn't find any broken bones, although she had little medical training. She shook him, feeling as though her heart refused to beat. "Striker, wake up."

His eyes fluttered open. He looked up at Aries as she cupped his head in her hands and smiled. She pressed her lips to his, feeling the warmth of his lips. Her mouth traveled along his jaw, spreading kisses until she reached his ear and whispered, "I love you, too."

...

A gentle sun warmed her back as Aries stepped onto the meadowland of Refuge. Dust-sized insects blew by on a mild breeze as she took in a deep breath of fresh, unpolluted air. The dove-white grass looked as slender as hair strands and as soft as a whispering wind, with wisps of seeds reaching up to the pale blue sky. Aries stepped forward and the strands brushed up against her pant legs like worshipers reaching for their god. All at once she felt as though she belonged to this world, as if it had beckoned to her in her earliest dreams. All her life, Aries had thought she'd longed for old Earth, but it had been Refuge calling her instead.

Aries had each orphan who was strong enough carry out one of the precious alien eggs. They placed them in the rays of the golden sun, nestled in the long stems of grass.

As the first volunteers journeyed out to search for water, food and a place to build shelter, Aries stayed behind, tending to the eggs. Like she'd watched the aliens do in the video, she smoothed her hands over the tops, dusting off the cosmic particles possibly built up over hundreds of years. As the afternoon wore on, the rays of the sun grew stronger, and she could almost see the tiny bodies inside if she held the shells up to the light.

"No luck yet?" Striker walked up with a bottle of water and an armful of purple fruits shaped like pears.

"No." Aries accepted the water and gulped it down.

"That's from here, you know." Striker boasted as if he'd made it himself. "The kids found a lake past the meadow, and they found these growing on trees."

He handed her a purple fruit. "We think it's edible because we saw one of the bird-like reptiles chomping on it. What does my favorite biologist think?" Aries brought out a knife and cut through the thick skin. The inside felt like the creamy texture of an avocado. "You're sure you saw birds eating it?"

"Something like birds, but not quite."

She cut a piece and smoothed it between her fingers. "I'll run some tests. If it's edible, let's call it a pearvacado."

Striker laughed. "Whatever you want. We'll set up camp, explore the region, and once we find the most suitable place to establish a colony we'll name it Aries, after you."

"What a silly name for a colony!" Aries tried to think of a better suggestion when she saw a crack in one of the eggs. "Oh no! Look, this one is damaged." How had she not seen it before? She ran over to it and traced the crack with her fingertip.

Striker joined her, kneeling by her side. "It can't be. The kids were so careful bringing them out."

"Maybe the landing damaged it?"

Aries glanced at the others. Cracks ran down the length of each egg near her. She panicked, feeling like she'd failed, until she heard a sound from behind her, a light cooing like a morning dove.

Striker walked toward the noise and bent down, scooping something up from the ground. He turned back to her, with his arms full, cradling a small body with ivory skin and glimmering wings.

Around her, winged creatures shot up in the sky like fireworks set off by the blazing sun. They spiraled and dove over her head, gliding and dancing in the air. Filled with pure joy, Aries lifted both arms up to the sky and smiled. The being in Striker's arms joined the others in the sky. Striker ran over to Aries and picked her up, twirling her around in the sea of broken shells. She had never felt more loved or more free.

Acknowledgements

I'd like to thank my agent, Dawn Dowdle, for believing in my manuscript and finding such a wonderful publishing company. Also, Liz Pelletier and Heather Howland at Entangled Publishing, for being so excited about Paradise 21. Thank you to Caroline Phipps, my editor who worked so hard to get this manuscript polished and find even greater meaning in each conversation and scene. My beta readers come next: the best sister in the world, Brianne Dionne, and my mom, for giving me support and intriguing insights. My awesome critique partners deserve numerous thank yous: Cherie Reich, Theresa Milstein, Lisa Rusczyk, Kathleen S. Allen, Lindsey Duncan, and Cher Green. And lastly, my husband, Chris, for allowing me the time I needed to work on edits, do research, and most of all, write.

Aubrie Dionne lives in New England with her husband and her two miniature doxens, Jedi and Leia. When she's not writing, she plays flute in orchestras and teaches at the university level.

Visit Aubrie at www.authoraubrie.com, and on her blog at www.authoraubrie.blogspot.com, and her Twitter page @authoraubrie for updates. Readers can e-mail her at aubriedionne@yahoo.com.

CPSIA information can be obtained at www.ICGtesting.com
Printed in the USA
BVOW041132020112

279598BV00008B/4/P